A MATTER OF
ADULTERY

A MATTER OF ADULTERY

DON LEE

CUTTING EDGE

ISBN-13: 978-1-957868-33-2

Published by
Cutting Edge Books
PO Box 8212
Calabasas, CA 91372
www.cuttingedgebooks.com

CHAPTER ONE

The scream of tires and the smell of burning rubber jerked me to reality. The beautiful girl had disappeared.

I had been watching her in a speculative sort of way as I followed her along the street from my office building.

I liked the way her little rounded buttocks jiggled at the end of each step and her long black pony-tail joined happily in each little jiggle. Her prettily shaped head caught the light rays which slanted down between the buildings as though they were seeking out her virginal thoughts under that crown of wavy hair.

I decided she must be very young from the way she tripped along, but I wasn't able to see the front of her because she was walking faster than I cared to.

I love to look at pretty girls in the same manner as a gardener loves to wander through a perfect flower garden feasting his eyes on the exquisite blossoms and smell their heavenly fragrance.

My mind was wandering over her delectable loveliness when she stepped off the curb. Suddenly she wasn't in sight. I leaped to the corner of the street and looked down.

There she was, lying in a crumpled heap under the front bumper of a Cadillac. She looked like a rag doll that had lost all its sawdust. Limp and disheveled, her dress twisted awry at her waist. Her long shapely legs, bare to her panties had several deep scratches from which small drops of blood were already starting to drop. I stooped and felt under her breast for a heart beat. She fluttered an eye toward me in half consciousness, then opened her eyes wide and whispered fiercely, "Leave me alone, you dumb cluck. And keep your mouth shut." I leaned over her in amazement, and for a second I was sure I hadn't heard right. She looked so disheveled and battered it didn't seem possible she had spoken in that fierce, angry voice. At that instant I was roughly shouldered aside by someone, and I felt a sharp stinging pain on my ankle. I stepped away and I knew damn well she had kicked me. I hadn't been stepped on. I had been purposely kicked.

A big crowd of people gathered around the accident space and I allowed myself to be unobtrusively pushed to the outer edge where I took a firm stance and watched to see just what would happen next. Something screwy was in the making and I wanted to see what it was.

A policeman appeared from nowhere and, exerting his authority, he partially cleared the street and asked someone in the crowd to call an ambulance. There was a man bending over the girl and I surmised it must be the driver of the Cadillac because he was almost crying in his throat as he talked to the policeman. However, no one touched the girl until with a wail of a siren clearing the way, an ambulance pulled up beside the Cad. A couple of white-dressed attendants spilled out of the machine, hurried to the back door, opened it, and slid out a business-like stretcher which they set on the pavement beside the girl and tenderly lifted and rolled her on to the thing. They lifted it into the ambulance, closed the door after them, locking themselves inside with the girl on the stretcher. Then the ambulance swung away and with the siren screaming like a banshee, it headed toward the hospital.

After the ambulance left, I got a good look at the driver of the Cadillac. He had features like a squirrel—small bright eyes, sharp pointed nose, his mouth drawn down like he was about to burst out bawling. Not that I blamed him. Anyone would feel the same who had just hit and knocked down a pretty girl. Besides I recognized him. He was Wilson Connely, the owner of the biggest banking system in the state and a tight-fisted old skinflint if one ever lived. He was also a power in politics and had a reputation as a kind of overlord of all the rackets that were running wild in the country. That reputation was only hearsay however, as no one had been able to pin anything on him. He had too much money and he was able to practically control the elections to the point where unless you were a Connely man, you didn't get elected.

The policeman practically got down on his knees in front of Connely. He then asked him a few questions and waved him back to his Cadillac. Connely got in the car and drove off. The policeman began to make like an officer of the law as soon as the car was out of sight, took out a note book and began asking questions of the people still standing around.

I wanted no part of that business, so I eased out of the crowd and walked back to my office.

I was curious as hell. A young pretty girl gets clobbered by a banker's car and refuses help from the first person on the scene, which was me, and then insults my manhood by kicking me on the shins and calling me a dumb cluck. She had no right to kick me. I was only admiring her before she got run over and besides, I never saw her before. Some women are the strangest people.

I'm in the Public Relations business, which is a fancy title for the purpose of selling anything to the public for a stipulated sum of money. I was doing right well, too.

I had just had my biggest year, money wise, and I felt I was on my way to bigger and better things—like more money and a bigger car with a fancy garage in the country to park it in.

I discovered last year that there was a hell of a lot of money in getting some jerk elected to a public office by selling the gullible voters on the idea that such and such a man would be the best prospect for the office of dog catcher or other allied offices. There seemed to be an abundant supply of good hard cash always available to finance the campaign of the candidates. The trick was to get the voters to believe in your choice. That year I had been lucky. Two of my clients were now nestling on the edge of the public trough, and because they gave me a proper amount of credit for their success in hoodwinking the voters, I was fairly swamped with offers to guide another man who was ambitious, if not smart, to the successful goal of a state office which he thought might fill his pockets with public funds and keep him off the relief rolls.

Between you and me, I hate politics. I was raised in a back part of the country on a farm and my father was a kind of hit or miss politician. He was always running for some office and if the Democrats were in, he got the job. If the Republicans were in, we went hungry. The whole state was solid Republican so we were hungry most of the time. But in spite of its drawbacks, my father was a politician every day of the year. He talked politics, breathed politics, and lived politics. By sheer force of his fervor, he was elected just often enough to keep him running after the political plums like a dog on the race track chases the electric rabbit. When the Republican machine broke down, he caught the rabbit or rather the office he was running for at the time.

This is not my story, but I wanted to show you why and how I came to be mixed up in such a whirligig which I hate.

For some unknown reason I seem to have a knack for the way the voters feel and I seem to be able to dig out the devious ways of presenting my clients to them in a light most favorable to catch their votes at election time. Besides, I love money, not for itself but for what it will buy for me.

I also love women, and money and women are synonymous. Ever try to catch a woman without any money in your pocket? She will outrun you every time. Most of my life I've been outrun. Some other fellow always got into the winner's circle and had the garland of flowers draped around his neck, which in this case, was the arms of the woman I had been panting for. It was a bit frustrating to say the least, and hard on my ego.

Now I was on my way. I hoped.

I entered my office with my little mind busy as a hive of bees swarming around the queen bee which, in my case, was the cute trick that got her dainty torso bruised by a Cadillac. Why a Cadillac? Why Banker Connely's particular Cadillac? There are a lot of bankers in this country that own Cadillacs. Why did she kick me on the shins where it hurt. I wasn't about to make improper advances to her in her condition, even if her dress was scrambled above her—Well never mind. She was sure an eyeful.

As I walked past my secretary's desk, she cornered me with a glance then opened her eyes in a full piercing look and murmured sotto voice,

"My. My. What nice doggy bit you on the leg?" She leaned toward me in mock pity. "Tch, tch, did it hurt? I hope."

I answered as gently as I could, "No nice doggy. And, no."

I passed on into my private office without another word.

My secretary is one of my more serious problems because she is a woman. But what a woman. All curvy, lush, twinkling, brash, sweet as apple cider and competent as a secretary should be. Sometimes I have an idea that she is waiting for me to bat her on the head with some hard instrument like a stone-age club and drag her into my office by her hair, throw her on the couch and ravish her exactly like a stone-age man would have done to one of the wild maidens he had captured.

So far I had only had the impulse, I knew full well if such a thing came to pass I would find myself the unwilling participant at a wedding with her clinging possessively to my arm while the minister made us man and wife for everlasting.

She had a way of stirring me up inside every time I looked at her walking about the office. Damn it. She didn't seem to walk at all. She seemed to just float around like a blossom wafted by the wind, and she smelled just as sweet.

There were times when I thought it would be perfectly all right to take her in my arms and consider myself well paid by becoming lost in her enchanting flower garden of delights. Then I could sense another odor of drying diapers hanging in rows and rows on a line back of a small cottage in some new real estate development while I struggled to make the payments on the cottage and pay the doctor and hospital bills for the continuing flow of offspring and smelled more drying diapers.

The very thought of such a monotonous way of life caused me to keep hands off of her, and at the end of her first year as my secretary, she was still in possession of all her maidenly virtue as far as I was concerned. But at times the situation was most trying.

I settled down to work out a sure fire campaign to hoist my latest client into the public fancy enough to ensure his election to the House of Representatives. His name was Finley. Arthur P. Finley. He had started when he was a punk kid and had bulled his way up in a trucking firm until he owned it. Finley's Interstate Lines. You've seen his trucks everywhere coming at you on the highway with the big signs on the front of the cabs reading, "Here Comes Finley."

I always thought he should have added to the signs the words, "Get out of my way or I'll smash you off the highway."

He was that sort of man. Now he wanted to get to the legislature for the purpose of getting the taxes cut on truck lines so he could buy more trucks and make more money to buy more trucks without having to give a cut in his profits to the government. He had a roll of dough to spend on his campaign so I was willing to give him a run for his money to the best of my ability. I honestly tried to concentrate on my work but the thought of that luscious female lying under the front bumper of banker Connely's Cad kept sneaking into my mind like a persistent mosquito.

The thought just kept buzzing around that here was a small mystery that was opposite of the odor of roses.

I caught myself making marks on the sheet of paper in front of me. I looked at them closely. Why? Why? Why?

I gave up the afternoon work in disgust and stomped out of the office, giving my precious secretary a casual nod and a mumbled,

"Good night, Miss Dahl. You may go home whenever you wish. I'm through for the day."

She gave me a beautiful smile and said softly,

"Bur-r-r, what an unhappy man. What you need is a good—"

I heeled the outer door shut and I never heard what it was she thought I needed.

Down on the street a newsboy was calling out the headline of the afternoon edition of the paper. He garbled so no one could understand what it was he said, and when he saw me he came running, a big grin on his freckled puss.

"Paper, Mr. Howard? You're early tonight."

I fingered in my pocket for a coin and gave him a quarter, "Keep the change, Jimmy. But don't expect that to become a habit. You might become one of the idle rich."

"Gee. Thanks, Mr. Howard. Some day I gonna be rich like you."

I stuck the folded paper under my arm and walked on feeling pretty good. One person thought I was rich, anyway. I might make it yet.

I went into my favorite restaurant, a little place run by a big fat German woman who, in my opinion, was just about the best cook in the city. The concoctions which came out of her kitchen were out of this world and I had been eating most of my meals there since I had established my own business. When I was broke I could sign a tab and walk out, when I was flush, she would feed me up with oversize orders of tempting, delicious meals which I ate and suffered afterward from an overstuffed stomach.

She was sitting on a high stool behind the cash register so I went up to her, leaned over, and chucked her under her generous chin.

"How's my baby tonight? Ready to give this dump away and marry me?"

She opened her mouth like a baby hippo and gurgled.

"Ach. The man says I should marry him. What for, I ask? So I could starve while he chases the young floozies. Nah. Get along to your dinner and mind you keep your hands off the new girl."

She gave me a belligerent look and waved me away. I found a vacant table near the back and spread out the evening paper and began to look for an account of the accident I had inadvertently been a party to earlier in the day.

Hands set a glass of water on the table and at the same time part of the paper was brushed aside and a paper napkin was placed beside the glass. An assortment of silverware was neatly laid on the napkin. I looked up and barely repressed a whistle. New girl was right. Inches from my face was just about the prettiest pair of breasts I'd ever seen, and they were almost bursting out of the white uniform blouse. I was almost tempted to reach right out and taste them with the tip of my tongue. Then, their owner leaned back and they were out of my reach. My popeyes followed on up the rest of her. A round chin with a deep dimple in the very center was poised just below a warm moist pair of the reddest full lips. The tip of a tongue stuck peepingly out between the lips like it was trying to see what was going on. Her nose was oddly pugged but fitted perfectly just below her wide set eyes which were deep blue, nearly black, and were they shining, right into my own which were still popping. Her hair was coal black and piled on top of her head like a kind of edible bun.

I just stared, what I mean, is I stared until her lips kinked up at the corners and she said, amused like,

"Do you wish to order now? Or just think about it"

I looked at her meaningly, "If I think about it, I won't want anything to eat. What time do you get through work?"

She bubbled delightfully, "My husband will call here for me at ten o'clock."

I felt the tension go out of me like air from a leaky tire. I asked her disgustedly,

"Why in hell do I always see them last? Why am I always too late?"

She bent forward to move the silverware a fraction of an inch and her proud breasts just whispered against my shoulder, as she said softly,

"Don't feel too badly. He is out of town a lot of the time. That is why I went to work here. I never worked before, but I get awful tired of being cooped up in an apartment all alone."

She stepped back, and very businesslike poised her pencil over her order pad, "May I take your order, sir?"

I leered at her, "You already know what I want, but for the moment just bring me something to eat. I suddenly seem to be very hungry."

Her eyes lingered on mine for a moment, then she swayed toward the kitchen, dragging my eyes after her.

When she passed from sight behind the kitchen door my eyes resumed their proper place in my head and I continued my hunt for the report of the accident in the newspaper.

I found it on the second page. Just a short column.

"Prominent Matron Hospitalized After Car Accident.

"Mrs. Jennifer Morley was taken to the General Hospital this afternoon suffering from shock, when hit by a car driven by Wilson Connely. Attending physician, Dr. Ralph Smith, reports there is no serious injury, but is holding the patient for observation. Mrs. Morley is the wife of Bart Morley, who is prominent in civic affairs."

As I reread the notice I could see the fine hand of Wilson Connely bearing down on the reporter who wrote the account. Sure. Write it, if you must, but be damn careful what you say.

I wadded the paper in disgust and threw it on the floor. So. She was married to a big-time lawyer and part-time politician, with an ambition to be a big politician and part-time lawyer. I knew he had run for States Attorney General at the last election and had been beaten by a mile. I also knew he came from a wealthy family and would probably try again when he learned how to spend his money where it counted. He was forty if he was a day. How he could have latched onto that young wife was beyond me.

I made a mental note to learn more about Bart Morley and that conniving little chick who was his wife. I might pick up a buck or two. There was no two ways about it, her getting smacked by banker Connely's car would bear looking into.

About that point in my thinking, the pretty waitress came and placed my dinner in front of me. As a waitress she was no great success, but as a relish to the food she left nothing to be desired. She puttered around the other tables all the while I was eating, and I can truthfully say I don't know to this day what I ate. She didn't look at me once but I could see her, even when she was behind me.

When I was finished eating she came quietly to my table, laid the check on the table, breathed, "Thank you, Sir." And before I could say a word she went away. I followed her with my eyes but she didn't even give me a hint of a glance. I put a folded dollar bill under my plate and stalked to the cash register in high dudgeon.

My fat German girl looked at me pityingly, "Ach. Such a fine one you are. She is not for you, that one. Ashamed you should be for eating at her with your eyes all the time. I see you look and look. But she sees you not. For that I am happy. You should be ashamed."

I said in retort, "If you would marry me, I would not care to look at other women."

She jabbed the cash register viciously and handed me some change.

"I should live so long. All you think about is women, women, women. Ashamed you should be."

I reached over and patted her gently on the cheek and went to the front door. I glanced back. She was smiling, but when she saw me looking, her smile changed to a grimace of distaste. Beyond her I saw the pretty waitress give me a quick little nod and a sweet smile. I went home in a state of beautiful contentment.

I live right down town only a couple of blocks from my office and I usually leave my Plymouth car in the garage most of the time. It takes longer to find a place to park than it does to walk, so, I walk. My apartment is in one of the old brick buildings which was built at the turn of the century and has remained in the possession of the family which built it. Now it was owned by one of the spinster sisters and she is practically broke so she makes her living renting out part of the house.

The part I rent is on the second floor with an outside entrance from the side. I have five large rooms—two bedrooms, an elaborate sitting room, a large room I use for a den, a very efficient kitchen which I never use, and a fine bathroom where there is always plenty of towels and lots of hot water. I pay a hundred and fifty bucks a month for the place. When I'm broke, I live there anyway and the old spinster hopes I'll pay her at some future date. The arrangement is very satisfactory to me. At the moment my rent is paid in advance.

When I turn off the street and walk towards the entrance to my place I'm at peace with the world and I love everybody in it. I even manage a small whistle of a tune I love,

"Happy days are here again."

At the foot of the entrance I saw a shadow beside me, but before I could move, I was impolitely grabbed on both sides and my arms nearly jerked out of their sockets, while some bastard swiped me across the mouth, which almost left me toothless and put a severe crick in my neck.

I'm not puny by any means, but I was helpless as a new born babe in the grip of those two thugs who held me. I kicked and twisted but it was wasted effort. For my trouble, I got another roundhouse alongside of the head. I fully expected to see my head go bouncing along the side of the house and was surprised to feel it still anchored on my neck as I slumped down. They didn't let me fall down, however, but propped me against the side of the house, and a third son of a bitch began methodically trying to drive my belly through the hard bricks, one punch at a time.

I felt one rib after another give way under the punching and the last I heard was one of them say,

"This is only just a little warning, Buster. Be like the Three Monkeys. Hear nothing. See nothing. Tell nothing. You might live to a ripe old age."

As I went out I heard someone screaming. It was me.

CHAPTER TWO

There was a loud roaring sound as a bulldozer came grinding down the street and a crushing agony in my chest as the tracks on the bulldozer ran diagonal across my prostrate body. I could feel, but not see, the blood oozing out of the gashes left by the mud cleats on the tracks as the bulldozer went on down the street and out of hearing. Then, it was quiet as death. I opened my eyes as far as the swelling permitted and looked out. I could see stars far above me and the moon was hanging lopsided in a perfectly clear sky. I discovered I was lying on my left side with my head half tilted up against the side of the brick wall. A stair loomed upward in front of me and I thought how foolish it was to have a stairway leading to the sky when I was in no shape to walk up there. Then I began to yell.

When I could open my eyes again, the first thing I saw was my spinster landlady bending over me, clucking like a setting hen.

"Oh, you poor boy. Oh, you poor man. Oh, your poor face." She turned her face aside and called, "Oh, Doctor. His eyes are open."

A man bent over me and I went back to sleep.

I could see a whole room full of beautiful women dancing around me, naked from the waist up, and fastened on each of their pink tipped breasts there was a long piece of iron pipe which swung in cadence with their dancing. When they danced by me, the pieces of pipe would swing out and hit me in the face a

terrific blow. I kept trying to duck the blows but they hit me anyway, then they started on my chest, banging the damn pipes in a
steady rhythm in time to some distant music. On my bare flesh,
they kept doing it up and down on my whole body. They were
wearing shoes with heavy iron soles which cut into my tender
skin at every step. I begged them to stop dancing but they danced
over me with pounding steps. When they passed over my face,
they would bend down and kiss me, and each time one of them
kissed me, she would bite out a chunk of flesh from my cheeks
and spit it into her hand, then hold it out for me to see. It would
be a perfect apple. I could feel my apple tree being torn apart by
inches. I started screaming again.

They danced away one by one and soon I was left all alone so
I opened my eyes and looked around.

I was in my own bed, in my own apartment, and my beautiful secretary, my darling secretary, Miss Dahl, was gently holding my hands and crying big round tears while she murmured,

"Never you mind all the beautiful dancing girls, you ugly
brute ... they are all gone now. I won't let the nasty old girls come
back any more to torment you. Just lay quiet."

She slipped her arm under my head and as I went back to
sleep, I swear she was singing a lullaby.

When I awoke again I felt fine. I cautiously looked around.
My landlady and my secretary were sitting at a small coffee table
parked in the center of the room and they were talking a mile a
minute. Between them were arranged everything necessary for a
cup of tea—a tea pot, cup and saucers, half a lemon, and a bowl
of sugar.

I watched them for a moment in fond admiration, but my
kidneys were bursting and I wanted to go to the bathroom, so
I had to get them out of the room in a hurry. I groaned audibly
just to see what they would do.

They sprang up like startled pigeons and flew straight to the bed and me.

My landlady whooped, "Glory be. His eyes look normal again. See. He's looking at your legs."

I didn't know the old girl had it in her to make a remark like that and at that moment I could have kissed her if I hadn't been in such a hurry.

I said as gruffly as I could, "You gals get out of here so I can go to the bathroom."

My sweet little secretary giggled, "Just lay right there, big boy. I'll bring you a bed pan and you can go potty in that. No getting out of bed for you."

Really, and I mean really. I threw back the covers and found I was wrapped up like a mummy from the armpits clear down to my hips. I couldn't move my legs. They were bandaged too. Well—I had to submit while they giggled and chucked a cold white enameled bedpan under me and then they discreetly left the room while I filled the damn thing full.

I was barely finished when they came tripping back, looking as pleased as little cherubs. My landlady took the enameled monstrosity away while Darleen fluffed up my pillows and made herself quite at home fastening my pajama top close around my throat and tucking the covers around my naked lower body.

For some reason she seemed to be particularly happy, so I asked her,

"Just how do you come to be here, Miss Dahl, making like a nurse? Is that part of your work as a secretary?"

She answered with a small smile and quite formally.

"Your office is closed temporarily, Mr. Howard. I thought I might as well continue to earn my small salary." (She emphasized the small.) "I once studied to become a nurse before I became your secretary and when your landlady called to tell me you had been in an accident, I came right over, and have been here ever since."

I broke in, "What do you mean, ever since? How long have you been here?"

"Four days now. You have been quite a problem … what with all your talking about your beautiful dancing girls, and your screaming about some automobile accident." She giggled, "and you sure can mess up a clean bed. Aren't you house broke yet?"

If I hadn't been so shocked I would have slugged her. Four days. Dead to the world. For the first time I wondered why I had been beaten up. And by whom. All I could remember was some guys holding me while another mug beat me half to death. All for nothing. I didn't know a single thing about anything that could deserve a mauling like that. But by the Holy Gods, I would sure find out and then I'd tear someone apart a thread at a time. I struggled upright in my righteous anger, cursing.

Darleen pushed me back on the pillow.

"My goodness. What a ferocious man. Lay down or I'll bop you one. Want to tell me about it? You probably got just what you deserved, fooling around with some married woman."

I looked at her in a new light. So that was what she thought, but still she came to me and waited on me, cleaning up my messes and worrying about me like a wife. Quite a gal that secretary of mine.

I said carefully, "You may not believe me."

She said quickly, "I sure won't, but tell me anyway."

I said plaintively, "You might hear me out, with an open mind."

"Go ahead, I love fairy tales."

"I left the office the other night early as you may remember, and went to the German restaurant." She interrupted me and said tartly,

"Where you tried to make a date with the new waitress and ate her up with your eyes all the time you were in the restaurant. But she wanted no part of you. Go ahead."

She sure made me smart, but I continued.

"I walked home. Alone. You know that too, huh?" She barely nodded.

"At the foot of the stairs a couple of thugs grabbed me and held me, while a third one beat the hell out of me."

She said delightedly, "Good, three husbands all at once. You sure get around."

I tried to slap her pretty puss, but she ducked her head and I missed. I glowered at her.

"That's the honest God's truth. I don't know who they were. I never saw any of them before. I don't know why they chose me. I haven't been fooling around with any married women, as you so delicately point out. Nor do I have any pregnant girls' daddies chasing me. I'm a very respectable citizen and I don't like being beat to a pulp for any reason. It hurts my feelings."

She looked at me in a kind of wonder. "Well, this time you got more than your precious feelings hurt. You nearly got killed." Then of all things, she started to blubber. She vigorously shook her head to throw away her tears and said tenderly,

"I was so scared. We all were, but I was sure I was going to be out of a job. And I like working for you."

She picked up a corner of the bed sheet, wiped her eyes and blew her nose on the thing. She said,

"Now tell me again. You are not mixed up with any married woman at the moment whose husband wants to kill you. About the pregnant girls, we'll let that pass for the moment for how could you tell. Now think, if that's possible for you, have you been mixed up in anything shady I don't know about?"

I considered, she acted exactly like a wife, but for the time being I could not correct her on that point. She obviously wanted to help. The perfect secretary.

"The last thing I remember was one of the bastards telling me to act like the monkeys. You know. Hear no evil, Speak no evil, See no evil. Hell. I don't know anything to hear, speak, or see about. But, by God, I will."

She sat for a long time in pensive thought, presently she sighed,

"You know, Mr. Howard. I almost believe you are telling me the truth and you really don't know why they beat you."

She asked, "You going to tell the police?"

I shook my head.

"No. What could I tell them? That I was beat up just for the hell of it? They'd laugh at me. The publicity wouldn't do me any good, either. I'll just keep my mouth shut about the whole thing and see what happens. Tomorrow you go to the office and bring me the layout on Finley, and we will work here till I can maneuver under my own steam. That is if you don't mind living here in sin with me."

She answered archly, "Ha. That's a good one. You couldn't sin right now if you had help. By the time you are in shape to do so, I will be out of your reach, believe me."

She rose to her feet and leaned over me to straighten the covers, and kept right on leaning till her lovely lips covered mine in a breath-taking kiss which lasted all of a tenth of a second, and before I could get a hand out from under the covers to hang onto her, she jerked away from me and ran toward the door.

I yelled at her.

"Just remember, you started it. You kissed me first."

CHAPTER THREE

For four days I was kept in bed by the doctor whom my landlady had called when she found me lying at the foot of the stairs screaming my head off. She told me she was asleep at the time I must have been been getting the beating, but was awakened by my moaning and yelling. She had slipped on a robe, opened her bedroom window and looked out to see if she could locate the racket. She had seen me at once, lying under the window, and for a few minutes she had been deathly afraid to do any more about it. She didn't know it was me, of course, and debated whether to call the police first or investigate.

She had finally made up her mind to have a look, and when she recognized me, she had called the doctor and together they had carried me to my room and put me to bed.

I can imagine the shock in the old girl when she saw her star tenant in such a state of disrepair. I'm sure she suffered both mentally and physically that first few hours almost as much as I did. But these old-timers are made of stern stuff and her only thought was to keep me alive. In the morning she had called my office. Miss Dahl had answered and had come on the run to my apartment.

The fourth afternoon the doctor came to see me and after a few grunts and poking me here and there, he said,

"Well, son, it looks like you are going to live. I'll take these bandages off your legs and you can try walking. No going out of the house, though. Just take it nice and easy and probably you will be all right again."

He proceeded to unravel the bandages from my legs and when they were naked, he tilted me on the side of the bed and helped me to stand upright. He stepped back and said, "Now, take a step."

I did, and fell full length on the carpet moaning.

"Jesus Christ, doc. I'm paralyzed from the waist down."

He grunted and helped me back to the edge of the bed and said again, "Now take another step and I'll hold you up."

This time I made a better effort and managed to take a few steps with his support. He laughed.

"Your legs are just asleep. The circulation has been partially shut off under the bandages, but you will be all right in a little while. Sit down and stretch out your legs and kick them. Get the blood circulating."

I sat on the bed and kicked my legs out and around for about fifteen minutes until all the prickly feeling had left them. I found I could stand alone and walk to the bathroom. Thank God, the ordeal of the bedpan was behind me. Two giggly women and a bedpan are hard to stomach.

I recovered fast after that. Miss Dahl came to the apartment each morning, cooked my breakfast, cleaned up the place, and then we worked on the Finley campaign the rest of the day, only taking time out to eat delicious meals which she cooked.

As an employer, I am not an easy man to work for. I'm exacting and I don't spare myself when I'm engaged on any enterprise which I feel is worthwhile. At first our relationship was of employer and employee. I expected her to be helpful with ideas and to take an attitude of collaborator instead of employee. When evening came she was always worn out.

Yet she continued to cook for me and cater to my wants without question and gradually we melted toward each other.

My apartment being on the second floor was a big advantage as far as view was concerned. The side windows looked out on a beautiful vista of leafy green trees and the great lawn about the house was a carpet of velvety smoothness.

She loved to stand at the windows in the evening with her back to the room and me. I would go over to her and stand beside her, enjoying the closeness of her instead of the view.

I didn't touch her until about the third evening she had stood there. I touched her shoulder tentatively and she threw her head back and her hair fell over my face and hand.

Slowly she turned her head and offered me her mouth, keeping her lips together like a girl of six or seven.

Her act was so winsome and delicate I could only press my lips to hers in silent wonder. None of the harsh, fierce, desirous and demanding passion was in my thoughts at the time. I simply kissed her. In that instant I knew she was virginally pure and had never known the feeling of a man with animal passion weighing her down.

While our lips were still clinging, I moved my arms around her and cupped her breasts in my two hands. She caught her breath softly and stepped out of my embrace easily and surely, moved gracefully to where her purse and coat were lying on a chair and turned, her mouth trembled just a bit as she said quietly, "I will see you in the morning, Mr. Howard. Good night."

I barely nodded as she left the room. Her withdrawal from my arms left me with a sense of terrible aloneness. I didn't feel like reading, so I took a hot shower and went to bed.

I slept badly all night and in the morning I woke up feeling washed out and limp. I was in a fever of impatience waiting for her to come back to me. When she finally arrived I was exhausted from the strain.

She came in as usual with a cheery, "Good morning, Mr. Howard. I'm hungry, how about you?"

I realized instantly she was a bit shy and frightened at being alone with me, and wanted no allusion to what had happened the night before. I covered my feelings by saying gruffly,

"It's about time you got here. You are letting me starve to death. Be a busy little housewife and get me some breakfast in a hurry."

Instantly her whole face blossomed and she hurried toward the kitchen. I could hear her singing softly along with the burbling of the coffee percolator.

She served me a delicious breakfast and I ate all of it with relish. There was no strain between us, and she apparently had no further thought of the fears she had harbored through the night.

After breakfast we concentrated on the business at hand and except for a hasty sandwich at lunch time, the day sped by in a flurry of concentrated endeavor by both of us to prepare a winning campaign for our client, the unworthy Mr. Finley.

Winning a political campaign for a well known professional politician is no cinch in either party and when the man running for office is completely unknown, like our Mr. Finley, the odds against his winning are tremendous.

However, in this case, the office of State Representative for which he was running, was more of a title than an important post. His opponent was weak in the city, and I could count on the labor vote almost to a man. We could get a lot of publicity by simply putting posters on his many trucks which covered the entire state daily and that bit of advertising was free.

In a layout for a big campaign affecting a major office, there are a thousand and one things to which I give my undivided attention. I use every medium of advertising possible within my budget, such as newspapers, radio, television, and throw-away posters.

In addition, I make all the appointments for my client to speak at every gathering in the state—club meetings by the hundreds, regional picnics, grange meetings, farm and ranch barbecues and midweek church gatherings. In short, I try to have my client on the spot at every place where he can meet the voters on their own ground.

Plane schedules, train timetables, and hotel accommodations must be planned far in advance so there will not be a minute wasted once the actual campaign gets under way. I even go so far as to coach my client on the proper clothes to wear at a given location. I know my state like the palm of my own hand, and in practically every precinct I have a friend or two who will get behind me and help willingly.

I prefer to have my client find his own money for such a campaign, but when the money begins to run short, I am not above getting out and helping raise money to sweeten the pork barrel.

Such a campaign as this, we were planning for our Mr. Finley, on a smaller scale, and he was footing all the bills. The sky was the limit.

At the end of the day I was frazzled and my head throbbed from the mental exertion. I decided to take a nap before dinner, so I lay down on the couch and was instantly lost in slumber.

Darleen must have let me sleep a couple of hours because it was quite dark when she gently nudged me awake.

"Please wake up, Mr. Howard. By the time you shower I will have dinner ready."

I yawned gustily and looked at her. She was fresh as a daisy and fairly blooming. Twinkling, that's what she was. Twinkling. Like a happy star. Even after a long hard day's work she fairly glittered. She nudged me again.

"Hurry. Dinner will burn."

I trudged sleepily to the shower and went at it. After my shower I felt better. I dressed in my underwear, socks, old T-shirt and a pair of slacks, stuck my feet in a pair of beat up slippers and went in to dinner. Thank God, I was beginning to feel normal again.

She had moved the kitchen table into the living room, covered it with a white tablecloth and had put a tiny vase of flowers in the center. I sat down in one of the chairs she had placed beside the table, tucked a napkin under my chin, and then I banged a fork on my water glass for service.

She came out of the kitchen with a little dinky apron tied on the front of her, carrying a tray. She set the tray on the table and placed in front of me a steak fit for the gods, good old pan fried potatoes, creamed peas, a bowl of crisp salad and wonder of wonders, a plate full of hot biscuits.

I know my mouth must have gaped open like a dying fish, because she laughed merrily.

"Just eat your dinner, Mr. Howard. I can cook, too."

For once I rose to the occasion. I untucked my napkin, laid it on the table and walked around to the other side. I gallantly pulled out her chair and said, "After you, my dear."

She gurgled, "You are so kind. But don't you think I should get my dinner on the table before I sit down?"

I paused to look. There was no food at her place. I said, "Pardon me. I'm not a well man, you know."

She danced to the kitchen and came back carrying another tray filled with the same goodies, but on a smaller scale, which she placed at her place at the table. Then she allowed me to slide the chair under her cute little bottom.

I kissed her tenderly on the top of her precious head and returned to my own place at the table.

We didn't talk all through the meal. I was too busy feeding my face. Golly, it was good. She watched me eat every morsel she had prepared, with a smug look on her face.

When I finished eating, I suddenly wondered where all the food was coming from. I asked her.

"Where are you getting the money to pay for all the groceries?"

She looked away for a second, then faced me.

"I have a little money saved up. I've been spending that."

I leered at her.

"You live with me. Nurse me. Bathe me and feed me. Good. I always wanted to be a gigolo. I sure like this kind of life."

She cracked right back.

"You will find all the items on my expense account at the end of the month, Mr. Howard. I might as well put down my overtime also. You're a real stinker."

She pushed her chair away from the table and walked to the window dabbing at her eyes with a napkin.

I would have been happy if she had slapped my head off. I knew I was the rear end of a horse and I was a plain fool to try to kid her about something like that. She had loved waiting on me and I had broken her heart.

I went to her, and stood for a long time beside her just patiently waiting until she could sense my thoughts, begging for forgiveness.

She turned toward me, laid her head on my chest and wept. Her eyes got all red and her nose had the snuffles, but she didn't seem to care. I let her have her cry. After a time she snuffled against my neck in a little child's voice.

"I'm such a fool. Such a fool. But I wanted to wait on you. I liked waiting on you. I thought you would be glad." She drew away from me and raised her voice, "From now on you can damn well get along without me. I'm through. Through. Damn you! Through."

She fought me like a cat but I couldn't possibly let her go feeling like she did. I held her tight and gradually she quieted. She said angrily,

"That's right. Use your strength to overpower me. I wish I could hurt you." I had her arms pinned so she was unable to strike or scratch and she subsided ungraciously.

I held her in the crook of one arm and gently stroked her hair and the back of her head for a long time. Gradually the tumult which possessed her passed away, and she continued to lean against me of her own free will.

I gently tipped her head back and bent to her lips, just a soft tender pressure. Her body responded, but she remained immobile. I continued to nibble at the corners of her mouth and her cheeks until she joined me in a long sweet kiss that left us both trembling. She turned her mouth and said wonderingly,

"I like your kisses. You are so sweet. I feel all melty inside."

Her arm slid around my neck, pulling me down to her lips again. Her kisses were not very expert, but they were sweet and obedient to my own. Her hand kept stroking the back of my neck. Sending little waves of delight down my spine.

I picked her up, sliding my arm under her thighs and carried her to the couch. I held her for a moment, our lips still closed on each other, then tenderly laid her full length on the couch.

I knelt beside her, burying my face in her breast, murmuring fragments of sound. After a long time I eased her away and bit her gently at the corners of her mouth and on her cheeks. Sliding the top of her dress down over her shoulder, I followed the exposed flesh with my lips. She sighed softly and quivered in delicious enjoyment as I caressed her legs. Whispering against her ear, I said, "You have such beautiful legs, so smooth and silky."

She pressed her face against my throat, and kissed me.

"Do you think so? I'm glad you like my legs."

Almost holding my breath I told her, "I like all of you. I want to love you so much."

"Do you really?"

"Yes, very much."

"Oh, Chris. I'm afraid I want you, too."

"Precious girl." I moved my hand under her dress, up along the dewy flesh.

"No. No, Chris. I can't stand it."

"Why not, if you want me too?"

"No. No. No. I want to, but I just can't help it."

She rolled away from my arms sobbing. I reached after her, but she said breathlessly,

"No, Chris. We just can't. I know I'm acting like a bitchy bitch, but I just want the first time to be right, and this way isn't right. You know it isn't."

I straightened up and walked away from her. I thought furiously, girls like her are all the same. The only way to get into their sex circle is through the circle of a wedding ring, and suddenly I could smell diapers hanging on a line. I watched her licking my kisses off her pouty lips and wondered if it would be worth my solitary life just to have her around all the time.

CHAPTER FOUR

She squirmed around and placed her feet on the floor, sitting up in a crouched position. She said pleadingly,

"Please, Chris. Please try to understand. I love the feel of you, and I love the feel of your hands on me, but I just can't let you love me that way. I would be just another easy pushover to you and it would spoil what we have together. I like to work for you, and if I let you love me that way, I couldn't face you any more. I would be too ashamed. I know I've been a bitch allowing you to think I was willing to go all the way, but I just can't"

She flung herself, face down on the couch, bawling in earnest.

I couldn't stand it. I went to her, turned her over and sat down holding her head against my chest.

"It's perfectly all right. I'm not so hard up I have to take something away from you by force. Your precious cherry is safe as though it was in God's pocket as far as I am concerned. But if you want to keep it, don't get yourself in another position like this with any other man. He probably wouldn't be so easy on you. You're a passionate little wench and the man who gets there will have something to remember. Now go wash your face and go home. Tomorrow, we will start at the office again and forget all this."

She snuffled a bit, then sat up away from me.

"Thank you, Chris. You're a sweet guy." She gave me a baby like kiss and went to the bathroom.

When she came back out she was again the perfect secretary. She busily picked up all our papers and stuffed them into my brief case, but I could see her mind was on something else.

I didn't say a word. She took her time putting on her coat, and then she turned to me.

"I suppose now you will go out and get one of your more willing girls and jump on her like a monkey on a coconut."

I grinned at her.

"Could be, I'll do just that."

She gave me a disgusted look and flounced out into the night.

I had a good laugh and went to bed.

The next morning when I walked into my office, she was already there and her typewriter was humming. She gave me the usual bright "Good morning, Mr. Howard. It's good to see you back in the office again."

She added, "A lady called for a ten o'clock appointment. I told her you would see her. She wouldn't give me her name."

"Thank you, Miss Dahl. You're looking very lovely this morning."

She dimpled, and resumed her typing without a glance as I went into my private office.

At exactly ten o'clock, she opened the door and said formally, "A lady to see you, Mr. Howard."

I looked up. The lady who came through the door was a doll. I sprang to my feet and put on all the charm of which I was capable. I saw Darleen smirk as she closed the door behind my visitor.

The lady hesitated for just a breath, then said,

"It was kind of you to see me, Mr. Howard. I know how busy you are."

"I'm delighted. Will you be seated?" I walked around my desk and swung a chair into position so I could look at her. She was sure an eyeful.

She threw back a gorgeous mink stole from her shoulders and sat down in the chair, primly crossing her feet at the ankles. She said, in a low husky voice,

"I'm Mrs. Bart Morley. I'm sure we have never met before. Formally, that is."

"It is a great pleasure—" Her last words sank in. I stared at her.

"Yes. That is right." She smiled a quick fleeting smile, and looked squarely at me.

She had read my thoughts like a mind reader. I grinned.

"That was quite a performance. How did you manage it without getting damaged beyond repair?"

"It took a bit of doing, I'll admit. However, the outcome was very satisfactory. It was necessary as you shall see."

She leaned toward me, in her eyes a look of polished steel.

"Mr. Howard, my husband will be the next governor of the state. Four years later he will be elected to the United States Senate. After that he will be nominated for the Presidency of the United States."

I clutched the edge of my desk and looked at her, flabbergasted. She looked into my eyes steadily, without batting an eye. My eyes were the first to pull away. She sat quietly while I rummaged in a drawer for my pipe, loaded it and got it fuming. Then, I asked,

"Just how do you propose to pull such a miracle out of the hat? Are you some goddess of sorcery, that you can wave a magic wand and all things will come to pass?"

Without a single change of expression she went on, "You might say so. I get what I want, and I want him to become a national figure in politics for a reason. We won't go into that at the moment, but you will learn my reason in time. I am quite willing to pay any price to see my husband become such a figure, and with your help, I am quite sure we will accomplish our goal."

When I am busy, I always forget to draw on my pipe and the damn thing is continually going out. I smoke more matches than tobacco, but a pipe to me is a wonderful consolation. I can fiddle with it and concentrate on thinking. While I scratched a match and fiddled with my pipe, she sat perfectly still.

I wondered why she had picked me and how she could be so cocksure I was going to take the job, for she seemed assured I was going to. I had an uneasy feeling I was going to get into something over my head.

Abruptly she stood up and turned slowly away from me and walked about the room, turning first one way and then another as she looked at the pictures on the walls, at some of my trinkets lying on a small table, always moving with a sensuous grace that gave me time to study the contours of her body without making the study too obvious.

I decided she was about twenty, old for her years, and a crackpot of the first water. I wanted no part of her and leaned back in my chair to tell her so.

As the chair creaked when I leaned back, she stepped quickly to my desk, leaned forward and braced herself against it with both hands.

"You are wrong on the last thought, Mr. Howard. I am thirty years old and I have lived fifty. I get what I want. I have come to you because of what you are, and of course you are going to help me."

What she had said was so unexpected, I tightened up like a hot drum, and I could feel a flush of sweat break out all over me. She laughed deep in her throat.

"You see, Mr. Howard, I know all about you. Born on a farm, rural education, left home when you were sixteen, worked your way through two good colleges, joined the Navy at the beginning of the war, received a commission in the battle of the South Pacific for valor above and beyond the regular duty, received the Navy Cross and the Purple Heart. When you were sent home, you went to Stanford and got your Master's degree in political science, graduating at the head of your class. You borrowed money from the government on your war record and set up in business for yourself. You have managed seven successful political campaigns without a single loss for any of your clients, which in itself is a small miracle. You are dedicated to your clients and fairly honest. At the moment you are out of debt and have a bank balance of one hundred and twenty-eight dollars. You like money and women, in that order."

She straightened up and turned half away from the desk so I could see the side view of her from her head to the tips of her toes. Tilting her head towards me and giving me a side glance, she said roguishly,

"I've got lots of money, and I'm all woman. Look at me."

I scratched another match and puffed it into my pipe. My hands trembled as I did that simple little chore. Now I really looked at her. She had on a funny little tight fitting hat that didn't begin to cover the mass of shining jet black hair that swept down to the back of her neck and curled up in saucy little ringlets. In place of the pony tail, small waves curled around the sides of her head. One round curl was loose and stuck out above one eye. I wanted to curl it around one finger, and tuck it back where it belonged, under her foolish hat.

Her eyes were blue, blue-black I think, and startling wide apart in her heart shaped face. She had kind of a Bob Hope nose, but on her it looked good. Her mouth was her best feature. Her lips were a bit too large for her small face, but they were in the shape of a cupid's bow and very red, kind of puffed. While I studied her mouth she stuck out the tip of her tongue and moistened her upper lip from the center both ways. I had a fleeting thought that I was looking at a pomegranate that I had just bitten into.

Her dress looked like it was painted on and the nipples of her breasts were round and firm tiny mounds where they stuck out. I could see that she didn't wear a brassiere. I could see the upper halves. Her stomach was flat as a boy's and she had a very small waist, but her legs were extra long for the rest of her and what I could see of them, they were rounded to perfection and the upper part of her thighs were a bit heavy, like a dancer's.

I sure took my time looking her over. She helped me by turning just a bit as my eyes traveled over her and she showed just a tiny bit of a smile when I looked into her eyes.

She queried softly, "You like it?"

I bit down hard on the stem of my pipe and nodded toward the couch across the room.

"Shall we talk about money first, or shall we wait until later?"

She threw back her head and laughed merrily.

"That's my man. Money and women. I'll always know just where you stand."

She caught the leg of the chair with the toe of her shoe and turned it around and sat down facing me again. In an instant she was a different woman. All business, eyes cold as an ice cube and just as unwinking. Again I had an uneasy feeling I was being a sucker. She could turn on sex as easy as pushing a button and turn it off like a light, but she was a sex machine if I ever saw one. I wanted some of it, even if it cost me my neck.

She opened her purse, rummaged around in it, and pulled out a piece of paper. She handed it toward me and said,

"Money first Here is a certified check for ten thousand dollars made payable to you. You will be paid a like amount for the next four years. Forty thousand dollars in all. You will have an unlimited expense account in addition, and you will devote your entire time to my husband's campaigns. When he is nominated for President of the United States, you will receive a bonus of sixty thousand dollars making a total of one hundred thousand dollars, and I want no slip-ups. As I said before, I get what I want. You may continue your efforts for your client, Mr. Finley, until he is elected. After that I will expect you to concentrate all your efforts on my husband's campaign."

She leaned back and smiled like an angel. Just like that. I felt hotter than a seven dollar bill. Ke-Rist. Forty thousand dollars. I could be sure of that, but the bonus was not even a possibility as far as I could see, but forty thousand dollars. I was in the swim and going strong. I'd see her damn husband got his money's worth if I had to kill off his opposition.

I suddenly realized she had done all the talking since she had entered the office. I slid the check under my ashtray, laid my pipe in the tray, and stood up and stretched. I felt good. Even ten thousand dollars is not to be sneezed at. I looked at her with a gleam in my eye, and walked around the desk.

She met me, standing up. I held out my arms and she took a step toward me and laid her mink stole across my arms. She said gently,

"Lay it around my shoulders, will you please? I will call you tomorrow. I am having a small party at my home in a few days and I will expect you to attend. You will meet the rest of the gentlemen you will be working with for the next four years. I am sure it will be a very pleasant and rewarding four years. Goodbye, Mr. Howard."

She fairly floated to the door where she paused for an instant, then came floating back to me. She said very softly,

"You have a very lovely secretary, Mr. Howard, and she is head over heels in love with you. Scandal is the one thing you

must not become involved in. Watch it. Also let the little waitress alone in your favorite restaurant. You have things to attend
to now."

I stood stricken dumb and immobile as she went out of the
office, closing the door behind her.

God damn her. She knew what I was thinking before I knew
it myself. What kind of a bitch had I become involved with?

In a daze, I walked around my desk and sagged into my chair,
trying to sort out the pregnant details of the last hour.

She had carried the ball. She had done all the talking. She
had set the price. She had even paid her money. The check was
already made out in my name. Ten thousand dollars. She had as
good as told me she went with the deal—arms, lips, body, everything. The works. I had been raped. Mentally, if not physically.
I had no doubt in the world that when the right time came along
she would rape me physically and even if I were not so inclined,
she would perform the act just as surely and impersonally as she
had dominated our interview. She was a luscious dish, too. She
was sexy as a woman could be and proud of it. She meant it when
she said, "Look at me." She knew well what she was cradling in
her warm body, the necessary things to make a man, any man, do
what she wished. I was a man she wanted—or rather needed—to
help further her schemes, whatever they were, so she turned on
the sex and I fell for it.

My glance fell on the check tucked under the ashtray. I pulled
it out and looked at it. At least it was the real thing. "Payable to
Christopher Howard. Ten thousand dollars." It was drawn on the
Bankers Trust. A sudden light burst. That was Connely's Bank.
She had promoted Connely into backing her husband. That was
the pratfall in front of the car. A little skin rubbed off her lovely
little ass and she had the biggest politician in the state tied to her
by the checkbook. I'll bet that was a dandy show she put on in his

office while the old bastard looked at her and licked his lips wondering how little he would have to pay and how soon he could get her on a bed stark naked. I laughed out loud at the thought of him paying her ten thousand as a campaign gift when she put on the pressure. How he must have squirmed. And that wasn't all. She must have let him have both barrels to get the promise of another thirty thousand over the next four years, including his help in getting her husband elected Governor and then Senator. What a woman she must be. I began to get excited about her for the first time. Even if Connely did get her in bed with him, there would still be plenty left over for me, and I made up my mind I was going to get mine, you can bet.

My secretary opened the door and leaned casually against the jam. She looked at me and said meaningly,

"Getting yourself lined up in the big time are you, Lover Boy?"

Because those identical thoughts were running through my mind, I turned red in the face, which she was quick to notice.

"Keep your hot little hands in your pockets, boss, and don't let your imagination run away with your better judgment. She's silky and soft to the feel, but she is pure unadulterated poison inside, believe me."

I picked up the check, endorsed it with shaking fingers, stabbed the pen back in the holder and waved the check toward her.

"Take this little memento to the bank and deposit it in my account, will you please?"

She came forward like she was walking on eggs, took the check and looked at it. It was the first time I had ever seen her register surprise, and it was beautiful to see.

Her eyes glowed, then she shut them, opened them, looked at the check again and licked her lips. Her mouth opened and shut as she looked at me wonderingly.

"What do you have to do to earn this? I didn't dream stud service came this high, even in the very best circles."

"Miss Dahl. You are being very facetious. For your information, that is only a small down payment on our very valuable services for the next four years. Mrs. Morley has just hired this firm to lead her husband in the right paths of the political forest to the Governorship of this great state and then on to the Senate of the United States and right on into the White House in Washington. Wipe that silly look off your face and come here."

In a kind of daze she started to obey. I left my chair in one leap and met her, swinging her around and around in a frenzy of excitement. She responded instantly to my mood and when our lips accidentally met, she pressed her luscious form against me and tightened her arms around my neck in a strangle hold, biting and bruising my lips with furious abandonment. I carefully steered us towards the couch and we fell lengthwise on it—arms, legs, and bodies pressed together in a sea of passion. Wild as an animal, I swept her dress upward from her long, slender legs and eagerly caressed the soft moistness of her femininity with my hand.

She slid her hot mouth away from my lips and a long moan of pure ecstasy came from her throat as her trembling body melted under my weight. In a flash she loosened her arms from around my neck and with a quick shove she rolled me off of her and I fell with a crash on the floor between the couch and the wall. I lay there for a long time sobbing, cursing, and moaning in sheer frustration.

I raised up on all fours, doggy-like, and looked at her. She was again leaning against the door jam with the door open and while she was slightly disheveled, she was the picture of pure innocence. She smiled at me and said brightly,

"Why, Mr. Howard. Whatever in the world are you doing behind the couch? Did you lose something?"

I was certainly in no position to answer that so I glared at her as I got to my feet and straightened my clothing. I moved meaningly towards her but she stepped through the door opening and slammed the door after her.

I went wearily to my chair and slumped into it feeling like I had just taken another beating. The intercom on my desk buzzed and her voice came floating out.

"I will go to the bank now, Mr. Howard, and deposit this lovely check. I can see now that I will never be able to afford you."

"Go to—" I shouted into the instrument, but she had already clicked the switch.

To hell with women. Every time I feel the urge, I'm pushed away like a puppy and left panting with my tongue hanging out. Bitches. Every one of them. Besides, I've better things to do. Make money. Lots of it. Money. That will show them.

The telephone rang stridently. I jerked the receiver to my ear.

"Howard speaking."

"Listen, Howard. Remember the monkeys? Lay off the Morley dame. You want no part of her scheme. You can't spend her money in hell. That's where you are going if you try to take her on. Just return her check and tell her you changed your mind. This is the last time we tell you. Lay off."

The phone went dead. I hung on a minute, then softly cradled the receiver. I thought for a second, then broke out in a cold sweat. So, it wasn't her that had me beat up, but someone else that didn't want me to handle her husband's campaign. Now I was committed to her and if I went ahead, I was likely to be a very dead duck. Why?

I wiped the sweat off my face and thought. I should have paddled her pretty backside and sent her home the minute she stepped inside the door. I had the feeling she was trouble but she had overridden my better sense with her damned display of potent sex. Someone was keeping a damned close check on her movements and apparently knew all about her plans to hire me long before she came to see me. It had to be someone close to her or else she was mixed up in something besides politics. I shook my head in misery. I was the patsy. Just a waggly-tailed lamb, bleating in the darkness. God damnit, this was my state. What was there about Bart Morley running for Governor that was worth getting killed for? Why would anyone want to kill me just because I was hired to run his campaign?

My anger and my ego flared up at the same time. I must be quite a fellow at that, if whoever they were thought I might have a Chinaman's chance of getting him elected. Enough of a chance that they threatened to kill me if I went ahead.

That did it. I would get Mr. Bart Morley elected to the Governor's chair if it killed me. Killed me. That was an ugly thought. I thought of the ten thousand dollars and the unlimited expense account. That's it. I'll hire a big tough body guard to live with me day and night, stay out of dark alleys, sleep alone, not trust a single person.

Right away I felt better. The old Howard spirit. Fight boy, fight.

The door opened abruptly and I cringed back like I'd been shot. Scared? Sure I was scared.

Miss Dahl came tripping toward the desk and laid a deposit slip in front of me. She was in exuberant spirits.

"There, Mr. Howard. All in order. Now how about paying me my back salary?"

I mentally shook myself and said,

"Come around here. I've something to tell you."

She dimpled and said breathily,

"No, thank you. I'll just stay on this side of the desk. Once is enough for me, if you don't mind."

I lost my temper. I shouted at her.

"Come around here and sit down. This has nothing to do with your sex appeal. I'm in trouble. Big trouble."

She sobered instantly and said softly,

"Goody."

She came hesitantly around and perched on the edge of the desk like a bird poised for flight. Under other circumstances her attitude would have boosted my ego, but right now I was scared and she was the only one I could trust or confide in.

"Remember I told you I had no idea why I was beat up? Well, now I was just threatened I would be killed if I didn't leave the Morley campaign alone. Some bastard called me on the phone and laid it on the line. Lay off the Morleys, or else.

"The man on the phone told me to take the check back to her and tell her I'd changed my mind. How in hell did he know she had a check for me? I didn't, until she told me. Then he told me I couldn't spend it in hell and that was where I was going unless I laid off the campaign."

The Dahl slipped off the desk in a hurry and I grabbed her skirt and hung on.

"Sit still. I'm not through yet."

She slapped at my hand.

"Oh, yes you are. You are going to take that money right back and throw it in her sexy face. I told you she was poison, but all you could see was her slinky form and smell her. The bitch." She fairly spat the word.

I towed her close to me by her skirt and put my arms around her. She resisted for all of two seconds, then sat down on my lap and started bawling, shaking all over.

I held her tight and let her cry awhile, then wiped her nose with my pocket handkerchief, gave her a fatherly pat on her head and sat her back on the desk.

"We're going to keep the money, and we're going to see Bart Morley elected to the Governorship of this state. No damned hoodlum or passel of hoodlums is going to stop us. You hear?"

"Yes, Mr. Howard. Maybe you, but not we. I've had enough. This is too much for me. I almost get raped, and a few minutes later I am told I will get killed if I keep on with my work. Plenty is enough. Get another female to work for you. I'm going to get another job as a parachute jumper. It will be much safer."

I took a firm grip on her ankles so she couldn't kick me in the face and went on talking.

"You little idiot, I need you. You are smart, honest, beautiful, and I'll double your salary and pay you every payday.

"I won't make any passes at you, I promise, and that's a hell of a promise for me to make, I assure you."

She squirmed around and in the process I couldn't help but see her dress creeping higher and higher. I shut my eyes in order to keep my mind on the business at hand until she decided I was going to hold on to her. She settled down and said matter-of-factly,

"All right. You can unhand me now. I'll listen, and you better make it good."

I opened my eyes and did a double take. The dress was higher than ever, but she was looking at me with such a concentrated look I knew she was testing me to see just how much I had meant. I let go of her ankles and she drew a long sigh of relief and sedately pushed down her dress, tucked it neatly around the calves of her legs and said,

"Now, tell me just what we are to do."

"First we will get a good reliable firm of private investigators to gather facts. I want to know everything about the Morley dame, her husband, where she was born and every single item we can dig up about her from the day she was born to the present Likewise, the same goes for her husband.

"Probably in the process we will find a clue to the pressure being put on us to keep us out of the campaign. In this state, anyone can run for any office he chooses. It's still a free country. This is Connely country and as long as he is going to pay part of the bills, I see no reason why he could be against Morley being Governor. Just the same, we will look into his connections and find out if he has been pressured into backing Morley by the simple method of blackmail. He may have his own ideas who he wants for Governor, and it might not be Morley."

The Dahl sat silent in thought for a moment, then said,

"I believe I have the answer to a private investigator. A friend of mine was in the Armed Services for a long time and right now is on vacation. The name is Captain Downs, and the Captain has a very successful record in the OSS, all kinds of hush-hush investigations and doesn't look in the least like a private investigator. Want me to call the Captain?"

"Sounds good to me, and we will pay a good salary. I can use a good man like that as a body guard."

Her eyes twinkled.

"I'll call the Captain right now."

She slid off the desk with a lithe movement and went into the outer office, closing the door behind her.

This deal called for plenty of thought. I knew nothing about Bart Morley except just what I had read at intervals in the daily paper, but I knew in a general way he was connected to money. Big money. The little sexpot who was his wife was something else.

Not a word had ever been printed about her that I could remember, yet she was so cocksure she would be the next Governor's Lady. I grinned to myself. My God how she would lord it over people if by chance she did occupy the mansion at the State Capitol. It stuck out all over her.

The intercom clicked and Miss Dahl said.

"The Captain will be in to see you in half an hour, Mr. Howard. Not much interested, but is willing to talk it over."

"Thank you. Please come in."

She came in with a wary look at me.

"Miss Dahl, draw a check on the bank for five thousand dollars and buy the full amount in one thousand dollar Government bonds. Five of them. That is going to be our mad money. Draw out another thousand and bring it to me in cash. We will need some expense money until I can set up an expense account with the Morleys. Also write yourself a check for the salary you have coming and add the amount you spent on me while I was at home. I have never thanked you for the time you spent with me and for your wonderful care. I just want you to know I'm grateful beyond words—"

She stopped me.

"Ah, shut up. I loved every minute of it—"

I stopped her, leering at her.

"Every minute of it?"

She blushed beautifully and whispered,

"Yes. Every minute of it," and fled like a startled deer into the outer office, kicking the door shut with her foot.

What a gal. Just looking at her made my senses reel. I had seen all of her, and it was all good. Perfect. But I had a promise to keep, but what the hell, promises are made to be broken under certain circumstances, and sooner or later she would forgive me if I broke my promise. I felt sure I could hold out as long as she could.

The intercom clicked and I heard a soft giggle, then,

"The Captain is here, Mr. Howard."

"Come in."

I looked up as the door opened and caught my breath. Captain? She was about five foot six, long black wavy hair worn shoulder length, round perfect face, dimpled cheeks, blue eyes, full curvey mouth, ripe juicy lips turned up in a half smile—all this topped off a figure that would cause a stampede on any street corner in the world. Captain, hell. No wonder the Dahl had smiled when I said I could use the Captain as a body guard. The Captain had a body I'd love to guard.

Miss Dahl said,

"Mr. Howard, Captain Amy Downs. And don't get any ideas. Captain Downs has been a judo instructor for the last five years."

I turned on all my charm and walked around the desk.

"This is indeed a surprise, Captain. My secretary is full of surprises for me, but I believe this is the prize one."

The Captain smiled and I felt myself turn to jelly.

"Darleen has talked about you for a long time, Mr. Howard, so I feel I know you quite well. We grew up together and went to the same schools, so I also know her quite well."

"You have the advantage of me there, Captain. I thought I was beginning to know her a bit myself, but I see I was oh so wrong.

Please sit down."

Miss Dahl smiled like an angel.

"I will go to the bank now, Mr. Howard, and leave you two to get acquainted. Amy is my dearest friend and I would trust her with my life." She gave me a steady look and added,

"Which is exactly what I'm doing."

As she went out the door she turned, and over the Captain's shoulder she raised her hands shoulder high, closed her fists and gave them a quick twisting motion like she was wringing out a wet towel. I got the point. I could easily get my neck twisted, from one or the other of them.

Seated securely behind my desk, I looked at Captain Downs. This was something else. I wanted a big tough man, and here was a beautiful helpless-looking woman. The more I looked at her the more I realized I would need a body guard to keep me away from her. One luscious female in my office was already too much for me and with two, I would be lost for sure.

My thoughts must have shown on my face because the Captain said,

"Don't worry about me, Mr. Howard. I have been around men all my adult life and I am still unmarried. I have been devoted to my work with no time for romance. Now I am on vacation and Darleen asked me to come in and talk to you. Just what sort of problems do you have?"

"Just what exactly has Miss Dahl told you?"

She smiled.

"Nothing whatsoever about your business. But she has talked a great deal about you personally, with a dreamy look in her eyes. I have been planning to meet you accidentally so I could make up my mind about you myself. I don't want her hurt and would go to any lengths to see that it would not happen. She is a very dear child and I love her. Just what kind of a business do you operate?"

"Do you mean to say she hasn't even told you what?"

"She has never told me what you do. In some ways she is very secretive for which I admire her. What is your business?"

"Captain Downs, I am a specialized public relations man. I handle only political figures, and for a good sum of money I try to get them elected to public office. The office of their choice. Right now I am promoting a Mr. Finley for the office of State Representative, and have just taken on a client for the office of Governor of the state. That client also expects to be elected to that office and the next election year he is going to run for Senator—and get elected of course. He also has dreams of being nominated for the Presidency of the United States. That is the contract I have just taken on."

Captain Downs leaned forward.

"You are really in the big time, Mr. Howard. No wonder Darleen is so excited about working with you. Just how do you accomplish these things?"

"In a way, it is very simple. I have friends and co-workers in nearly every precinct in the state and we have built up a very close organization. We are neither Republicans nor Democrats, but purely promotion experts and work for the candidate who is willing to pay the way. So far, we have handled seven public figures and have won every election."

The Captain gave me a look of admiration.

"I never realized political campaigns were handled that way. Is there no chance of you ever losing?"

"Yes. At best it's always a gamble. The wrong man, a public scandal that makes the papers just before election, a general trend of public thinking across the nation when the voters just want to vote those out who are in, and many things beyond our control. Of course, we choose our clients and try not to get suckered into a bad deal."

"It certainly sounds interesting. Just why do you use private investigators?"

"Frankly, I never have before. But in this case, I know nothing about my client except what I have read in the papers. His wife came in here with a check for ten thousand dollars, laid it on the desk, and went right ahead on the assumption that I was her boy. Before she came in, I was cornered near my home and beaten half to death by some thugs and warned to leave the deal alone. That was even before I knew I was being considered for the job. Immediately after I cashed her check, I had a phone call warning me to return her money and forget the whole thing or I would be roasting in Hell with no chance to enjoy the money.

"Somewhere in the background of my client, there is some reason why certain interests don't want him to run for Governor. They figure with my organization behind him, he has a mighty good chance of getting elected and upsetting a basket of prize apples.

"I hate getting beat up. I like money and I love my work. If I get killed in the process, I'm going to leave behind me some mementos of my own. I was wounded six times in the war and I don't die easily. I'm just plain mad as well as scared."

Captain Downs looked grave.

"May I presume and ask what your rank was in the Armed Forces?"

"Certainly. I was a Commander in the Navy at the end of the war. I came up from the enlisted personnel."

"My, an impressive record. I've been in the Intelligence section of the Army for ten years and promotions don't come easily—Darleen has been holding out on me. I have taken an indefinite leave of absence from the Army, and I'm becoming restless already.

"Just exactly what would you require of a private investigator?"

"To tell you the truth, I have no definite plans beyond learning everything about my client and his wife from the day they were born up to now. I even want to know what they eat three times a day, who are their close friends, what they do in their spare time, all about their sex habits, just how faithful they are to each other, children if any, state of his health, education and all affiliations with clubs, lodges, and any other facts that seem pertinent."

She smiled.

"In my kind of work, that is routine. May I ask who your client is?"

I studied her.

"Are you interested in working with me or just curious?"

She answered promptly.

"Your getting beat up for no apparent reason, then being threatened for a routine job of promotion adds up I think to dirty politics. It's going on all over the country. I've had a small hand in similar cases where the offenders were put out of circulation for a long time. Yes, I'm interested. Now, who is your client?"

"Mr. Bart Morley, only son of one of our most prominent families."

She fairly jumped, "Colonel Bart Morley?!"

"You know him?" I asked, puzzled by her ruffled response.

Then in complete control of herself she stated, "He was one of the most decorated war heroes of the entire European Theater."

"I didn't know he was a hero, I never met the man. I know nothing about him. His wife is just a plain little sexy bitch in anybody's language. She came in here, waved her sex appeal all over me until I was stupid, told me her husband would be the next Governor, then Senator, and then he would be nominated for the Presidency.

"She laid down ten thousand dollars in a certified check made out to me, promised she went with the deal personally and as often as I felt the urge, and walked out. Miss Dahl said I was a fool and said the Morleys were plain poison.

"Now you know. I love money and women. The Morley dame told me she had all the money I could use and she was all woman. And she gave me plenty of opportunity to examine her closely. Believe me, she is all woman."

The Captain laid back her head and her laughter rang like bells. She presently sobered up and said cuttingly,

"I see you don't always pick your clients. It seems in this case you were picked, and I do mean picked."

"Captain. The ten thousand was only the down payment. I mean in money. There is to be thirty thousand more, and an unlimited expense account which could run to a quarter million more. Think about that for a moment."

I said it smugly and watched for her reaction. It came promptly. Very satisfactory, too.

Her eyes fairly popped and her mouth opened and stayed that way. She had beautiful teeth and her red, red tongue just moved slowly back and forth across her lower lip. Now it was my turn to laugh and I made the most of it. All the tension went out of me as I laughed like I was half nuts. I went around the desk, knelt beside her and picked up her purse and gloves which she had dropped and I laid them back in her lap. She looked down at me and murmured a soft,

"Thank you."

"Well, very cozy indeed. I see you two got acquainted in record time."

We both jumped, startled, and I lost my balance and sprawled on the floor. Miss Dahl was standing by the open door, her face ablaze. If looks alone could have burned me at the stake, I'd have been fried to a crisp.

The Captain said gently,

"He just handed me my purse and gloves which I had dropped. Nothing more."

Darleen glanced at me and said to her,

"I'm quite sure you are right. But he was up to his sneaky tricks. Take my advice and keep your skirts fastened down with safety pins whenever he gets that close to you, or better still, don't let him get that close again. He has the idea he is the only thing in life a woman could possibly want, any woman, as long as she is female and can walk under her own power. He's a real stinker and, oh, hell—"

She ran out of the office and we could hear her heels beat a tattoo down the corridor.

I jumped to my feet to follow her, but the Captain held out her hand.

"No, let her settle down by herself. I've known her a long time. I had no idea she felt that way about you."

I said angrily,

"What way? I'm just her boss and I need her. She can't fly off like that. I've got work for her to do. Besides, she has six thousand dollars of my money and I want it."

The Captain looked at me in amazement.

"Do you mean to stand there and tell me you don't know she is crazy in love with you?"

CHAPTER FIVE

"What do you mean? In love with me? That's impossible. Sure I've loved her up a couple of times but she made sure it went no further than some kisses. But I sure tried. She wants some decent fellow with a wedding ring and a houseful of dirty diapers, and believe me, that is not for Howard."

Downs looked at me steadily for a moment.

"Thank you. Now to business. I can tell you, without any research, all you wish to know about Colonel Morley.

"He is a fine man, honest—there isn't a crooked bone in his body—very, very rich, proud, and above all the kind of a man his officers and enlisted men loved. You can be sure if he is going to be Governor of this state, he will be the very best Governor the state ever had.

"His wife, I know nothing about. We can find out about her easily."

"Miss Downs, you amaze me. You look so very feminine but I can well imagine you are anything but that. Ten years in Army Intelligence has been a rough school, and I can say from the bottom of my heart I'm happy to have you aboard.

"If Bart Morley wants to be President, we'll make it possible."

Her lovely face glowed as she smiled and I noticed the dimples in both cheeks winked happily, then I noticed her eyes.

Dark blue, cold as a chunk of ice, and just looking into them made my temperature drop way below normal. This was one gal

I wasn't going to sneak a quick feel around or play peeping games with when she wasn't looking. Not this boy.

"As I told you, I will have an unlimited expense account and out of that will come your salary. How much?"

"Mr. Howard, I will leave the salary up to you. You can pay any expenses I incur. But for Colonel Morley, it will be a labor of love."

"Good. How about twenty dollars a day when you work and all expenses. We will even pay for your living quarters and I will have an office desk set up in here for you. Or you can work on an hourly basis, as I realize you may work at odd times. If you need other operatives to help you, go ahead and use your own judgment. All I require is complete reports, and I want a line on the opposition to his candidacy as soon as possible. I don't want to get killed before I know who is doing it to me."

She raised out of the chair, tucked her purse under her arm and said smartly,

"Yes, Sir, Commander. I will get right at it. I'll have a report ready for you by tomorrow morning."

We looked straight at each other for a second and both of us burst out laughing. I said quickly,

"You're a grand girl, Captain."

She answered just as quick.

"So are you, Mr. Howard."

Then she realized what she had just said and she had the grace to blush. On her it looked darned good.

She went quickly out the door and I swear I never saw a person look less like a private investigator.

The intercom came to life.

"Mr. Howard?"

"Yes?"

"I have the bonds here."

"Good, come in."

She came in, fairly flying across the floor and laid two large envelopes on the desk.

She said in a kind of hushed voice,

"I never had a thousand dollars in cash in my hands before. Isn't it lovely?"

I ignored the envelopes and looked straight at her. She turned red from the neck up and blurted,

"I'm sorry I rushed out a while ago, but I suddenly remembered I hadn't had any lunch, so I thought it would be all right if I ate lunch while you and Amy were talking business. I brought you a sandwich and some coffee. Would you like it now?"

Once again my ego was deflated, like a ruptured balloon.

"Yes, and thank you."

She hurried into the outer office and returned in a moment with two man-sized sandwiches and a steaming carton of coffee. I bit into one of the sandwiches and opened the larger envelope with my free hand.

The bonds were in order, payable to bearer, with spaces left blank to be filled in by the owner. I signed four of them with a flourish and handed the fifth one to Darleen.

"Sign your name on this one, Miss Dahl, and then go and tuck it away in your old teapot or wherever you keep your valuables. That is your bonus for the first year's work with the Howard firm and it will give you a little nest egg in case the firm is suddenly put out of business. The other four, please take to the bank, rent a deposit box in my name and file them inside it. That will be my down payment on my uncertain future. Here is two hundred and fifty dollars. Give it to Captain Downs and do not get a receipt. I don't want any record of expenditures where her work is concerned, at some later date it might be embarrassing for some eagle-eyed politician to learn there was a staff of private investigators connected with us.

"Her salary will be twenty dollars a day when she works and she will keep her own time and hours. List her on the record as a stenographer and pay her regularly. As soon as the Morley expense account is set up, we will make a proper accounting of all expenditures to the Morleys.

"Captain Downs says she has known Bart Morley, either personally or by reputation, for many years and she thinks he is God's gift to the American political scene. She says we will certainly have no trouble, either with him or his spotless reputation. She heartily endorses him, which is a lucky thing for us. Our trouble will come from his opposition, which is apparently strong and vindictive. Why? We don't know, but we will find out. That will be Captain Downs' work. Order a desk from some firm and have it set up where the couch is. Have the couch taken away and put in storage. I'm afraid I will have no further use for it, and the temptation to use it will be removed.

"If the Captain wants a telephone, have one put in on a private wire with an unlisted number. I imagine she will want privacy in her conversations. All clear?"

"Yes, Mr. Howard, except for one thing. I couldn't possibly accept this bond."

"You little idiot. Keep it. There will be more like it for you in the next four years if I make it that long, and if I don't, I won't need them anyway."

She looked at me long and solemnly, closed her lovely eyes and big round tears trickled down her cheeks from under the tightly closed lids. She straightened up like a sleep-walker and came around the desk feeling her way and literally fell into my lap. Her arms crept around my neck as her moist lips searched for mine. Surrender was in every fiber of her body which trembled and pressed hard against me. I held her close and whispered softly against her mouth.

"The couch is still here."

She murmured softly,

"Yes. Yes. Now, carry me."

I picked her up, carried her to the outer office and dumped her unceremoniously into her chair. She screamed,

"I hate you. God, how I hate you." I stepped back,

"No, you don't. Right at the moment you've got hot pants and in five minutes you'd be sorry. Let it go."

She looked at me furiously for a second and then her face softened.

"Oh, Chris. How could you do this to me?"

I grinned wryly.

"Tain't easy. You can bet. It's going to take ten women and a week for me to get over it, but I'll do it."

She looked at me from under lowered eyelashes and said smugly,

"You never will get over it. I know now." She added, "I'll wait."

I know when I'm licked so I beat it out the front door and headed for the nearest bar. Behind me, I could hear her ringing laughter follow me down the corridor.

I walked purposely down the street and turned into the Pony Bar, thinking what a damn fool I had been to leave her when she was ripe and ready after all the time I had spent building her up to that point, but I well knew it was no good. I'm just not the marrying kind.

I paused a second inside the door of the bar to get my eyes accustomed to the light and looked around.

The first person I saw was Captain Downs sitting at a table with a man. His back was toward me and I saw her give me a quick eye and a tiny shake of her head, so I headed for the bar and ordered a double Scotch and Soda.

I watched her in the mirror and presently she got up and went out on the street without a single glance at me.

I finished my drink and decided the thing for me to do was go home, have a hot bath, end it with a cold shower and go to bed. I felt wrung out, even if it was still daytime.

I went out the door. Some sixth sense made me hesitate, pull my pipe out of my pocket, fill, and light it. During that time I noticed two men staring into the window of a ladies' dress specialty shop. That struck me as odd. I moved carefully toward home and past them. They never even glanced up so I walked on, but I hadn't walked a block before I saw they were slowly walking my way. Rank amateurs as far as shadowing was concerned, or else they wanted me to know they were there.

On the next corner the policeman on the beat was slowly walking along so I fell into step beside him. He was an old friend.

"How's the wife, Joe?"

He glanced at me.

"Hello, Chris. Just fine. We're going on vacation next week and she is spending all her time getting ready. The junk she is going to take will require a truck. What in hell a woman wants to take so much stuff along for two weeks beats me."

I laughed.

"As long as she takes you, let her be happy."

He grinned.

"All she is letting me take is one fishing pole, says we can buy more fish than I'll catch."

As I turned into my place, he hesitated and said,

"Just got the word to stay in this neighborhood and look out for suspicious characters. You seen any?"

I looked back down the street. It was empty.

"Nope, but stick around. They might show up at any time."

He laughed,

"Keep your pants buttoned. S-long."

I went upstairs to my apartment thinking what he had just said, "got the word," and then suddenly I remembered the man with whom Captain Downs had been sitting. He was an Inspector of Police in our fair city and an old time army man. That gal sure got around. Apparently now I was under the protection of the Police Department, thanks to her.

I went inside. It was cool, quiet and very peaceful. I stripped off my clothing, had a shower and went to bed. I thought of female beauties for all of one minute and dropped off to sleep.

When I woke the sun was pouring in the windows. I took a quick look at the clock by my bed. It was nearly ten o'clock and I had slept sixteen hours. Holy Mackerel. I must have been half dead. In ten minutes flat I showered, shaved and dressed, then made it to the office on the run.

Miss Dahl greeted me sarcastically,

"Good evening Mr. Howard. Now that you are in the big money I suppose you do not feel the need to work any longer?"

I gave her my number one smile.

"I did sleep a little late this morning, but if you will recall, I had a hard day yesterday."

She gave me a very nasty look,

"Was she a very entertaining bed partner?"

I said loftily,

"The best. The very best." I went on in to my office with a glow of satisfaction just seeing the wave of fury which swept over her lovely puss. I was my own man again.

There had been some changes made in the office arrangement. The couch was gone and in its place stood a very efficient desk with a padded chair pushed up to its gleaming side.

I looked at the chair. Padded yet. Can you imagine? I'd never owned a padded chair so I tried it on for size and decided to have one just like it. The desk was complete with typewriter, reams of paper, carbons and a vase of fresh flowers. I thought sadly what a pretty penny all it was costing me besides the twenty dollar a day girl who was going to occupy it. I had to get the Morley expense account set up pronto or I would be a quick candidate for the unemployment line.

The intercom buzzed,

"Mr. Howard. The Captain waited two hours for you, then went out. She left a report on my desk. Do you wish to see it now?"

"Please, bring it in."

She stopped just inside the door,

"Is everything satisfactory?" She indicated the new furniture with a wave of her hand.

"Yes. Only I'm going to take the new chair and give her my old one."

Her face flushed and she bit her lower lip then said angrily,

"You wouldn't dare."

"You may order another one just like it for her and one for yourself. I want you to protect a very tender part of your anatomy for future use." She spit out her words like a cat,

"You are the most impossible man I ever knew. You don't have a shred of decency in your whole body."

Then she barely whispered with stars in her eyes,

"But there are times when you are wonderful."

I chuckled.

"Now that you are happy again. May I see the report?"

There were four pages of typewritten words, with the cryptic heading,

Prem. Report.

Subject.————— Female.

Age, thirty last birthday. No living parents. No known living relatives.

Born in Tula, Florida. Town population, 110.

Father, fisherman. Mother, housewife.

Mother deserted family when child was two years of age.

Child raised by father to age of seven. Father lost at sea. Family always extremely poor.

Child taken into foster home, comprising of man, woman and three boys. Boys ages, nine, twelve and fourteen respectively.

Subject lived with this family until she was twelve years of age.

Very little education to this point when suddenly the subject became interested in education. Attended local school.

Teachers report abnormal attention to studies. Reports disclose inner compulsion for education. No known reason.

Subject finished eighth grade at head of class. Disappeared from Tula, immediately following end of school term. No known reason.

Next activities of subject picked up in New York City two years later.

Resident of fashionable girls school. Tuition being paid by wealthy Uncle. Dresses expensively. Participates in all sports. Above average in studies. Subject at this age of sixteen is well developed physically, poised, confident.

Secretive. Has no close friends. Spends week ends at Uncle's place on Long Island.

(Making check on Uncle)

Suddenly left girls school in mid-term of second year to enter theatrical boarding school. Apparently stage struck.

Same pattern follows. Excellent student. Hard worker. Visits Uncle every week-end.

Small parts in summer stock, good future in sight. Again disappears without reason for two years.

Next activities picked up in same city.

Subject is consort of well known racketeer, Tony Athens.

Has lush apartment, high priced cars, personal maid. Cash money to spend. No bank accounts.

Minks, sables, charge accounts at the best shops.

Secretive. No friends.

Tony Athens killed in gang war. Subject resumes visits to Uncle on Long Island week-ends.

Again starts to work in theatres. No headway. Starts dancing in club spots. Fair. No great success.

Suddenly marries Colonel Bart Morley. (Damn her)

This is all I could do on short notice. Still checking.
            "Downs."

Ke-rist. I'd sure hate to have her checking into my past if she could do this in one day.

I read the report through again and was struck with the one fact that stuck out like a sore thumb. The wealthy uncle who had given no thought to her until she was a grown girl, then suddenly he was trying to make her a lady and apparently succeeding. Witness the fact that she had married Bart Morley.

Think of her, I knew she was no lady or else she had outgrown it.

The telephone rang. I lifted the receiver,

"Howard speaking."

Dulcet tones wafted out,

"This is Jen Morley, Mr. Howard. Good morning."

"Good morning Mrs. Morley. Nice of you to call."

"Thank you. We are having a small gathering at our home tonight. I will look for you about eight. Good-bye-e-e-e."

The line went dead and I slammed down the receiver,

"Bitch."

Ordering me to wait on her like one of her lackeys. Me, Howard. I reached for the phone to tell her to kiss my—then thought better of it. I knew damn well that from now on I'd jump like a bull frog everytime she said jump. I'd hate it, but I'd jump.

I was hot clear through, but at the same time I was anxious to meet her and her husband on their own grounds. Maybe I could get her in a corner before the night was out.

CHAPTER SIX

I clicked the intercom.

"Yes, Mr. Howard."

"Will you see if you can get in touch with Captain Downs and have her come into the office if possible?"

"Yes. I can find her."

I needed some information quick. I didn't relish the thought of going to the Morley mansion alone. I'll gladly take on any man my size and weight anytime, anywhere, but I want to be able to see the bastard I take on and not be cornered in the dark by two or three.

I gave a thought to what I would wear to the party and decided to go all out and wear a tuxedo. Might as well go whole hog and put up a big front. Besides I always thought I was kind of handsome in a rugged sort of way in a tuxedo. Might make my chances better with the Morley dame. I sure needed a woman. My libido was boiling over.

I made some phone calls to my friends in the city precincts regarding the Honorable Finley. All the reports were to the good. Barring an accident, Mr. Finley was a shoe-in, come election time and I would still have a perfect record of getting my man elected.

I leaned back and thought for two solid hours about the coming Morley campaign. This was going to be a tough one.

He had no previous record of public office and was practically unknown to the voters of the state, yet he was heading for the top office the voters could bestow on him. The challenge was enormous. That was right up my alley. If I could help him win I would be set for life.

Captain Downs came in with a rush. She also made the blood rush to my head. She was a doll. I don't see why in hell I can't look at a pretty woman objectively. Every time I see a good looking woman, right away I imagine how they would act in bed. I must be some sort of a monster.

My flush must have been quite obvious because she said with a twinkle,

"You should be arrested for what you are thinking, Mr. Howard. However this time I will take it as a compliment."

I was quite willing to concede the point.

"You are very lovely, Captain. How you can be so efficient I don't understand. Your report amazes me. How did you dig up so much information in such a short time?"

"Such reports are routine in my work. I know a lot of people in the right places and a phone call here and there usually brings quick results. There were some things about the lady I did not put on the report. They would not look well written down in black and white. How Bart Morley ever married a woman such as her is beyond my understanding. He is such a fine man. So clean and good."

I laughed,

"No doubt the lady had hidden talents not apparent to the eye."

She said vindictively,

"None of her main talents have been hidden for a long time. In plain language, she is a whore of the first water."

I was amused at her fierceness.

"It looks like she has been able to keep her head above the water for a long time and now she is headed for the Governor's mansion and will be the first lady in the state."

"God forbid. Colonel Morley loves her and the poor man has no idea what she has been. I checked very closely on their personal relationship and I find he is convinced she is the most perfect woman alive. They have no children simply because she has had so many abortions she is unable to conceive."

My mouth dropped open.

"My God. How do you know?"

"That was one of the things I didn't put in the report. The first one was just after she left Tula, Florida, when she disappeared the first time. She was just fourteen at the time.

"The second one was just after she left the girls school in New York. She had a bad time over that one and was hospitalized for a week. I have a copy of the records coming in the mail. We will get it probably tomorrow. She had another one after that and nearly died."

I shook my head in bewilderment.

"You realize, Captain Downs, if any of this gets out your Colonel Morley is a dead duck as far as politics is concerned. It would probably break his heart as well."

"Yes, I know that. There are other things that are even worse. I decided to find out everything possible and then we will be in position to combat them. The Army teaches you to find your enemy's strong points and his weaknesses, then hit him with everything at your disposal."

"May I ask Captain, if there is anything to the lady's good?"

"Yes. First, she is married to Bart Morley which should be enough for any woman. She has had fools luck in being able to keep out of the newspapers in spite of her bizarre activities.

"For instance. When her gangster friend was killed on the street, she was at a church social surrounded by hundreds of fine people. How she came to be there is one of the mysteries of all time. She was not even questioned by the police so she slid out of that one, pure as a lily.

"When she was attending the theatrical school she never made dates with anyone. A strict loner. In her dancing career, (which was a short one) she never mixed with any of the other performers. Once again she kept to herself and that was no doubt the reason for her not being much of a success. Where she and Bart met, I don't know. Why he married her, I suppose only he knows. She couldn't have told him she was pregnant. She couldn't get that way. Since they have been married she has been to all intents and purposes devoted to him and is determined for some obscure reason of her own to see him become a national figure in politics. He admits freely he has never had any idea of becoming a big shot politician until the last couple of years. He says and I quote, 'I just want to make my lovely wife happy.'

"The answer to her driving ambition lies somewhere in her devious past. She has been heard to say on several occasions,

" 'My husband will be the biggest man in the country and then we'll show them.' Unquote. Just who she wants to show is pure conjecture."

"Thank you, Captain. We will do our best to keep her out of the limelight in the future and map out a campaign for the Colonel based on his personal integrity and honesty.

"We will try to represent his wife as a loving homebody not interested in publicity. If she won't maintain that role we will fall flat on our collective faces with a thud that will be heard around the state. Continue to dig up everything possible on her. We can use the stuff as a lever to keep her in her place, which is out of sight and sound."

"One other thing. This uncle of hers. Any ideas?"

The Captain snorted expressively,

"Uncle. My sainted aunt. She never had an uncle, least of all a rich one and on that I'll bet my life. I think when the report on that gentleman comes in we can go to work. Remember she was pregnant at fourteen and even in the best circles a man can go to the booby hatch for life for a misdeed like that. I suspect she was smart enough to capitalize on that event and set herself up for life because at that tender age she was no shrinking violet. It is not beyond the realm of possibility the same man was responsible for the second event, or at least was made to assume the responsibility and as she was still only sixteen she may have engineered the event with malice aforethought. If so, it has kept her in luxury all these years and now she feels she can turn around and spit in his eyes."

"Captain you make me realize how really ignorant I am of the facts of life."

She laughed merrily,

"You are just young. There are millions of good women who would be delighted to take you in hand and give you a delightful and liberal education along those lines."

I stared at her boldly,

"Any idea where I might find one in the near future?"

She didn't hesitate,

"Under the proper circumstances and in the right place you just might find one who was willing to make a tentative attempt at furthering your education. I only hope that her efforts might prove satisfactory enough to keep your lecherous mind from dwelling on Darleen. She is very dear to me."

My ego gave an exuberant leap. She wasn't as unattainable as I had imagined,

I said happily,

"I hope she shows up soon. A monastic life is not for me and circumstances have forced me for far too long to lead just that sort of life. I can't remember when I've—"

Her ringing laughter stopped me,

"Spare me the details, Mr. Howard, and hope for the best."

"May the time fly until she shows up. I have almost reached the breaking point and that could be dangerous to my well being. I don't think I could stand another session lying in bed for weeks with Darleen as my nurse. She is very efficient, but also very distracting."

She laughed very softly and looked at me with a roguish look. "Be patient. You may find her at any time."

I pressed my luck.

"Could it be tonight, you think?"

"You might find her tonight, and again you might not. As you say, you have been waiting a long time, and a few weeks one way or another wouldn't make any difference, would it?"

"Few weeks. In a few weeks I'll be too old to care one way or another. But I'll not give up hope for a day or so."

"You have a one track mind, Mr. Howard. Now what did you want to see me about?"

I dragged my mind back to reality, or rather I put her out of my mind temporarily.

"Mrs. Morley called this morning to tell me to come to a party at their home tonight at eight. Mind I said told me. She didn't even have the tact to invite me. Just come. I am a bit wary of being alone after dark for the moment and wondered if you would be kind enough to accompany me. After all I did tell Darleen I wanted to hire a bodyguard."

"Mr. Howard, I have always made it a policy never to appear at social functions with any man who I was associated with in business. However, I know about the party and I will take steps to get invited."

She smiled at my questioning look.

"Remember I have known Colonel Morley for a long time."

I needled her.

"Just how well have you known Colonel Morley?"

She said with emphasis,

"Let us say we are old friends. Nothing more."

I answered abashed,

"Excuse me. I'm naturally interested, as you can imagine."

Now it was her turn,

"All men are not like you, Mr. Howard. Some are gentlemen."

"I stand corrected, Captain."

She thought a moment, then continued,

"At seven forty-five tonight, get in your car and drive at a moderate speed to the Morley residence. Do not make any side trips or make any stops, just drive straight there and go inside immediately. At some time through the evening we will no doubt be introduced. Act natural and if you are so inclined, you might act delighted to meet me.

"You might even try to be a little on the make towards me later. We might cause some attention to be focused on me and in that manner draw the men who are opposed to you out into the open."

I asked seriously,

"Wouldn't that be dangerous to you?"

"I'm used to such situations. The main thing right now is to play for time until we find out why you were warned away from the Morley campaign. If they decide you might become interested in me, they may hope to get at you by threatening me, also. Then we will get them."

I raised out of my chair and walked around to her. She merely looked at me, puzzled.

"How anyone can look so beautiful and helpless and still be so damned matter-of-fact and efficient is beyond my comprehension."

I tried to take her hand but she brushed me off.

"I am neither beautiful nor helpless. I'm tough and mean. I've had to be, to survive. I could put you down for the count before you knew it was coming, as easily as a child plucks a flower and with as little effort. I've had years of training." She smiled at me in a sweet sort of way and stood up facing me, took a quick step which brought her close against me, and with one arm around my neck she kissed my lips in the most scorching kiss it had ever been my pleasure to receive. I could feel it clear down to my feet. She stepped away before I could make the slightest effort to hold her and said, from the vicinity of the door,

"Be on the lookout for that teacher, Mr. Howard. You never know just when you will meet her." With that, she was gone, leaving me feeling foolish and bewildered.

I shook the gremlins out of my mind and decided it was time for me to get some food. Perhaps that was the reason I felt like a wet rag. I was hungry, empty, except a part of my anatomy and that was full to overflowing, and that kiss had helped to build up the pressure still more. My groin ached.

On the way out I stopped beside Miss Dahl,

"I am going home now. You may close the office and take the rest of the day off."

She said sweetly,

"Thank you. Is the Captain working out satisfactory?"

"Yes. Yes, indeed. She is very efficient. Thank you for asking her to come in. She is exciting to work with."

She half smiled.

"Exciting is she. I think it is only fair to warn you I have heard her tell how she nearly tore a man's arms off when he thought she was exciting. I'd hate to think of you without any arms."

"Good night, Miss Dahl. Be sweet and have only sweet thoughts."

After a good meal, I went home, lay down and slept for a couple of hours. I awoke refreshed, shaved again, showered, and dressed in my very smart tuxedo, admired my very good looks in the door mirror, and was ready to beard the lion in his, or rather, her den. It was exactly seven forty-five when I walked out the door of my apartment. I stood for a moment at the top of the stairway and looked carefully around the garden. Beautiful. One of the night patrol officers was leisurely walking past the house. I went to my car, unlocked the door and slid behind the wheel. At the first touch of the starter button the old crate purred to life. The officer gave me a wave of his hand and I drove down the street. At the first stop light the light was red and I stopped. When the light turned, I eased ahead. Out of the corner of my eye, I saw headlights appear with blinding suddenness at my left. I floored the throttle and for once the old Plymouth responded. She dug rubber and took off, but the rush of wind behind her made her sway like a drunken sailor on leave. The car missed me by a whisper and kept right on going. Another car behind me made a turn after it and that was the last I saw of either one of them in the rear view mirror.

I caught my breath and drove on. The bastards. I prayed fervently one of them would come within hand's reach. Suddenly, I had another moment of panic. Another car was practically riding my rear bumper. I slammed on the brakes, and jumped out of the door on my side, prepared to jerk the driver of the car out in the street and beat his brains out. I caught a quick glimpse of the passenger in the front seat, frantically waving me on.

I was sure I could see a dimple so I got back in my car and drove to the Morley house without further incident.

The Morley grounds and house were lit up like a power plant. A couple of acres of beautiful lawns and shrubbery clipped and pruned like a new hair cut surrounded a two-story house that must have contained a dozen bedrooms on the second floor alone. Hidden lights reflected the beauty of the old-fashioned architecture, and I was reminded of the old Currier and Ives prints I used to see when I was a kid.

It was a beautiful home. It would look well in pictures, showing where the candidate for governor was raised and lived. It looked substantial and would give a feeling of security to everyone who looked at the pictures. I stood by my car for a moment, drinking in the beauty of the scene. I felt better about the campaign than I had at any time since I had become involved in it. Another car came up beside mine and parked. I heard a rough voice say softly,

"Go on in. Don't just stand there."

I walked to the open door. An elderly gentleman dressed like the pictures of butlers met me with a hard look.

"Your name, Sir?"

"Christopher Howard."

"Welcome, Mr. Howard. Go straight ahead to the drawing room. You will find Mr. Morley there."

I went down, or rather along, a long hallway from which high arched doorways opened into several large rooms which were all lit. They were apparently empty of people, but all were beautiful beyond description. I won't make any effort to describe the majestic and old-fashioned beauty of the house right now.

Suffice to say, it resembled houses used in motion pictures and topped them all. My acquaintance with such houses lay only in my imagination, and that was beggared by the beauty of this one.

The drawing room was about the size of a public ballroom, and there were so many people there it was crowded. Small gathering. I'd love to see one of her real large ones. The beautiful liar. Think of the devil and she appeared at my elbow like a floating moonbeam, and she had just about that much on. If she had worn less, she would have been overdressed. I could see over, under, around, and through it, and it was all good to look at. I knew I was going to enjoy my work and a minute later, I was absolutely certain of it.

Her greeting was a pleasure to listen to.

"Why, good evening, Mr. Howard. How kind of you to accept our invitation to our home."

She took my hand and turned, pressing it for a whisper against her pouting breast, covering the gesture with her turning body. She then looked me full in the face and chuckled deep in her throat.

"I would like you to meet my husband, the next Governor of the state."

She released my hand and I held it out to one of the handsomest men I had ever seen—above six feet tall, wavy slightly greying hair, rugged, chiseled face, broad shoulders, trim waist, slim hips, and straight as a pine tree.

"Welcome to our circle, Mr. Howard. It is kind of you to come to our home. My wife," (his look at her was eloquent of his adoration) "tells me you have been interested in managing my political aspirations."

"This is indeed a pleasure, Mr. Morley. Usually I take plenty of time to get acquainted with the clients I work with, but in this case, the time would have been wasted. I can only say, I sincerely hope you will not be disappointed in my efforts."

He laughed good naturedly.

"Oh, we spent considerable time and money in studying your background before you were approached by my wife. We feel you are the man for the job. Now that I have met you, I feel good about the whole thing, and Jen is certain you are the man. I trust her judgment, as well as my own."

She said contentedly, but with firmness,

"Now that you two handsome brutes have both finished with your mutual admiration compliments, no more business tonight.

"This is a night to play, and enjoy yourselves. After the campaign gets under way, I'm afraid I won't be able to see either of you. This is an order. Both of you stay close beside me tonight and make the evening one I will long remember."

CHAPTER SEVEN

He said softly,

"Nothing I would like better, sweetheart, but you know we have other guests. Excuse me, please. I see an old friend has just arrived," and he turned towards the entrance door.

Jennifer squeezed my arm, whispered close to my ear,

"Good. Now you are all mine. Be damn sure you stay that way."

I leered at her,

"After a man like your husband, wouldn't it be like drinking branch water instead of champagne?"

She said fiercely,

"There are times when I think I will die unless I can get a drink of branch water. Champagne is too strong for a steady diet. I love to wallow in branch water. I love to bathe my whole hot body in cool branch water, soak it up."

Her meaning was clear in every word she uttered, and the pictures it conjured up in my mind nearly drove me nuts.

"I know where there is a stream that runs clear and deep. Deep enough to drown yourself in—"

She interrupted me.

"I know. I'll be in it, bathing in the nude at the very first opportunity. Now allow me to introduce you to our friends and some of the men who will work with you in the next four years. My husband is going to be the biggest man in the country, and then we'll show them."

The danger bell rang long and loud in my mind.

She had said, "We'll show them." Who did she want to show? Why?

She led me toward a corner, merely greeting her guests with a word or a smile, but didn't bother to introduce me to any of them until she reached her chosen objective.

Wilson Connely sat on a luxurious divan like a fat toad in a mill pond. I barely repressed a chuckle.

She cooed at him.

"Dear Mr. Connely. I want you to meet Mr. Howard. This is the gentleman who is going to manage my husband's successful campaign for Governor. Mr. Howard, I would like you to meet Mr. Connely."

I extended my hand downward toward the fat toad, and when his moist paw touched mine I felt quite justified in the comparison. A toad had just squatted on my palm. I almost glanced at it to see if there was a bit of residue sticking there. He grunted,

"Hu-ump. Should have hired you long ago, young man. Made a mistake. I hate to make mistakes. You came up too fast. Must try to remedy the situation. Come see me tomorrow."

Jennifer glanced from one to the other of us and her face was deadly white. She said softly, bitterly,

"He's on our side now, Mr. Connely. The best public relations man in the country. I know you will be happy to help us with everything in your power to make my husband Governor and then United States Senator."

She leaned over him and gently stroked the side of his repulsive face with the back of her hand.

"You know you will be glad to help us, don't you, dear Mr. Connely?"

He sagged down and I swear I almost saw tears in his eyes.

"I may be able to add my small efforts to your husband's campaign when it gets rolling, but only for your sake, my dear. It must mean a great lot to you."

Her voice came out strong and confident.

"It means everything in the world to me. I want my husband to be nominated for President of the United States. Only then will I be satisfied. We will have all the power we need. Then I will be satisfied."

Through half-shut eyes, Wilson Connely slowly looked her over from her tiny feet to the top of her head, and nodded silently, then closed his eyes, as though ready to take a nap.

She tugged at my arm. As we walked away, I saw her wipe the back of her hand with her handkerchief.

She led me to another part of the room where a group of men and women were standing in a noisy group. She approached a big heavy set man and spoke to him, ignoring the rest.

"Mr. Flynn, I would like you to know Mr. Howard, my husband's campaign manager."

He roughly took both her hands in his hairy hands and said loudly,

"Little girl, you know I am happy to meet any friend of yours." He just looked at me and said,

"Hello, Howard. Know all about you. Up and coming young pup, full of vim and vinegar. Lucky, too. You must live right. Little girl here seems to think a lot of you. Hope her confidence is not misplaced."

His eyes betrayed his jovial manner and I knew he wasn't on our side. Far from it. I would look into the Mr. Flynn and his associates. He was the kind of a man dogs bite at first glance. I wanted to be damn sure I got the first bite.

Jen said sweetly,

"Mr. Howard, Mr. Flynn is the big political boss around here. He is going to work very hard for my husband's election, aren't you, Mr. Flynn?"

He gave a surreptitious glance across the room at Connely, and lowered his voice.

"Why don't you come to my office in the next day or so, little girl, and we can talk it over?"

She answered quickly,

"We will be happy to, Mr. Flynn. Then you can tell Mr. Howard just how much you plan to give towards the campaign fund and also give him some of your valuable pointers about winning a campaign. You have had so much experience along that line I know he will listen gladly."

He mentally gritted his teeth but he was not the boss of the state for nothing. He said, for all to hear,

"I know more ways to win elections in the state than any man alive. You just do that. I'll be mighty glad to talk to you any time. A pretty little girl like you will make my day brighter anytime."

However, the look he gave me was far from political. In my mind, he was another jackal feeding on the public carcass.

We spent the next half hour circulating among the guests. There were so many of them, I could not remember all the names of the men and women Jen introduced me to. They were practically all of the leading citizens of our city and many I knew already from past association, or knew by reputation. In all it was a worthy gathering and I was delighted to meet most of them. They gave me a royal welcome and I felt I was accepted. The fact that I had been chosen to head the Morley campaign gave me unusual status.

Jen's obvious personal attention to me didn't hurt, either. Through the evening, I had plenty of opportunity to study her.

She had learned her lessons well and with all the Morley money at her command, she was in a position to capitalize on her charm. She sure had that in overflowing quantities. She stood out in the crowd like an orchid in a weed garden, and there were plenty of beautiful women present.

I found myself unwillingly changing my opinion of her. She would be a big asset to her husband in spite of her lurid past.

She was a delightful companion as we moved about the room. Not for a moment did she let me forget her potent sexual attraction. A dozen times when we were in a crowd she managed to press her hips against me or sway her round little rear end against my upper thighs, and each time the feeling was electric. She kept my desires at fever point, and her flushed face and smouldering eyes told me plainer than words her whole body was tingling in anticipation.

She was a woman in which sex was a cultivated appetite and she could never get enough of it. She was made that way.

She suddenly spoke close to my ear.

"Look at that undressed bitch my husband is holding on to. I wonder which whore house he dragged her out of."

I followed her glance and started in amazement. Colonel Morley was standing close, with one arm around Captain Downs. Undressed was right. She had on less than Jen, and what a figure. She was absolutely stunning. Jen pinched my arm and said viciously,

"Wipe that candy-licking look off your face, you bastard. I'm all the woman you'll ever need. Come on, I'll fix her right now."

She swung away, and I followed her apprehensively. She stopped in front of Bart Morley and cuddled against his chest.

"Darling, introduce me to your lovely friend. I didn't know you knew such women."

Bart Morley said, with evident pleasure,

"Miss Downs, I would like to present my wife, —Jen, this is Captain Downs. We were in the Army together. She is one of my very dear friends."

Jen's honeyed words dripped out.

"How nice, Miss Downs. So you have been taking care of the Army. You look quite capable."

Amy Downs never batted an eyelash. She said sweetly,

"Thank you, Mrs. Morley. I'm quite sure had you been in my position in the Army, you would have done far better than I."

Jen imperceptively stiffened and murmured,

"It must have been exciting, working under all those fine Army men like my husband."

A fleeting smile crossed the Captain's face.

"Your husband was never my commanding officer, Mrs. Morley, although it would have been a pleasure to work for a gentleman like Colonel Morley."

Jen's tone changed slightly,

"It's nice to know you and my husband were not co-workers. I might never have met him. May I present our friend, and the manager of Bart's campaign for governor, Mr. Christopher Howard."

I started to extend my hand to take the Captain's, but Jen accidentally bumped against me and half turned me away. She said quickly,

"Oh, pardon me. I'm so clumsy," but she was directly between the Captain and myself.

Over her shoulder, I winked at the Captain.

"I'm delighted to meet an old friend of Colonel Morley. Perhaps you will be able to help with his campaign."

"It would be a pleasure, Mr. Howard. You say he is going to run for Governor?"

Jen answered,

"He is going to be elected."

Bart laughed.

"Jen is almighty sure, Captain. She thinks Mr. Howard is the best man in the state to manage my campaign and with the two of them working together, I'm sure to be elected."

"I'm positive they will work well together, Colonel. They both have one track minds, both dedicated to the project at hand."

Bart Morley said soberly, completely missing the point,

"Yes, it is a big project. I have never had much interest in politics until the last couple of years, but Jen insists I will be successful, so we are going all out to win. After all there is no use, in not winning battles, is there, Captain?"

The Captain's look at him told me much.

"You will win, Colonel. Remember you always did."

Jen said caustically,

"I see you two have old times to talk over, so I will take Mr. Howard and show him the rest of our home. Come along, Chris."

Bart said,

"Show him father's rooms, Jen. Perhaps he would like them for an office during the campaign."

Jen faced him for an instant, and caught her breath.

"Why Bart, that is a wonderful idea. You two could be together all the time. What a wonderful idea."

She wrapped her arms around his neck and gave him a kiss that even shook me. Captain Downs gave me a cryptic look over a half smile. I almost laughed out loud at her expression.

Jen tugged at my arm.

"Why, it's just the place. We can put in telephones and desk, and it's big enough to hold conferences. Why it's ideal."

She babbled on, leading me down the long entrance hall until we entered a large open door, just to the right of the main entrance. Jen heeled the door shut with a bang and in a flash she was in my arms sobbing and moaning like a wild cat. She writhed and turned against me in agony, biting my lips and crying between bites and moaning,

"Oh, Chris. Oh, my God. Oh, Chris." Her hands dug into my back as she strained to hold me tighter.

Her fury set me afire, and I almost mashed the breath out of her against my heated body.

A loud knock sounded on the door. We sprang guiltily apart and Jen leaped to the far side of the room, leaving me standing just inside of the room. She motioned me to open the door. I took a firm grip on the door handle to support my weight and opened the door. A man and woman who I had not met were standing there. The woman entered, gushing,

"Oh, Jen. We were just admiring your beautiful home. Do you mind if we look at these rooms?"

Jen answered in a perfectly controlled voice, though I could see her bosom heaving,

"Make yourself at home, Mrs. Wilson. This is Mr. Howard, my husband's campaign manager. We are going to turn these rooms into an office for Mr. Howard, and we were deciding what should be done to make them appropriate."

Mrs. Wilson gave me her hand and said,

"We have been hearing about you all evening, Mr. Howard. We all wish you every success. Bart and Jen are such dear people. I'll be very happy to visit them in the Governor's mansion. What a thrill that will be."

Jen spoke up,

"You will be very welcome, Mrs. Wilson. We will call on you for a big amount for the campaign fund at the proper time, and I know you will be generous."

Mrs. Wilson said cautiously,

"I will give what I can, Jen. You know that."

"Thank you, Mrs. Wilson." She walked up to me and took my arm, leading me out of the room.

In the hallway she leaned against me, her body still trembling, her voice steady,

"I can't wait much longer, Chris. I'm nearly crazy. It must be soon. Real soon."

"Jen." She placed her hand over my mouth before I could say more.

"Don't say a word. I'll make the time and the place."

A man met us in the middle of the hallway. With a bare glance at me, he said to Jen,

"I would like to talk with you, Mrs. Morley."

Jen stiffened against me and turned pale. She seemed to be thinking furiously, then she stepped towards him and laid her hand on his arm and said to me,

"Please excuse me, Mr. Howard. Join Bart and his light of love and see if you can get her away from him. I will see you later."

She and the man walked rapidly away toward the main entrance.

I remembered the man well. He had been indicted for tax evasion the year before and his pictures had been in all the papers. He was a racketeer with a hand in all the vices of the city, but he had beat the case and was back in business. He knew Jen Morley well enough to practically order her to talk with him. Jesus Christ. What next.

I boiled inside as I watched them walk out the front door and into the garden. Jen Morley was dynamite in more ways than one.

Colonel Morley and Captain Downs were the center of an admiring group when I found them. The Captain's eyes were cold as a frozen fish when she saw me. Bart greeted me with,

"How do you like the arrangement of the rooms, Mr. Howard? Will they be satisfactory as an office?"

"Yes, indeed—if you wish to turn such magnificent rooms into a cold office. There were so many people there, I didn't get to see much of them, but if you think such an arrangement is necessary, I bow to your wishes."

"Good, it is settled. May I leave Miss Downs in your company while I attend to some of my other guests? Miss Downs just arrived in the city and surprised me today. We are very old friends. Take good care of her."

"I will do my best, Colonel." He nodded and was gone.

I faced her. Her eyes were shining and she moistened her upper lip with the very tip of her tongue. I gently took her hand and led her towards an empty divan in the corner of the room, partially hidden by a huge plant. We sat down, side by side, and I could feel the length of her leg from my ankle to my hip—warm, wonderful.

She said softly,

"I thought perhaps you had met the woman who would be willing to become your teacher."

I answered in kind,

"No, I'm still waiting. Impatiently. The night is nearly ending, and she is just as far away as ever."

She laughed, and it made me think of honeysuckle and mocking birds. Sweet and haunting.

"Be patient, Mr. Howard. She might be nearer than you think."

I tried a bold course.

"Feel my forehead. Don't you think I have a high fever?"

I leaned my head down and she obediently placed her hand on my head and rested it there for a moment.

"No. I think you are just in a fever of imagination. Nothing serious."

She moved away slightly and said quietly,

"That was close tonight. Too close. We had two cars there and had driven around and around the area several times. All was clear. The car was parked two blocks away and two men were watching the street intersection. We have them in custody at the central police station on a reckless driving charge. That is all I know at the moment. When you leave here tonight, drive straight home and do not make any stops. Go straight to your apartment. Just be careful. In twenty-four hours it will be all over."

I started to say something, but she shook her head.

"Just do as I say. You will be safe."

I raised her hand to my lips and kissed the palm, and as I did so, I saw the man who had led Jen into the garden watching us intently from across the room. I whispered,

"The man in the shiny tux across the room, curly hair. He seems interested in our intimacy."

She instantly laid her cheek against mine and nuzzled me affectionately. It made my toes curl. She turned her head toward me and I thought for a moment she was going to kiss me. She said,

"He just turned away and is walking out. Who is he?"

"He is just a racketeer and knows Jen well enough to order her around."

She said through clenched teeth,

"Well, a real problem child. Whore, faithless wife, up to her scrawny neck in racketeers. If you ever make her the first lady of the land, you will have to create a greater miracle than Moses did when he opened the Red Sea. If it wasn't for Bart, I wouldn't touch her with a mine detector. She would blow it up."

I laughed so loud we drew attention from all parts of the room. We went to the buffet table together and there she slipped away in the crowd. I filled my plate with food and went back to the corner divan to eat it in lonely silence, if that were possible in a crowded room. It wasn't.

Big Boss Mike Flynn joined me almost at once with a heaping plate of food. Without a word, he sat down beside me.

He stuffed a half a sandwich in his face and mumbled,

"What you getting paid for this job, boy?"

"Enough to make me happy and my client satisfied."

He gulped the other half of the sandwich and said,

"Not enough for a bright boy like you. I'll double it if you want to resign."

"No. I'm honest, and so is my client. He will make a splendid Governor. He will probably clean up the crooked rackets in the state and send a lot of men to the penitentiary. He has a lot of support along those lines."

He went on chewing his meal.

"He won't get elected. Johnnies come lately never do. It is good for the voters, though. Gives them something to do with their time and leaves the running of the state to us. We're doing a good job. Hate to see the administration upset. Might feel inclined to do something about it. Good-bye, boy."

He ambled away as though we had just had the most casual chat in the world. He left me with a chill running up and down my back. A real mean son-of-a-bitch, that Mike Flynn.

CHAPTER EIGHT

I finished my food in moody silence, keeping my eyes roving around the room looking for the Captain, but she had left. At least, I couldn't find her. Bart Morley and Jen were, as always, in the thick of the crowd, and every man and woman seemed to be hanging on with bated breath to hear what Bart was saying. I could tell by their expressions how much they admired him. He might not be much as a Governor, but he would be one hell of a candidate. If his wife was of his caliber, they would be unbeatable. I hated to think about the consequences if we were not able to keep her under control.

I set my empty plate on a nearby end-table and went to join them. At first glance, Jen seemed bright and happy, but I saw her face was slightly pale and her eyes had a haunted look. She was forcing herself to be normal. The look she gave me didn't have the same come-on it had earlier in the evening. She was badly upset by something that had happened since we had been in the room together. Even her first words to me didn't have their usual verve,

"Have you met everyone, Mr. Howard?"

"Yes, I think so, except one of your friends who I am quite interested in," I said significantly.

She flushed slightly.

"All in good time, Mr. Howard. We will call you tomorrow."

She placed her hand on my arm and steered me out of the room, casually touching me with her hip as she walked.

When we were near the front door, she whispered with pure venom in her words,

"Chris, you must know I will not let anything stand in Bart's way. Nothing. I always get my way, and I want Bart to win at all costs. I've always known there were rotten men in the world, and tonight I learned just how rotten some of them can be. Oh, Chris, I need you so."

"Tell me all about it, Jen. Perhaps it is not so bad as you think."

Her hand clenched on my arm, hurting.

"How I would love to lay in your arms and tell you, tonight. I will, just as soon as possible. I promise."

There it was. Out in the open. Even though she was my client's wife, I knew she was a complete fool. If she was willing to get into bed with me, she would do it with any other man who happened to strike her fancy and sooner or later, the fat would be in the fire and Bart's chance of becoming Governor would be gone forever, as well as ruining any private career he might have in the future.

Right at the moment I wanted her, more than I had ever wanted a woman in my life. She would ruin me and all people around us.

She felt my withdrawal and quickly said,

"Chris, you won't be sorry. I'm all woman and I always get what I want. I want you. We will call you tomorrow and give you more money for the campaign than you ever had before. Good night, Chris. You're quite a man."

The clever bitch. She poured on the inducements in a single breath. Money. I love money. Herself. A luscious, passionate woman. I love that kind. And she fed my ego.

Quite a man, Howard. It all had a pleasant ring. She glanced down the hallway and backed into a door opening, pressing the entire length of her hot body against me, both her hands digging in my rib section under my coat, her mouth covering mine, searching, promising. It only lasted for a second, but in that second I knew I was committed. She left me and walked rapidly back towards the drawing room. My legs almost refused to carry me out the door and across the garden to my car. I knew I had to have a woman, or I would act like a farm boy in the hay mow with a busy right hand. I tried to think what place I could go and pick up a girl, then I remembered Captain Downs had told me to drive straight home and go straight to my apartment. I got in the Plymouth, started the motor and spun the rear wheels getting away. I slowed down because there was no reason to take my feelings out on the car. It couldn't fight back.

I drove less than a block when a car passed me, pulled in ahead of me, slowed down, but went on at a steady pace. I followed it trying to see the occupants. It was too dark in the other car, and then I noticed another car following me. Either I was damn well covered, or I was in a hell of a jam. I floored the gas pedal and tried to pass the front car, but the driver deftly swerved out and blocked me. I drew a long breath and settled back, ready for anything. I might as well have saved my worry. The two cars stayed with me until I parked in front of my place, then they both tore off down the street and turned the corner of the next block. I sat in the car a moment and watched a uniformed officer leisurely walk toward me. As he passed my car, he glanced in and nodded a "Good evening," and went on his way.

I locked the car doors and climbed the stairs to my front door. In the darkness of the entrance way, a shadow moved and I braced myself and rushed in, grabbing at the form standing there. A soft voice cried out,

"Chris, Chris, you're breaking my ribs. Let go. You're hurting me."

My heart gave a leap. I eased up the pressure, but believe me, I still hung on. She moulded herself against me and whispered,

"Open the door. Do you always greet your guests so roughly?"

I chuckled exultantly, burying my face in her hair.

"Only beautiful women. Only adorable women. Only Amy."

I fumbled the key out of my pocket and unlocked the door with one hand and pulled her inside. Still holding her close, I closed the door and locked it.

"Now, beautiful prisoner, suffer the consequences."

There were no consequences to suffer. Only joy of man and woman blending into one wonderful world of passion and ecstasy, mingled with the scent of flowers and woman, and the sound of birds in the distance. It ended quickly, with the crash of applause from thousands of throats of the great lovers who watch from their places in the universe beyond the ken of mortal man. Slowly the tumultuous sound died away, and we were in each others arms, filled with the sweet rapture of blissful contentment, lying on the carpet just inside the door.

I lifted my mouth from her bruised and trembling lips and looked down into her eyes—eyes which were warm, sultry, filled with tenderness. I closed the lids with my lips and kissed each one slowly and softly, traced the curves of her cheeks, each in turn, until again I found her moist lips, hungrily begging for mine. The flame leaped high and her body arched against my weight seeking fulfillment. Thus, for an instant or a year we lay, moulded in perfect harmony. She moved slowly and breathed against my mouth.

"Not here again, Lover. Not yet. I'm uncomfortable."

I sat up, drawing her into my arms.

"I know now, precious woman. Forgive me."

She kissed me long and tenderly.

"It was wonderful, so wonderful. You are wonderful."

She lay quiet, while I caressed her glowing body with gentle hands, finding each intimate spot respond to my touch. She trembled with pleasure as my hands roamed over her, her hands finding their way under my clothing with a knowing will.

She sighed softly, and a small laugh bubbled out,

"My, what an impatient man you are. You didn't even take my shoes off."

I lifted her in my arms and carried her to the bedroom, laying her full length on the bed. Small sounds came from deep in her throat, soft words,

"Undress me first. Please, undress me."

I made a ritual of it, removing her shoes and rolling her sheer stockings down her shapely legs. As each garment was removed, I followed the revealed warm flesh with my eyes and kissed each part of her, until she lay nude, tiny beads of moisture clinging to her loveliness, and she was murmuring pleadingly,

"Lover. Lover, please. Love me now."

That night passed in a moment. In my life, which had been empty without knowing complete surrender in a woman, the night was one of wonder. She gave me everything. She withheld nothing. Even in sheer exhaustion from our violent love making many times through the night, when morning came, we still clung together, the flame still burning brightly, but physically unable to continue. Sleep claimed us, as the birds outside the windows began their busy little lives to the accompaniment of their melodies.

The strident ringing of the telephone bell became louder and louder as I came out of my drugged sleep. I walked wearily into the living room and answered the damn thing.

"Mr. Howard, it is almost twelve o'clock. Are you ill?"

I mumbled sleepily,

"No, Miss Dahl. I'm fine. I guess I overslept."

"That is bright news. Overslept. How nice. Could you send her home now and come to the office? Mrs. Morley has called several times and seems a bit impatient."

"Yes. Yes. I'll be there in an hour."

Her tart rejoiner was to the point.

"Be sure she is fully dressed before she leaves you. You must not create any scandal, must you?" and the click in my ear was eloquent.

If she only knew. Scandal. Wh-ew.

On my way to the shower, I glanced in the bedroom. Amy was dead to the world. Flat on her back, she was smiling in her sleep.

I perked up. Quite a fellow, that Howard.

I showered, dressed, and hurried to the office. Miss Dahl smiled at me and said sweetly,

"You apparently did all right for yourself last night. The party must have been a great success." She looked at me intently for a moment and added,

"Are you going somewhere, Mr. Howard?"

I must have started in surprise, because she laughed wickedly,

"I just wondered, because the bags under your eyes are well packed."

I sheepishly grinned.

"The party was late in breaking up. I'm still tired."

I walked into my office and she said behind me,

"I understand these all night parties are rather tiring."

I slammed the door. She was just shooting in the dark but her shots were too damn close for comfort. I hoped she never found out Amy had been the cause of it all because it would hurt her immeasurably, but I didn't see how she possibly could. Even I hadn't known about it until it happened.

The phone rang. Damn telephones. They ring and ring.

I spoke into it.

"Howard speaking."

Jen's voice was anxious.

"Chris, are you all right?"

"Sure, Mrs. Morley. Shouldn't I be?"

"Chris, I've been so frightened when you didn't get to your office as usual. I thought all sorts of things."

"Be specific, Mrs. Morley. Why should you be frightened?"

She answered tartly,

"Well, don't be so God damned smug about it. I just was. Come out to the house. Bart will be here, and our attorney. We will have your contract ready for you. Also money. You like money, don't you?" Before I could answer that one, she hung up her receiver, the echo of a laugh preceding the click.

I needed food, great quantities of it. I was weak from hunger, but only for food. Otherwise I was drained and laid away.

Passing Miss Dahl on the way out I said,

"If you want to find me, call the Morley residence. I'm going out there to sign the contract with Mr. Morley and get a lot of money."

She squirmed around in her chair and I noticed for the first time she had a padded one. She looked cute wriggling about in it.

"It's so soft to sit in. Thank you Chris. It's very protecting. I hope it will make you happy to know how gently it holds me."

I hurried out the door. Ke-rist. All my life I had been panting after women and now I had three falling all over themselves, offering me their all. Dream gals, too.

I decided to have a double order of oysters for breakfast and let nature take her course. I couldn't possibly fight them off.

An hour later I drove to the Morley house. It was even more beautiful in the day light than it had been the night before when it was artistically lit up with flood lights.

It was a home of grandeur to live in and not up to. No one could possibly live in its years old magnificence and not get a feeling of goodness and humbleness living within its protecting walls.

I prayed some of the feeling I had for the place would rub off on Jennifer Morley. She was a fool if she let one single act of hers bring unhappiness to the Morley mansion. To me, even on such short acquaintance with it, I felt it was something vital, alive and proud.

I rang the door bell. It was opened at once. The butler said pleasantly,

"Come in Mr. Howard. You will find Mr. Morley in the first room on your right. He is expecting you."

The door was closed. At my knock the door was opened by Colonel Morley. He smiled and I liked his smile. Friendly, welcoming and his handshake was hearty. He said,

"Good morning Mr. Howard. This is my old friend and attorney, Kurt Avery. Kurt, my campaign manager, Chris Howard."

The gentleman who stepped forward to take my outstretched hand was a fitting companion to Bart Morley.

Big, handsome, easy moving and straight as an arrow. His clipped, precise speech denoted his Princeton education.

"My pleasure Mr. Howard. I know as much about you as you do yourself. For a young man on his own since you were sixteen, you have built up an enviable record."

I looked him straight in the eyes and grinned,

"Thank you Mr. Avery. I know a bit about you too. You have never lost a case in court. The attorney with quicksilver for blood."

They both laughed, and Bart said,

"What did I tell you Kurt? I'm as good as elected right now. Quicksilver for blood. Ha! By God now I know what makes you so damned righteous at times."

Avery chuckled,

"You could stand a small amount of righteousness in your own soul once in a while, Bart." He continued to me,

"You will find him a plain bastard at times, Mr. Howard, but on the whole a fairly good man."

Bart grunted,

"Pay no attention to him Chris. If he gets out of line I'll give you some information on his past misspent life you can blackmail him with."

I felt right at home. This was the kind of conversation I had heard many times just before the men went into battle to perform heroic deeds or to die trying. These were the kind of men to follow.

Bart motioned me to a seat and Avery handed me a contract.

They sat in silence while I read it through from end to end.

I reread it, penciled out one section and handed it back to Bart Morley.

"That is a very generous contract Mr. Morley with the one exception. I can have no absolute check on my expenditures.

"You must realize there are times when I want an item covered by a separate entry other than the one the money was actually spent on. I never for a moment overstep the legal line. However there are items which if they were recorded in black and white would not be to the best interests of my client should they become known."

Avery gave me a peculiar look and bristled,

"Do you mean to imply you skirt the legal edge in procuring votes for your clients, Mr. Howard?"

"Not for a moment. But I do require certain information and I get it any way I can. Usually with money or by investigation which costs a lot of money. In either case I must refuse to be held strictly accountable as to the whys and wherefores."

"In that case. What is to prevent you from pocketing sizeable amounts and running in a dummy receipt to account for it?"

"None whatever." I eyed Mr. Avery so steadily he dropped his eyes then said belligerently, looking at Bart,

"Damned sure of himself. Isn't he?"

Bart looked at me with a thoughtful grin,

"Yes. Either we trust him or call the whole thing off.

"Wipe out that clause in the contract and put fifty thousand dollars in his personal account at the bank."

His eyes slid from my face to Avery's and he pounded his knee,

"I'll bet you a new hat he accounts for every Goddamned cent even to your penny pinching satisfaction."

I said gratefully,

"You have just won yourself a new hat, Colonel. Be sure he buys you a white one. It will look good on the hatrack in the Governor's mansion."

Avery made one last gesture,

"What do you estimate this campaign is going to cost, Mr. Howard?"

I cocked both barrels and let fly.

"About two hundred and fifty thousand dollars, give or take a few dollars either way."

The full charge floored the genial Mr. Avery. He gave up, gasping and waving his hands in resignation.

Bart Morley laughed in sincere appreciation of the spectacle.

"Jen wants a husband and a Governor in the same man. By God she can have them. Excuse me gentlemen, I'll go tell her."

Kurt Avery grinned at me sourly,

"Bart has had a lot of expensive hobbies in his time, but that damned wife of his tops them all."

I said guardedly,

"She seems devoted to him."

He answered promptly,

"She is. She is a fine woman. A wonderful wife. No other man can lay a hand on her. A bit too ambitious. However she is good for Bart, he is inclined to take things too easy.

"Always had too much money for his own good. She will drive him into becoming a first class politician. You will have your hands full in this campaign. After all, we know next to nothing about how to win votes. We are in your hands."

He produced a blank file card from the depths of his brief-case and handed it to me saying,

"Sign this. It is a signature card for the National Trust Bank records. Any time after tomorrow noon the money will be at your disposal."

He watched me sign my name on the card then said,

"Mr. Howard, Bart Morley is one of the finest men I would ever hope to know. I would not like to see him disappointed in his trust of you."

"Rest assured Mr. Avery. Bart Morely will be the next Governor of this state. With a quarter of a million dollars to spend on a campaign I could elect myself."

He said dryly,

"I should hope so."

"There is one thing more Mr. Avery. Place this money in an account labeled 'Howard Trust.' Have it subject to withdrawal by Bart Morley's signature. In the event of something beyond my control he could get the remaining amount back."

He gave me a keen glance and his face wrinkled into a smile,

"I've had some doubts about you Mr. Howard. That settles those. Call on me at any time you are in need of legal advice.

"I am on a substantial retainer from Bart and I will include you in the service. Good luck and may I say, I think Bart has made a wise choice in a campaign manager."

"Thank you Mr. Avery. I'll be on my way. We will start our publicity and buildup as of now. In less than sixty days the Governor will begin his scheduled visits throughout the state. The first of August he will be known to most of the voters by sight and after that we will see he meets them all. Good-by, Mr. Avery."

He nodded absently as I went out the door toward my car. I looked for Jen, but she was nowhere in sight.

I cranked up the old boat and set sail for home riding the top of the waves.

For the first time in my life I had plenty of money of my own and fifty thousand dollars to start a campaign, with more to come when I wanted it.

My dreams were coming true. A big house in the country, a new car and women. Ah, beautiful women. How I love 'em.

The windshield splintered into a hundred pieces, blinding me. I instinctively jerked the wheel and the old car twisted off the road and we went rolling side ways, over and over, the rending, tearing screeching sound of tortured metal crashing about my ears.

Silence. Deadly silence. The deadly silence of death. Only I was alive. I knew I was, because I could see light between my legs shining through a space in the wrecked car below me. Then I realized I was upside down, jammed under the wreck and looking up at the sky.

Then I was sleepy. Just sleepy. I closed my eyes and blissfully the world faded away.

CHAPTER NINE

Sleep and sleep. I never wanted to wake up. I opened my eyes. Bleary, blowsy world. Lop-sided world. Hazy. Filled with distant voices, ringing voices. Big noses. My nose. Big enough to see way out in front of me. A monstrous big red balloon. I tried to touch it. No arms. Nothing. Just a big red nose. Whole world filled with nose. One sided. See only one side. One eyed. God in heaven, only one eye sees one side of big red nose. What the hell. Sleepy. Just sleepy.

Voices. Shut up Goddamnit I'm sleepy. Be quiet. Round and round. Got to hang on or I'll fall off. Fall. Falling. Thump. Thump. Ye-e-e-e-. Going to hit bottom. Soft. Warm and soft.

I listened. Low voices.

"He is conscious now, Doctor."

Voice way off calling,

"Mr. Howard. Mr. Howard. Mr. Howard."

Got to yell. Tell 'em where I am. Yell. Louder.

"That's fine Mr. Howard. Just lie quiet. You got quite a bump on the side of your head. Nothing serious except your right eye is swelled shut. You're tough, boy, and damned lucky."

I opened my eye and looked up. The room spun around and then it was all clear. A man in white bent over me smiling,

"I'm Doctor Brill. You bumped your head when your car rolled over. Probably hit the steering wheel. Otherwise I can find no damage. You will be sore for a few days so take it easy. I always wonder at the abuse a fine body like yours can take. Wonderful thing, a man's body."

I said as best I could,

"Thanks Doctor. Where am I? My nose feels like a potato."

"In the hospital. Your nose is just swelled up. It is not badly broken and you have no cuts on your face. You are a very lucky man. My nurse will pack your face for a few hours and then you will be good as new."

He walked away and a nurse bent over me murmuring,

"Turn your head on your left Mr. Howard. This will feel good."

She gently laid a cold compress over the side of my head and almost instantly I went to sleep.

I woke at a gentle pressure on my shoulder. The nurse was saying,

"You have some visitors, Mr. Howard. Do you feel up to seeing them?"

I rolled my head from side to side to see if it was still fastened on. It was. I said easily,

"Sure. I'm not dressed for visitors, but if they can stand me, I can see them."

She smiled, her eyes twinkling as she went to the door,

"They have been waiting for hours. You must be very popular."

She opened the door. Captain Downs and Darleen came in with a swish of delight. A lovelier pair of visitors a man could never wish for. The nurse gave me a wink and closed the door behind her.

Darleen took one look at the bulge on the side of my face and big tears rolled down her lovely cheeks,

"Oh Chris. How could you be so careless as to run off the road and get all banged up."

I grinned at them one-sided,

"It was easy. Just closed my eyes to think of beautiful women and there I was, upside down."

I almost ducked, I was so sure she was going to hit me.

She wiped her eyes and said with bitter sweetness,

"That figures. If the Doctor had cut your head open he would have found it full of naked women."

Captain Downs bent over in laughter,

"Darleen. The man is hurt. He needs kind words and consolation instead of a caustic rundown on his character."

Darleen said tartly,

"The only consolation he wants is a naked woman in bed with him. Just ask him."

She lifted the corner of the compress and peeked under it,

"At least you won't be handsome enough to attract any of the nurses around here for a few days. I love your beautiful shiner."

She patted the top of my head and said,

"Mr. Morley has been calling you since yesterday and wants me to see him as soon as I've seen you. Is there any message you would like to send him?"

"Just tell him I'm all right. Get the contract and be sure his signature is on it. Then go by Attorney Avery's office and pick up a deposit slip."

She queried,

"Deposit slip?"

"Yes. There should be fifty thousand dollars in the National Trust Bank deposited to my account."

Her eyes grew big and round,

"Fifty thousand dollars. Did you say fifty thousand?"

I nodded. Her dreamy look vanished and she said briskly,

"I'll attend to everything at once, Mr. Howard."

She turned just before she went out the door,

"Be very careful Amy. Even in his condition he will try. Keep away from his hands."

Her look at me was far from friendly as she closed the door.

Amy was on top of me in a twinkling. Her soft mouth moved over the good side of my face like a butterfly hovering on a flower.

"Chris lover. My God. I nearly went crazy when I heard on the radio you had an accident. I was waiting in the apartment to surprise you when I heard. I never dreamed they would shoot at you in broad daylight."

"How did you know I was shot at?"

"I called a police car. I was there before they moved your car. We went all over it. You were fired at by a hi-powered rifle. The bullet struck the corner post of the windshield and was deflected. We have the bullet and are tracing the gun. There are a dozen men out there now checking the whole area. There is a man waiting to see you now.

"I'll go get him."

She covered my ugly face with kisses, passionate and demanding. She breathed softly,

"Hurry home Chris. I'll be there waiting."

She left me panting, and went out the door, returning in a minute with the Inspector. She said formally,

"Mr. Howard. I would like you to meet my uncle, Inspector Rodgers."

He grinned at my surprised stare,

"Hello, Howard. Amy is my favorite people altho we didn't intend for the relationship to become known just yet."

He glanced at her affectionately,

"Wipe your face. Your lipstick is showing."

I wiped the side of my face with the corner of the sheet and glanced at Amy. She stood with her hands folded in front of her with a demure look on her reddening cheeks. She muttered,

"You damned detective."

He ignored her, saying,

"Amy said she told you it was a rifle bullet which struck your car and broke the windshield. That what made you run off the road?"

"Yes. It blew up in my face and I lost control of the car. I don't know where it came from."

"We'll find out. Amy is sure it ties in with your business connection with Colonel Morley." He hesitated,

"Or his wife. You been fooling around with her?" He asked bluntly.

"Not for a minute. I've only seen her twice. Once in my office, and I was at the party in their home night before last. The Captain was there."

He said to Amy,

"You are right as usual, but I wanted to be sure. You saw no one when leaving the house?"

"No Sir. I just got in the car and drove off. I remember I looked around the garden before I did too. No one in sight."

"All right, Howard. We will take it from here. Stay here a couple of days. Maybe we will get a break."

He touched Amy's arm.

"I suppose you want to stay and finish your, —er— conversation?"

She stood on tiptoe and kissed his cheek.

"Yes, Inspector Rodgers. In fact, I'm going to live in the room right next to him. I'm very ill and must have a few days rest in this nice hospital. They were even kind enough to give me a room with a connecting door."

He was as surprised as I was at that bit of information, but he never blinked.

"How very convenient. Happy convalescence, children." He walked out the door without a backward glance.

Amy bent over me and I pulled her down to my lips. A few minutes later she said firmly,

"Enough is enough. Right now, let me go."

I wasn't at my best, so I had to let her get away.

"There will come a time when you won't be able to stop. Remember that young woman."

"What a wonderful time that will be. You get some sleep and I'll be right next door. Hungry?"

"No. Just for some more of you. No food."

She fluffed up my pillow, laid her warm hand on my head and I went to sleep with the feel of it still lingering.

My next conscious moment came with a struggle. I wanted to wake, but my body seemed to refuse. My God how I ached. It was plain misery to lift my arms. My legs were heavy as lead. The only thing functioning was my kidneys and guts.

I spotted the call button fastened on the head of the bed and held it down. In a minute the nurse came in, carrying a bedpan. She said cheerily,

"Good morning, Mr. Howard."

I cut her off roughly.

"Get me to a bathroom and forget that damned thing."

She shu-s-s-hed me like an infant.

"Just raise up, Mr. Howard. This is a very useful instrument." When she had it placed to her satisfaction, she hurried out of the room. I did full justice to its usefulness, and right away the world looked brighter. Once again I pressed the bell and she came in promptly and took the thing away without any comment, for which I was thankful. The first time I have a few minutes to spare I'm going to invent something more comfortable than a bedpan, because I'll have the thousands of unsatisfied customers to buy my invention. If you don't think so, just walk down some hospital room and watch a big husky man jousting with nature atop one of them. He'd buy mine, sight unseen.

My nurse came in in a few minutes and without even asking, she stripped the bedclothes off me and began busily to give me a bath, or what passed for a bath.

I closed my eyes and let her have at it. I wondered if she was enjoying it. I peeked at her out of my good eye. She was kind of cute in a motherly sort of way, and I was tempted to ask her if I could return the compliment some night when she was off duty, then decided against it because I was going to be busy for a long time if Amy kept her promise.

When she finished bathing me, she spread some clean sheets along the side of the bed, rolled and tumbled me first one way and another, and presto, I was all comfy in a clean bed, pillow and all. She gave my hair a few strokes with a comb and said brightly,

"Now, your breakfast, Mr. Howard. Captain Downs said to tell you she will join you."

She gathered all the pans, towels, and bed linens in her arms and went away.

"May I come in now?"

The connecting door to the next room was slightly ajar and Amy was peering through the crack with one eye. Bless her little heart, she even wanted to look like me. One eyed, but hers was very mischievious looking. I beckoned with a forefinger and she came on the run and plumped into my arms.

What a delicious way to begin a morning. I just barely tasted her lips when she squirmed out of my arms and stepped back. The door opened and a hospital orderly came in, pushing a food cart ahead of him. He merely glanced at both of us, placed the cart beside me, lifted a nearby chair and set it next to the cart, and walked out of the room.

That was the best breakfast I ever had in my life. Every other bite was seasoned with a kiss. I could have been eating hay and I wouldn't have known the difference.

Amy left me as soon as we had finished breakfast and I was left alone the rest of the day. I guess I slept most of the time because it was nine o'clock before Darleen came in.

She was dressed like a society queen and was lovely beyond description. Her tongue was just as sharp as usual,

"Good evening, Mr. Howard. Have you had a nice day leering at all these pretty nurses?"

I tried to trap her hand but she was wary as a chipmunk, standing well out of my reach. I told her,

"You know I have thoughts only for you."

She answered derisively,

"That may be when I am in sight. I would hate to examine them under the light. Your eyes give you away. You like my new dress?"

"I think it is gorgeous, and what you have in it is more so. It is simply ravishing. Come here and let me feel the texture of the dress."

"No, thank you. I'm dressed for a party, not a wrestling match. I'm going to a shower for one of my girl friends who is getting married next week."

She eyed me intently for a moment and added with all the subtlety of a sledge hammer,

"Marriage is that institution where two people in love are joined together for life and live ever after in bliss and happiness. Something your little mind is unable to comprehend."

I murmured fervently,

"Amen." The thought of a big house in the country with her waiting at the door to greet me when I returned at night, sitting across the table from me, and wrapped around me all through the long nights passed through my mind in a flash. My expression must have changed because she said softly,

"It will be heaven, won't it, Chris? Just concentrate on it a little each day. It will be good for what ails you and soon it will become your one desire."

I shouted at her,

"Get out of here before I make a fool of myself."

She stepped to the side of the bed, and with a quick movement she tucked the sheet under my chin and tightly pinned my arms beneath it. She kissed me thoroughly, gurgling between kisses,

"You already have, Chris, but you are too damned mule-stubborn to admit it. I'll wait."

With a soft, "Good night, Chris," she twinkled out of the room like a fading star. I was left alone with my thoughts spinning around and around. When they settled down, I was startled to find I was wondering what a marriage license cost.

I thought of Amy—desirable, fierce, gentle, aggressive Amy. Now there was a gal. My senses leaped at the remembrance of her passion-tortured body moulding itself to mine in a consuming fire. Marriage. NO. NO. Not for Howard. I'm happy just as I am. Love 'em and don't look back. That's for me.

I waited for Amy to come in from the next room, but there was no sound from there so I settled deeper into the bed. Just before I went to sleep, I imagined there was a bright smiling angel hovering near me, repeating over and over,

"I'll wait. I'll wait. I'll wait."

The morning sneaked up on me while I was asleep. The first thing I knew about, a pert little nurse was shaking me awake.

One look at her and I was ready for my bath. What a dish. She nipped my ambition in the bud.

"The Doctor will see you in a few minutes, Mr. Howard. Would you like a bedpan first?"

Sure I would, but I'd bust before I let a little doll like her shove one under me. I had other thoughts for her besides polishing bedpans on my sheets. I tried,

"When is your night off, Nurse?"

Her smile was terrific, charming, amused.

"My husband takes good care of all my nights off. He is Doctor Brill." She appraised me thoughtfully.

"It was a nice gesture, though. So subtle. Are you always so sure of yourself?"

"I've been in an accident, nurse, and my mind wanders."

She snapped,

"Well gather it in, Mr. Howard. You are leaving us today."

"That's fine. Do I start now?"

"No, the doctor wants to see you first. Here he is now."

Doctor Brill examined me from head to feet while the little doll of a nurse looked on. I felt like a calf at a country fair. They were as impersonal as livestock judges.

All through the process, I was naked as a plucked chicken and I watched her to see if she took particular notice of my manly attributes, but she apparently considered them just another uninteresting specimen. When he lifted away the compress from the side of my face, she clucked, "t-ch, t-ch," and that was all. The Doctor said,

"A few bruised places, otherwise you are all right. If possible, you might keep a compress on your face for a night or so. It will help to make the swelling go away. You may leave any time you wish."

"Thank you, Dr. Brill. Send your bill to my office and I'll send you a check."

He waved his hand.

"Not this time, Mr. Howard. Mrs. Morley left instructions at the office for the bill to be sent to her. Good luck."

He left the room with a glance at the nurse.

She laid my clothing on a chair and said briskly,

"Would you like me to help you dress, Mr. Howard?"

"I'd love it. But in this instance, I think I had better do it myself. You might run into difficulties."

Her mouth turned up in a cute little quirk,

"None that I couldn't handle. Do you always try so hard?"

"Only when my nurses are as beautiful as you. I'm a very lonely bachelor."

That amused her.

"I'll just bet you are. I've seen your visitors. Better luck next time, Mr. Howard. Perhaps the nurse will not be an old married woman."

"Thank you, Mrs. Doctor Brill. If you every wish to consult a Public Relations expert, I will be delighted to serve you. I'm very good at personal relations, too."

Her quick laughter filled the room.

"That will be a frosty Friday. You deserve an A for effort, but I assure you it is wasted. Good-bye, Mr. Howard."

In fifteen minutes I was dressed, found the men's room, and walked out on the street. I hailed a passing cab which delivered me at the front door to my apartment in nothing flat. I paid the cabbie off and entered the door to my place feeling like a million dollars—fat face, not withstanding.

Inside I received a shock. My landlady and Amy were having a cozy cup of tea. Tea. Of all the times for me to come busting in. They both looked at me and beamed, my precious landlady further added to my dazed condition.

"I see you didn't waste any time getting home to this lovely girl of yours, Mr. Howard." She studied me with an amused expression and continued.

"I've always thought you should have a sweet girl like her. I'm only sorry I saw you forty years too late."

I picked myself mentally off the floor and walked to her and hugged her frail shoulders.

"What a fool I've been. Here we've been living right in the same house for years and only now do I realize what a doll you are. You sure it is too late?"

She said softly,

"Yes, too late. Not long ago I would have fought this child, no holds barred, for you, but now I can only think how well you complement each other."

She arose gracefully, patted my cheek and went like a phantom through the door into her own part of the house.

Amy devoured me with her eyes, which were misty.

"She is grand, Chris. She came in to clean the rooms the other morning after you left and she found me in your bed. I woke and saw her tiptoeing out of the room, so I thought she was furious. Before I could get dressed she came back, carrying a tray loaded with ham and eggs, toast and a pot of coffee. She said she thought I should have a big breakfast after the night I had just gone through. Chris, do you suppose she could hear us?"

I grinned at her.

"If she did, she was probably dying of envy. I'll bet she has some wonderful memories, judging by her conversation."

Amy said,

"Yes, she told me she had lived the most wonderful life and wasn't sorry for one single minute of it. She said she never married because she felt marriage would be an anticlimax, and was just happy remembering."

I knelt beside her and let my hands wander. She pulled my head between her breasts, digging her fingers into the back of my neck.

"Oh, Lover, You're driving me crazy. It's been two whole days. Carry me into the bedroom and undress me. Don't you know how to hurry?"

An hour later she lay in my arms, contented as a kitten.

She said in a dreamy voice,

"What a wonderful thing this is, the mating of a man and a woman. In your arms I feel whole and complete."

For a long time we lay, thighs entwined, mouths seeking, as my hands wandered over her moisture softened flesh until she shuddered from the ecstasy of their movements. With eager arms, she pulled me over her, straining at my mouth with feverish intensity. Physically I was unable to respond, and I groaned at my momentary impotency, but she deftly helped me with her soft warm hands until suddenly my pulses were pounding, and she breathed triumphantly,

"Now. Again. Love me. Love me. Oh, my Lover."

Long minutes later, I fell from her arms into exhausted slumber. When I woke it was almost dark. I drowsily searched the pillow beside me for her, but she was no longer there.

I sat up abruptly, and then I saw a small note lying on the bed-side table. I read it with sinking heart.

"Chris Lover, I am going to Washington. Will be away about a week. Forgive me for not telling you before, but I didn't want to spoil our last hours. For a short time, think of,

Amy"

CHAPTER TEN

The damn telephone was ringing insistently. I walked into the living room and picked up the receiver.

"Hello."

"Howard?"

"Yes."

"Bart Morley. Could you please come out to the house? It is urgent."

"All right, Mr. Morley. I'll be there in thirty minutes."

"Good." The phone clicked. Now what the hell? I keep getting into trouble, deeper and deeper all the time.

I called a taxi and made it to the house in record time.

The entrance door was open, so I walked in. Bart met me just inside with outstretched hands and a piercing look.

"What a hell of a shiner. You feel all right?"

"Yes, and No. The world has a cock-eyed look at the moment. I'd prefer to see it out of both eyes."

He laughed.

"I understand. What happened?"

I decided to play it cautiously,

"The front wheel struck the soft gravel and the car rolled over. My head got banged against the steering wheel and the next thing I knew I was in the hospital. The car is a total wreck, but all I got was a shiner."

He shook his head wonderingly.

"You were lucky to walk away from that one. I saw the car."
He walked into the room. I followed, and looked around.

All the beautiful furnishings had been moved out and in their place was a very efficient looking office, complete with desk on which were two telephones, deep upholstered chairs, filing cabinets, desk for a secretary, typewriter, and adding machine. A big map of the state covered one whole wall.

He noted my approving look.

"Anything else you need, Mr. Howard, just order it. I want you to have everything necessary. Now look at the rest of your quarters."

He opened a door and led me into a small but efficient kitchen, furnished with every modern piece of electric equipment possible. He opened the door of a huge refrigerator and chuckled,

"There is no food in here, but there is plenty of liquid refreshment. You can choose your poison."

He opened another door and led me up a flight of wide, soft carpeted steps and into one of the largest bedrooms I had ever seen. Across one whole side of the room were windows, from floor to ceiling. The view was magnificent, overlooking the wide expanse of flowering garden and on to the farthest horizon beyond the city to the mountains.

He forestalled my question by saying,

"There will be times when we will work late and long hours. This will be your home. It was my Father's, during the later years of his life, and we have kept the rooms just like he left them. You can have your meals served in the dinette, or we will be happy to have you join us. Jen and I live much alone and will both be very happy to have you as a member of the household."

"Mr. Morley, you overwhelm me. I certainly didn't intend to impose on you to this extent. The idea of the office is fine, but to live here, that is something else."

He said genially,

"Oh, we don't expect you to live here all the time. You have your own life to live, but this arrangement should work out fine. It was Jen's idea in the first place."

I thought to myself. Sure it was Jen's idea. The conniving little jade. An extra stud right under her own roof where she could come and go as often as the spirit moved her with not a chance of being suspected of anything but business.

I wondered just how long it would be, before she availed herself of my services. His next statement gave me the answer.

"I must go to New York for a few days, Howard. I am chairman of the board of a firm making experimental timing devices for the government. Timing devices for bombs, rockets and kindred items.

"I will be gone about a week and since the party the other night, Jen has been in a highly nervous state. I would consider it a favor if you will stay here while I am away.

"We do not have many serving people and all of them have been with us a long time. They are very dependable, however I think you will be good for Jen. Add a little life to the old place."

My thoughts were galloping. A week alone in the house with the bitch in heat. I quickly decided against such a proposition which would place me in such a role.

"Why don't you hire a companion for her? A woman her own age would be ideal."

He chuckled mirthlessly,

"She hates women. Especially ones her own age. She has always lived alone and has had no women companions since we were married. She says she prefers to be with me alone." He grinned reminiscently.

"In fact, we haven't spent more than a dozen nights apart since we have been married. She is a wonderful wife."

His faith in her was absolute. Perhaps all her words and hot body temperature pressed against me was a come-on to keep me at heel. Just the same I had a cold chill running up my back as I answered,

"All right. I'll get to work among my people in the state. When you return we will start the campaign simultaneously in every precinct and in every newspaper. I would like to have all the information possible on your background from the day you were born up to the present. Every minute of it. We will put on the damnedest campaign the voters of this state ever saw and next January first, you can sit down to dinner in the Governor's Mansion in the capitol."

He laughed, but his face registered satisfaction.

"By God, Howard. You sound so assured I believe you can do it. Just ask Jen to give you all my mother's scrapbooks and my clippings from college. Also the book containing my war record. I've lived a rather quiet life, nothing exciting or spectacular, but fairly decent.

"I never wanted to climb mountains, rather I have always been content to wander at ease in the valleys. Now Jen wants me to climb the hills and sit on the top. With her by my side, I'm willing to try for the top. You show me the way and I'll follow you."

No wonder his men loved him. I made up my mind right then come hell or hi-water, bitchy wife or not, he would be our next Governor.

"Fine Governor. I'll work here as much as possible from now on. By the time you return I will have an image to place before the voters. They will know you by name in the next two months, then you will start meeting them in person. It's going to be a real pleasure to work with you, Sir."

His handshake left my hand numb. I'd have to remember to tell him to take it easy when he shook the voters' hands or they would be too crippled to vote.

"That wife of mine is a wonder. She said you were the man for the job and she is never wrong. Goodby Chris. I will leave this evening and I want to spend a couple of hours with Jen.

"By the way, I've left word with Kurt Avery that I'll be gone. So if you run into anything you need some help on give him a ring. He's not just my attorney, he's one of my oldest friends." Then with a chuckle he said, "And he wouldn't stop short of spilling some of the 'quicksilver' in his veins to help me out."

He strode out the door like a man on a mission. I thought gleefully of what Jen was going to go through in the next two hours. He might not stop her, but he would sure as hell slow her down for a few days at least.

I called my office. Miss Dahl's voice was very pleasant with just a slight rising inflection at the end of each word.

"Mr. Howard's office."

"Is this the home for wayward girls?"

The tone of her voice didn't change one note,

"If it were, you would be right here in the middle of them. Don't you work here any more, Mr. Howard?"

When I could stop laughing I told her,

"No. Mr. Morley has furnished a beautiful office at his home for me and I will be working here for a few days. We are planning the campaign. If you want to get in touch with me, call me here."

She replied with a long slow drawl,

'Ah suah undahstan, Mistah Howard. Ah suah do. Jest a little ole office in the magnolias. Well shut mah mouth."

The phone clicked and I was laughing into a dead line.

Three hours later I had finished sorting out all the various items in boxes stacked around the room and putting the desk in order. Bart Morley didn't do thing by halves.

There were enough office supplies to run a business for a year and as far as I could see he hadn't missed a thing.

It was dark and I was wondering just how about getting something to eat when Jen came in without knocking. She walked straight to a big chair and slumped back into it with her legs extended straight out in front of her. She laid her head back and looked at me from drowsy eyes,

"Wipe that know it all grin off your pulpy face, you bastard. Sure I've been having a champagne loving. I love it. Now Bart is gone for a week and there is just you and me.

"Show a little excitement and come over here and tell me how happy you are about it."

At the moment she was just about as exciting as a wax dummy. I sat still and asked,

"Would you care to go somewhere with me and have dinner?"

She instantly showed some of her old animation.

"I should say not. We have only a few days together and I'm not going to waste any time trotting around town trying to be a lady. I'm sick of being a lady. The rest of this week I'm going to be a hussy. You're no gentleman either. We'll eat here and spend our time in bed together. I've the best cook in the world and she loves to feed hungry men. In fifteen minutes come into the dining room."

She raised languidly out of the chair and swayed her rounded rear end out the door with just a small glance over her shoulder to see if I was watching. I was. That view of her was entrancing. But damn her, she was the Governor's wife and I was going to keep my hands off of her if I had to handcuff my arms behind me.

In a few minutes I wandered out in the hall, mosied along looking into the rooms. They were all beautiful and I fell in love with the house all over again. Some day I was going to have a house just like this one. Well maybe not as grand, but one I would be proud to live in. I idly wondered what kind of a woman might occupy it with me and in spite of everything, cute little Darleen danced across my mind. Damn, she had pretty legs.

I found the dining room by following the wonderful smell of food wafting out of the room.

A large motherly woman was just placing large silver bowls on the table which was as large as a banquet table.

Two places were set, one at either end of the table. Candles were lit and cast a soft glow over the room, winking and flickering at each other. I wondered for a moment if there was a lot of food or just all show.

The woman said happily,

"You are Mr. Howard?"

Before I could reply, she went on,

'You look half starved boy. I'm going to enjoy cooking for you and watch you fatten up. Anything special you like, just whisper in my old ear and you can have it.

"The Mr. and Mrs. don't eat enough to keep me in practice and me who has raised three fine sons. I tell you they could eat."

Jen came in, glanced at the setting and said,

"Mary. Move one of the places so we can sit closer together. I'm not able to shout at Mr. Howard tonight. And Mary. Don't try to romance Mr. Howard so soon. He is a bachelor and intends to stay that way."

Mary gave me a keen glance, smiling.

"He's such a handsome gentleman too. What a pity."

She placed another setting at the side of the table indicating with a jerk of her head it was for me, then hurried out of the room softly singing.

I held Jen's chair for her then seated myself. In so doing I touched Jen's knee beneath the table. She reached under the tablecloth and fiercely squeezed my upper thigh. Damn her, she never missed a single trick to keep me aware of her sexy body. The touch of her hand there was enough to set my blood pounding. She said throatily,

"Eat all you can hold, Chris. You are going to need all the strength you can build up. I'm going to tear you apart."

She uncovered the dishes and helped herself to generous portions of all of them.

I was so surprised I said kiddingly,

"You eat all of that and you will be a beautiful fat woman."

"Bart was right. He said you would be good for me. I'm hungry for the first time I can remember."

It was a perfect meal for a hungry man. Nothing fancy, just excellent food. If it hadn't been for the ornate silver, table linens, the candle light and the luxurious room I could have been at home on the farm at threshing time.

When I had stuffed myself to excess there was still enough food on the table to feed a large family. I was going to love living at the Morley mansion. Yes indeed.

Mary looked in from time to time and when I had finished my dessert and leaned back in a well fed kind of stupor, she marched in and stood with hands on hips scowling at us in mock fierceness.

"I didn't hear a single word out of you children all through dinner. Was it so bad?"

Jen waved her hand.

"You are the world's finest cook, Mary. You know it. I haven't eaten so much in years. Help me up."

Mary said in high glee,

"Help yourself up. I'll serve your coffee in the drawing room. Scoot now."

Jen led the way and I followed her into the lovely drawing room. She settled on a great couch and motioned me into a chair close by.

"Mary is one of the few people who have accepted me as Bart's wife. She bullies me all the time and strange to say I don't resent it. I was raised in the gutter and she treats me like I was a real lady. She'll bully you too, if you give her the chance."

"All women bully me, Jen. With her, I will enjoy every minute of it. You are a lady, Mrs. Morley. The Governor's wife. Remember?"

Jen abruptly sat up, her face drawn and tight. She clenched and unclenched her hands in nervous tension,

"What a dear you are, Chris. I will be a lady. I will.

"I've nearly gone out of my mind this past week just thinking what I might do to Bart. You know what I am. I'm a dirty slut. I have been a good wife to Bart since we have been married. Not once have I let a man touch me, except Bart. Now I have reached my limit. I've got a hell inside of me that is driving me crazy and you are the man who is going to put a stop to it.

"The moment I walked into your office and looked at your big bull frame I knew what I wanted to do. You think I'm utterly shameless. To hell with it. I am, and I don't care.

"I just know what I want. I think you are honest and good in every way but one. You are a woman chaser and when you catch her and use her, you are through with her. I feel exactly the same way. You are going to help me through this week, and we are going to use each other. Every time you love me, I will die a little, but each time I will live a little until I am living again. Then I will be the Governor's wife again and a lady."

I was absolutely shocked by her fierce words.

Never in all the time I had been in the Navy from Hong Kong to Bordeaux, in all the sink holes where women were to be had for a small price had I been told I was going to be used like a stallion. Not for the duty of procreation, but for the simple task of satisfying the lust of a female.

The thought appalled me. I love women. What healthy man doesn't? But damn it I like to choose my own partner for my love sessions. Not to be told to undress and perform like a trained monkey in a zoo.

She was watching me closely. I'm no poker player because my face shows all my mental reactions. Mine must have shown plenty right then. Her voice softened and she touched my hand.

"Look at me Chris. Look at my lips, my breasts, my legs. I'm more woman than you ever held in your arms in your life. You asked me once if I were some goddess of sorcery. I am. I believe I am. Years ago I studied Greek mythology. I studied it for years and I learned many things of which I unconsciously became a part. Much more than a part. I am just as sure as I live and breathe I am one of them thousands of years later, living in a modern world, but with all the requisites she possessed. Her name was Cir'e. She was a madame in a whore house which catered only to the gods who came to her, to purchase for one time only the choice virgins she brought to her house from all corners of the universe.

"In spite of these tempting offerings the gods preferred her. She was eternal beauty and youth.

"Her beautiful and seductive body and her wealth of experience gave the gods a satisfaction they could not get from the simple virgins. She conceived the idea she could drain from the loins of these gods a fresh and life-giving pollen then transfer it like a bee from them to another and lesser mortal whom she chose to rise to a position equal to the gods themselves.

"With this idea in mind she would rise from the bed of the god who had just filled her body to overflowing with the life giving substance and hurry to the arms of the other person and pull him over her, working in a frenzy to reverse the flow of sperm into his body hoping that one tiny atom might remain there and take life, creating in him some part of the powerful impulse that had made the god she had just left, a great and wise leader in the shaping of the universe."

Her voice sank to a whisper and her eyes closed. Her body slowly relaxed, and then she continued.

"I am that woman. I will make my husband a power in the country. I will take from the leaders their strength and experience and use them to further my dreams and ambitions for my husband. When he stands above them all, then only will I be satisfied."

For a long time my mind refused to believe what I had just heard. She was a monster in female form. What she proposed to do was to become a common whore to gain her ambitions. God help her. The means would be her downfall. Men do not give up their abilities, experience and dreams of a lifetime for the momentary pleasure of going to bed with a woman. Even a woman like Jennifer Morley.

If she tried by that means, she would be used and cast aside. She would lose everything. Her husband. Her home. Her way of life. Above all her self respect, and the respect of her husband who loved her.

I had been thinking with my eyes closed, my head throbbing. I opened my eyes and looked at her, suddenly aware of a deep silence. She had drawn herself up into a rounded ball of girlish innocence and was sleeping soundly. A quirk of a smile drew the corners of her lips and one arm lay over the edge of the couch extended toward me in a pleading gesture.

Mary came to the door carrying a tray with coffee and cups. I motioned her out of the room and followed after her. I closed the door saying,

"She is sleeping, Mary. Will you please take the coffee to my rooms."

She said softly, her voice filled with love,

"The sweet child. I'll let her sleep awhile before I awake her and put her to bed. She is a lovable girl Mr. Howard, good and kind. A perfect wife for Mr. Morley."

In the dinette, she said,

"I have put some cold meats and sandwich bread in the refrigerator, also some milk. If you want me any time just push that little button there. I will fill the box with all kinds of good things to eat, tomorrow. I want you to get filled up. My boys were always hungry and you're too thin. Sit here and drink your coffee. I'll pick up the dishes in the morning. Good night"

She turned at the door and said,

"It makes me very happy to have a boy around. You will be good company for Jen too. She is lonely in this big house with just us old folks."

Her soft singing voice as she went away reminded me of my mother.

I thought of what she had said about Jennifer Morley. Sweet child. Lovable girl. Perfect wife. God help us.

Just about as sweet as a wild cat crouching on a limb ready to pounce down on some unsuspecting prey.

CHAPTER ELEVEN

hated to go to bed not knowing when the door would open and I would have a visitor. Right now she would be plenty unwelcome. For the first time in my life I had an insight into what depths a woman would go to gain her ambitions.

Go to bed with any man who could help her and then blackmail him for all he was worth. That's exactly what she intended to do. I gritted my teeth. She had to be stopped or Colonel Morley and his political ambitions were a lost cause. Along with them would go Howard, Public Relations Counsel!

I phoned for a cab. It came shortly and I went to my apartment, hastily stuffed some night clothing into a bag and returned to the Morley house. It was still lit up and the front door was still unlocked. I sneaked into my rooms like a burglar, tip-toed up the stairs and in a few minutes I was in bed.

I tossed and turned most of the night expecting every moment for the door to open and there she would be, naked, alluring and bent on rape. My rape. In my state of mind I could call it by no other name. I wanted no part of her.

Weariness finally made me go to sleep. I woke to the sound of someone in the room. I opened my good eye, peered around. Mary. Good old Mary was throwing back the window drapes singing softly, happily. At my loud yawn she said,

"Get up, you big lummox. It's almost nine o'clock. You sleep just like my boys. I always had a fight with them in the morning to get them out of bed. Hurry now. Your breakfast is ready in the dinette."

I shaved, showered and dressed in nothing flat. The table in the dinette was set for two and Jen was already there.

She was dressed in the skimpiest shorts and halter I had ever feasted my eyes on. Bare footed too.

Her first remark was right up to par as she turned and twisted about in her chair for my benefit,

"Something to look at. Isn't it?"

I popped my eyes back in my head and sat as far away from her as the table permitted. I said calmly but my chest was heaving,

"You are the loveliest creature it has ever been my good luck to sit at the breakfast table with."

"Why Chris. How sweet. After the riotous night we spent together I was almost afraid you would throw me out."

She leaned back and her merry laughter rang out,

"Honestly, Chris. That was the first time I ever went to sleep before—." Her voice trailed off in more laughter.

Her merriment at her own expense made everything all right between us. No talk was necessary through the meal. Our own thoughts were enough stimulation. My spirits soared as I saw she was bubbling over with animation. Her glances at me were keen, her blue black eyes shining. She ate like she enjoyed every mouth full, and I know I did because I was plain hungry. My night had been hard on my nerves.

All too soon she pushed away from the table and said,

"Come on Chris. I want to show you the horses and the dogs."

She laughed at my quizzical look.

"Yes. We have horses and dogs. All over the place. I ride a lot, It's good for my figure." She took my hand and pressed it against her upper thigh,

"Feel how hard."

It felt just right to me, not hard at all. She tugged my hand and led me almost running out the door, across the garden to enter a long dog kennel filled with dogs of every size and color. She explained as they set up an unholy clamor at sight and smell of her,

"These are all Boxers. We raise them for breeding purposes only. When they are just puppies we send them to a training school. I tried training them myself but after I worked with them a year I couldn't bear to part with them, I loved them so. Now I just ship them away and forget them."

What a mixture of emotions this woman was? Hard as nails, childish, willful, yet I could well imagine her crying her eyes out when she had to give up a favorite puppy.

Like a child she went down the length of the kennel introducing me to all the dogs. She called each by name and made me put my hand on each wet nose and rub it.

"They will know and remember your smell, Chris. If you came here alone the first time they would tear you to pieces. Now they know you belong here. You can come any time you wish and play with them or take one of them for walks. They are wonderful companions."

I told her quietly,

"What an amazing woman you are, Mrs. Morley."

She closed the kennel gate, tucked her hand under my arm and said gleefully,

"I'm the most female you ever had, Chris Howard. Now come see my pets."

We entered a wide open barn door, walked between bales of hay stacked to the rafters, to another door which opened into a series of corrals. Beyond the corrals great pastures stretched flat green and unbroken for a mile to a line of timber.

Fences divided the pastures into smaller pieces in which mares and colts stopped grazing, threw up their heads and came galloping toward us at Jen's piercing whistle. She said with excitement,

"Just look at them come. I'm crazy about our horses and they seem to sense it."

She led me in a rush across a corral to the edge of the pasture where she opened a gate motioning me to stay behind.

Closing the gate she was among the wildly galloping herd. The horses came to a skidding stop almost on top of her, crowding around her. One after another she pulled their heads down against her, stroking them like they were her babies.

It was beautiful to see. Out of the melee she suddenly sprang on the bare back of a sleek trim animal and went racing off across the pasture, the rest of the band following at breakneck speed. I wondered how in hell she could hang on that racing animal without bridle or saddle, or even a rope to hang onto.

The thought crossed my bind, if the voters could see her now the election was in the bag and all tied shut.

She made a complete turn of the pasture at racing speed, returning to the gate, flushed and wild with excitement.

She slid off the horse, grasped the flowing mane and gave me a pretty bow,

"Like what you see, Mr. Howard?"

"That was the most amazing thing I ever witnessed. The voters will love you. How in the name of God do you hang on?"

She impudently lifted one leg and waved it in my direction,

"See this pretty leg. I can hang on to anything real tight with these."

She slapped a couple of the horses, then climbed the fence without any effort and jumped down beside me,

"Now I'll show you my stallion. I'm nuts about him."

She led me around the fence, opened a solid gate and we were in a tightly enclosed pen with the most magnificent animal I had ever seen. Coal black with just a trace of silver on his head and chest. Slickly groomed and proud. He came running toward us and plowed to a halt jabbing his head against Jen almost knocking her down. She shouted for joy in his ear, as he nibbled at her bare flesh. He knew a good thing when he had it.

She told me with eyes shining,

"I raised him from a colt. When he was a baby he was sick all the time. Many nights I stayed with him all night keeping him covered with blankets and keeping him warm with hot water bottles. He had every disease known to horses and some that weren't. Many times I thought he would die. I simply made him live. Now just look at him. One of the most beautiful animals alive."

I heartily agreed with her,

"The way he loves you, he seems to know."

She hugged his head fervently,

"I've always wondered what he would be like if he were a man. You should see him in action on a mare. He is a madman and a devil, but the mares always come back for more."

"Don't you ever think of anything else?"

She gave me a look from under lowered eyelashes,

"Is there anything else worth thinking about?"

On the way back to the house I asked her,

"Who handles all the work around this place?"

"There are several men who work here. The groom who cares for the horses lives in a cottage on the other side of the woods. One man cares for the dogs and we have a dozen or so who ran the farm. It is a big place.

"They are all ex-army men who Bart has pensioned off and he gives them their homes to live in and enough money to live

DON LEE

on comfortably. In the big house we just have Mary and another Army man who is combination butler and chauffeur. We live very simply. If we give a big party I call in caterers.

"I like to do housework, so I'm busy all the time."

Every moment I spent with this amazing woman I understood less and less. One contradiction after another. Housework was the last thing I could imagine her doing. I probed her,

"Do you mean to say you scrub, make beds and wash dishes?"

She faced me indignantly,

"Certainly I do. Is there anything wrong in that?"

I stammered,

"But you. Mrs. Bart Morley. Why do you do it?"

"Because I love it. I was a gutter rat. Gutter born. Gutter raised. I know the stink of the seamy side of life. Bart Morley took me away from it and I'm going to see he is one of the biggest men in the country to pay him for that.

"There is not one single thing I wouldn't do to make that possible. If there are any obstacles in the way you can bet I'll remove them. When he is on top of the world, then we'll show them."

I took a chance,

"I've heard you repeat that expression before. Just who do you want to show?"

She looked at me with cold eyes,

"Just stay close beside me and do the job you were hired for. You will learn in good time."

She struck out for the house, walking fast. At the door to my office I touched her hand,

"Jen. You are a woman apart from all the rest. I'll do my damnedest to serve you to the best of my ability. I will consider it an honor."

In a flash she was in my arms, pressed against me, sobbing,

"Oh Chris. I'm such a bitch. I know it. I know it. God what a bitch. Hold me. Hold me tight. Make it go away. I'm so frightened."

I held her like a child, no clamor of desire troubling me. Gently I placed my hands on either side of her face and tilted her chin upward.

"I will Jen. I will if only you will tell me how I can."

She bit fiercely at my lip then leaned back, fumbling at her halter. She murmured "Damn it," and stepped back. The halter was missing, caught on a button on my jacket. She was nude to the waist. She crossed her arms across her pert breasts and ran like a wild thing down the hallway.

An hour later she came in carrying an armful of scrap books. In a trim fitted cotton dress she was a lovely creature. She was all business.

"Bart asked me to hunt up all his mother's scrapbooks and other bits of information you might like to use. I will find the record of his Army life tonight if you need them right away."

She waited a second, thinking, then said,

"Chris, I want to help. I can run a typewriter like a real secretary and I don't want another pretty girl around you. Please, may I help?"

"Now she tells me she is a secretary. Is there nothing you are not good at?"

"Chris, I'm the best at everything." She threw a quick meaningful glance at the big lounge,

"You want to try me now?"

"No. Not that. Get some sandwiches out of the refrigerator and some milk for me. We'll get to work."

She obeyed instantly, humming softly. While she spread a napkin on one side of the desk and piled sandwiches, milk, glasses, and a dish of fresh peaches for each of us handy to our reach, I opened the scrapbooks.

Beginning with the date of his birth, there was a complete record of his every day doings. His mother had neglected nothing, even to little incidents like when he had skinned his knee, sliding down the banister in the drawing room.

It was all there. Grade school. High school. College. Graduation. Girl friends. Pictures and newspaper clippings.

Just an average boy growing up. With money to bum he had acquired no particular ambitions. In fact looking at the records I concluded he had been lazy. I concentrated on the work and the pile of food was gone with darkness settling in the room before I let up.

Jen worked without a word which was not necessary, her nimble fingers flying over the machine. She typed from my dictation if I spoke slowly saving the time of taking it down in shorthand. Her copy was clean, spelling excellent, and to her credit, she was as good as Miss Dahl.

I straightened up, stretched my back and said,

"We will call it a day now. You're wonderful."

She crossed her arms on the typewriter, laid her head down sighing deeply,

"Oh my back. Carry me out in the center of the room where I can lay down. Do you always work your women to death?"

I did as she told me, laying her full length on the carpet,

"I'm sorry, Jen. You should have told me you were getting tired."

She rolled over on her stomach,

"Now. Rub my back. I'll never walk again. I haven't sat behind a typewriter so long in years."

I kneaded her back gently at first gradually exerting more pressure as I went along. She said suddenly,

"Push my dress up above my waist. Your hands hurt when they cross my belt."

I gave it some thought. She said with a stifled chuckle,

"I have on pants. They're very becoming."

I lifted her dress and I'll admit I lifted it much farther than was necessary, but from that moment my mind was not on massaging her back. Her pants were transparent and trimmed in a frothy lace which didn't begin to cover the two cute little rounded apples in plain view. I hastily walked away from her before I began to pat them.

She sat up, leaning back on her elbows and drew her knees up. That view was even better. She mocked at me,

"Piker. You're a hell of a romeo. Help me up. I'll take a hot bath and be good as new. Dinner will be ready in half an hour."

She sprang to her feet without my help and trotted away.

Dinner that night was a repetition of the night before. Excellent plain food in great quantities, perfectly served in gleaming satiny finished silver. A sense of perfect contentment began to flow through me. This was the way I had always hoped to live.

Jen was a charming hostess although more like a companion. She allowed long silences between us, seemingly content with her thoughts. When she did say a few words they were sparkling and vivacious. For such a small woman, she ate an enormous amount of food.

Mary came in once in a while and when we finished her face beamed. She said with a smirk,

"Guess I haven't lost my touch the way you children ate. Just like my boys. They said I was the best cook in the country."

I patted my stomach,

"That was no exaggeration Mary my love. They must have grown ten feet tall and round as barrels."

Her laugh was delightful,

"It's a crying shame. They're less than six feet, and almost that big around. Roly-poly, all three of them."

Jen and I both laughed with her and Jen said,

"I haven't eaten so much since I can remember. If your cooking is going to make me that fat, I quit right now. At least until breakfast."

She raised slowly out of her chair and walked toward the drawing room. Mary blew me a kiss and winked as I followed.

Jen turned on the TV set, piled some pillows on one end of the lounge and lay full length, relaxed and content.

I sat in a chair near her thinking what a picture of domesticity we made. The hell of it was, she was another man's wife. I stole glances at her when I thought she wasn't looking.

I thought of the hard day's work she had put in, yet here she was, fresh, dainty, very feminine, very desirable.

She unexpectedly chuckled,

"Keep thinking about me, Chris, I love your thoughts. I can feel them kissing me all over my body. So soft and warm."

She shivered in pure delight as though I had actually touched her. She raised her arms and clasped her hands behind her head making her body arch and her breasts stand out proud and inviting. She whispered softly,

"I'm so close to you Chris. You could reach me if you tried real hard."

The instant pounding of my heart made my temples throb and my body tremble. My God how I wanted that woman. How I wanted to crush her lovely body deep into the pillows and bury my face in her proud breasts. The passionate woman smell of her made my emotions give way under the strain. I leaned toward her, out of the chair and kept right on going in a half running crouch out the door and into my rooms.

Her raucous laughter kept beating in my ears even after I closed the door and leaned against it dripping with sweat.

When the emotional fuzz cleared out of my head I thought what an ass I had made of myself. Her mind was made up and she was all mine. It was only a question of time until we would be tearing at each other like animals in the forest. Why had I left her?

It was simple. She was the Governor's wife. I had to leave her alone. Think of her as just another woman beyond my reach. What I needed was a cold bath, not a hot woman.

I went upstairs to my bathroom, undressed, took an icy shower and crawled into my bed shivering.

For the first time in my adult life I didn't think of beautiful women before I went to sleep. I was too mentally and physically exhausted to give a thought to the darlings.

In the morning I felt different. This was the day to tackle the real problem of placing Colonel Morley's name before the voters in a spectacular way. I had to think up some scheme to make all the newspapers sit up and take notice without knowing it was a publicity stunt. All newspaper men are wise, smart and able to smell a publicity action before it gets off the ground. I had to be very careful in my planning in order to break the announcement of the Colonel's intention to run for Governor as a surprise.

At present only a small group knew about his plans. By the pressure being put on me I knew they weren't talking. At present he was virtually unknown through the state. By some miracle I had to bring him to the front pages of all the papers at once. I had to create an image the voters would remember at election time.

I wondered if I could use Kurt Avery in some way to set the whole shebang off. My mind wandered, trying to put stray ideas together to form some sort of opening blast. Kurt Avery—prominent lawyer. Lawyer—crime. The state was crawling with hoods. Maybe Avery could take a mighty whack at these criminal operations with something concrete. He'd get good play in the papers—big man, no political connections for or against the machine. Then Morely steps in and—. No. Too gimicky. Worse than that, run of the mill. It's got to be something big—more than that, DIFFERENT.

But, I thought, I'll have to keep Kurt Avery in mind. Somewhere, with his dough and name, he'll fit in.

The sun was just beginning to show above the horizon when I went down to the office. I picked up the record we had made the day before of his entire life searching for some small item to hang a campaign on. After an hour of careful study I knew the situation was hopeless from that standpoint.

He was just not the kind of a man to do anything spectacular no matter how well I prompted him. He was a rich man's son, a rich man in his own right, a good business man since his financial statements showed he had doubled the fortune his father had left him.

I sat back and thought of a dozen ways to bring him to the attention of the public with a bang. Nothing I had done before would work. This one had to be a dandy or we were sunk.

I discovered I was hungry as hell. I went into the dinette and pushed the little bell button.

In about fifteen minutes the old butler came in carrying a tray loaded with ham and eggs, potatoes, tomato juice, and a big bowl of hot cereal. He set the tray on the table, saying,

"Good morning, Mr. Howard. The cook says to tell you if you want more she will send it right in."

There was enough for four people so I said,

"Will you join me for breakfast? I hate to eat alone."

He glanced at me from under bushy eyebrows,

"I sure as hell will. This butler business gets my goat. For twenty years I ate Army slumgullion and beans out of a messkit along with a thousand other guys and I got fat on the stuff." He rubbed his ample belly, and added,

"I'd sure like to have a mess like that just once more."

He held out his hand,

"My name is Wells. Sergeant Wells, late of the damned Army."

His handshake was warm and friendly.

"You don't look like a tough sergeant. How do you come to be a butler?"

"It was the Colonel's doing. When I retired he asked me to come see him. I was alone so I did. I had been with him ten years keeping him out of trouble one way or another so he cozened me into staying here. One thing led to another so here I am, fat, senile and lazy as hell."

I laughed long and loud,

"You draw a graphic picture. How is the Colonel to work for since he can't give you direct orders?"

"Him give me orders? That's a laugh. It's me that keeps him on the hump. He was born lazy. Too damn much money. If I didn't make him do setting up exercises every day he'd get so fat he couldn't waddle. An' him a Colonel."

"Sergeant. I know all the men who work here are ex-Army men. Was his outfit all from this state?"

"Yes. It was a National Guard outfit at first and when the war came along we went in as a unit. We had a lot of casualties and got split up some. Half the bunch got killed and were replaced with men from all over the country, but the Colonel tried to keep all the original men together.

"After the war was over and we came home the Colonel kept in touch with every man jack of us. He set, God knows how many of the old bunch up in business. They're strung from hell to breakfast in the state and some outside of it. They are all doing fine too, and they owe it all to the Colonel."

"Sergeant. Do you often see any of these men?"

"Once in a while, Mr. Howard. Especially if one of them gets in trouble. He calls the Colonel, we get in the car and hotfoot it to where the feller is. Mostly it's money trouble and poor business judgment so the Colonel pays his bills and the guy is on his way again. If the feller has been a damn fool and got himself in a mess of his own makin', I get him out in an alley an' give him a talkin' to by hand. I can still beat the Be-jesus out of most of them an' the rest are scared to death of me still, so we make out all right."

"Sergeant, how many of the Colonel's outfit are there in the state?"

"I don't know. A thousand anyway. The Colonel could tell you to a man. A few of us used to get together on his birthday but we gave that up long ago."

"Most of them married?"

"Yes. With a raft of kids. It was the woman chasingest bunch in the army."

I decided to kid him a bit,

"You ever been around a bunch of Navy men?"

"Never. The swabs." He eyed me suspiciously,

"You ain't Navy are you?"

"Yes. Commander Howard. Navy Air Arm."

He let out a gusty sigh,

"I'll be damned. You look like a decent guy too. What in hell made the Colonel put you up here?"

"I'm the Colonel's campaign manager for Governor. Didn't you know?"

He rared back in surprise,

"So that's it. Governor. You think he can make it?"

"Easy. You have just given me the biggest idea for a promotion stunt I ever heard of. I've often thought the Army must be good for something."

CHAPTER TWELVE

He jumped to his feet and squared off bellering,

"Just step right up Navy boy and find out damn quick just how good the Army is. I'll tear your goddamned head off."

I said soothingly, but I had to laugh,

"Sit down Sergeant. I'll give you a job big enough for a general. If you let me down I'll drag you astern of a boat till you are naked as an onion."

He eyed me with disgust but sat down unwillingly.

"You. Sergeant Wells, are going to give the Colonel a birthday party. The largest birthday party this state has ever seen. I want every man, woman and child, who ever had the remotest connection with the Colonel here. I want all his relatives, too. Find all you can out of the state and get them here, too. When is the Colonel's birthday?"

He answered promptly,

"The 27th day of May. He will be forty-five years old."

I flipped my desk calendar.

"The 27th falls on a Saturday. Three weeks from next Saturday. Plenty of time if you get the lead out of your pants and don't do any goldbricking."

He squirmed about for a moment then faced me,

"Mr. Howard I couldn't afford a birthday party for a sparrow let alone a bunch of Army men and their families. I just been figuring. Counting women and kids there would be around five thousand at the very least. Maybe six, seven thousand."

I shouted happily,

"Hurrah for you. The more the merrier. I'll give you ten thousand dollars to start the ball rolling. You figure out what you are going to do with that many people and how you are going to feed them. They should come in on Friday night and stay until Sunday. Feed them good, keep them happy and entertained, and I'll see you have all the money you want."

I watched him digest that for a moment and I saw him wavering so I let him have the needle,

"Could it be the Army is not up to such a big job? Should I call in some of my Navy friends to put it over?"

The effect could not have been different if I had landed a haymaker flush on the point of his jaw. He jumped up breathing fire.

"You dirty bastard. Put up your measly ten thousand dollars an' get out of my way."

I pulled my checkbook out of the drawer and wrote a check for the amount payable to Sergeant Wells and handed it to him.

"If you want more, just say so. Get at it."

He glared at me, picked up the phone and dialed a number.

"Operator. Get me Judge Brown at the State Capitol building. Yes. I'll hold the line."

While he waited I could almost see his mind at work. He twitched all over, squinting his eyes and rubbing his ears.

"Hello. Judge Brown? This is Sergeant Wells, Yes Sir. Just fine. I want to borrow a couple hundred Guard tents, ten kitchens and six thousand beds with transportation for the equipment, Sir." He listened attentively.

"No Sir, I'm not. I'm going to give a party for Colonel Morley. A birthday party."

He held the receiver away from his ear with a grim smile,

"No Sir, I'm not. I'm just as sober as you are. It's a reunion of all his old outfit. Saturday the 27th of May. About six thousand, Sir."

He listened for a moment then his face wreathed in smiles, "Thank you, General. Yes, I'll pay all expenses. Thank you, Sir. You can be the guest of honor General. Saturday, May 27th. Goodby, Sir."

He dialed another number and said gruffly to me,

"I raised the General from a second lieutenant an' nursed him along till he was a real officer. He commands the Guard now."

He spoke into the phone,

"May I speak to Mr. Michaels, please?

"Hello Mike? Wells. Close that damn bank of yours, pack a bag for extended duty and get your ass over here. We got a mission. Three weeks. Yes. Three weeks. What? Oh hell. Just tell her the mission is confidential. Tell her to have another kid or buy a new hat. Shake it up boy. We're pressed for time."

He looked at me sourly,

"Mike is president of the National Trust Bank an' don't have anything to do but count his money. He needs the exercise. Besides his wife drives him nuts."

He dialed the phone again,

"Mr. James, please."

He held the receiver away and said softly, to me,

"This guy owns the Mortgage Company and half the land in the county.

"Fred? Wells here. Need a mess sergeant. Know where I can get a good one? Six thousand. Three times a day, women and kids, too. Ten kitchens—. Three weeks from now. Bring her along, she can wash dishes, besides I want to love her up. Right now. On the double."

He turned from the phone and said belligerently,

"We get things done in the Army. We don't float around in bathtubs wearing little blue aprons. By dark I can tell you where they are going to sleep, what they are going to eat, and what pot they can piss in."

He studied thoughtfully then asked,

"You got a lot of paper and envelopes?"

"Yes. But use the telephone."

He grinned broadly,

"Sure I'll use the phone, but half the fellers will think I'm nuts unless they get a letter, too. There has been times when I stretched the truth just for the hell of it. They got memories like elephants."

I suddenly had a thought,

"Will all these men be able to leave their businesses and homes to come here for three days? Can they afford it?"

He thought for a moment,

"Most of them can. Since they will be out only their transportation, it won't cost them much. They'll bust a gut trying to make it."

"All right. If you hear of any of the men who are short of transportation, send them tickets for themselves and their families or arrange for them to charter a bus. Pay the bills and get them here. I want the Colonel to be really surprised."

He looked at me dumbfounded,

"You mean to tell me the Colonel don't know about this hassle? You are doing all this on your own?"

"Goddamnit, Sergeant. I told you this was a surprise party. You, Sergeant Wells, are giving a party, not me. If you even mention my name I'll boil you in your own stinking juice."

He threw back his head and roared,

"Old Wells throwing a party for the Colonel and paying all the bills. Not a son-of-a-bitch in the outfit will believe it. Not for a minute. I got a reputation for hanging onto my money. They're not going to forget that."

I decided it was time to jab him again.

"If that is the kind of a man you are, we'll call off your part right now and I'll get my own Navy men in. At least we trust each other."

I reached for the phone. He was over me in a second, his fist cocked,

"Touch that phone and I'll jerk your goddamned arm off and beat you to death with it. You got the nastiest way of saying words."

I waited expectantly while he sat down and simmered. His face broke into a quick grin.

"The Army lost a good man when you joined the Navy, Commander. You got a cute trick of goading a man to fighting pitch. Not many men know how. You have done it to me three times today and each time I wasn't looking for you to hit me. I know an officer when I see him. You just give the orders, Sir, an' give me room."

He chuckled,

"Surprise hell. The Colonel will know all about the shindig two minutes after he walks in here."

I walked around the desk and held out my hand,

"Shake, Sergeant. I've been wondering where I could find a good right arm. You sure fill the bill. With a little training you would be a fairly decent Navy swab."

He got red in the face but looked at me and laughed,

"Nope. I know better now."

I told him,

"The Colonel will know all about the party, but at the proper time he will be surprised as all hell. Leave that part to me."

I had another thought,

"Is there some room in the house you could use for three weeks as an office?"

"Yes. The den. It is just down the hall on the other side. It is seldom used any more. The Colonel keeps his guns there and the furniture is old. More like a storeroom."

"Just the thing. Have a phone put in right away, get a typewriter and call the employment agency for a stenographer to do your typing and help you with the paper work."

He laughed shortly,

"I'm way ahead of the Navy this time, Fred James' wife was secretary of the Women's Auxiliary for a long time and knows every ex-soldier by his first name. Why did you think I wanted Fred to bring her along? She will do the inviting and half my work besides. Fred was mess sergeant for the Colonel for five years. The Colonel set him up in business after the war and now he is worth a couple of million."

I decided to hit him again for the fun of it,

"How come you can order all these guys around when they can buy and sell you? The peanuts you make here leaves you out of their class?"

He gave me a crafty look and shook with laughter.

"You missed that time, Commander. You're off balance."

Then it hit me like a baseball bat on the head. Sure as hell. The largest office building in the city. A million dollar building. The Wells building. Next door the Wells Hotel. Another million. The Wells Theatre. I mentally walked around the block. All Wells enterprises. I could only look at him in astonishment.

He wore a fatuous grin but said kindly,

"Straighten up. Push out your chest and suck your belly in Commander. We all have to start someplace. You are in the right place. The Colonel gave me a push an' I been running ever since. You got your push from him now dig in. I might be able to give you a little help if the going gets rough.

"If he says you are OK, that's good enough for me. If you let him down you'll wish to God you had sunk in one of your stinking bathtubs in the Pacific."

He added a simple bit of information.

"I have a suite on the second floor and only butler for the fun of it. I can look after the Colonel easier that way and keep him out of trouble."

I had one more question that had to be answered.

"When the Colonel is Governor, how do you think his wife will fit in? Will she be content to leave this lovely old house and mix in the dirty game of politics?"

He replied without reservation,

"She will fit any place the Colonel wants her to.

"She is a wonderful woman, a good wife and a charming companion. Before she married him she led a hell of a life. He don't know just how hard. She has told me parts of it. I admire and love her like she was my own child. She is young and full of fight and in my opinion the Colonel couldn't have picked a better wife. She hasn't been unfaithful yet. That answer your question?"

The last part of his answer was loaded, his look was grim and deadly. I nodded,

"Yes. I had formed my own opinion but I wanted to be sure. She is a magnetic woman with tremendous drive. We must channel it into an image of the perfect housewife and Governor's lady. That is what will bring in the votes in November."

He gave a growling laugh,

"Jesus, you are innocent, put her up front where the men can get a good look at her and they'll come running with their tongues hanging out. You ever see such a sexy woman?"

"No. You are right there. But the women would turn out en mass to vote against her in that role. They would hogtie their men at home to keep them from voting. Her role must be quiet and subdued. The loving wife behind the man."

"Maybe you ain't so innocent. How come you know so much about the way women would think about her?"

"Well Sergeant. The Colonel gave me the tipoff. He said she hated young women around her. If that is so women will instinctively hate her too. Her face and figure gives her a predatory look. She can't help the way she looks. They see in her a rival for their own men and resent it. We must keep her in the background. For that I will need your help.

"She must appear sweet, shy, and just happy her great big husband is going to be Governor."

His laugh was from his heart,

"Man. I can just see her in that role. She'll bust out all over when you tell her to be sweet and shy. I want to be far, far away when you tell her the news. Take my advice and send her a letter on asbestos, and take the first train out of town. Believe me I know her."

"Never mind, Sergeant. You attend to the details of the party. I'll make her sweet and shy."

He gave me a parting shot,

"I was just beginning to like you swab. Too bad you're not going to live long enough for us to become better acquainted."

"One thing more Sergeant. I want no uniforms or flag waving. This is a party for old friends only."

He laughed,

"There ain't one in a hundred could get into his uniform because they've outgrowed 'em." He eyed me keenly,

"You have a devious mind, Commander. I hope when the corkscrew quits turning you come out on top. I don't savvy what's going on an' I never questioned an order in my life, but right now you can't blame me for wondering if you have all your marbles."

"That is all, Sergeant. On your way."

"Yes Sir." He strode out of the room like he was on parade. He was a hell of a man.

I phoned my office, and Darleen answered at once,

"Mr. Howard's office."

"Good morning Miss Dahl." She started talking, the angry words tumbling out of the receiver,

"I quit. If you think I'm going to sit in an empty office and read True Confessions all day long, you think again.

"You haven't been near the place in a week. I just read in the paper where Mr. Morley has gone to New York. No doubt you are too pooped by now to attend to business. You will find my key in the outer door."

I shouted into the phone,

"Don't you dare hang up on me. I've too much on my mind to argue with you."

I listened to see if she was still there. She murmured sarcastically,

"I know what's on your little mind, but go on."

"Miss Dahl. I want a complete list of every newspaper in the state, including weeklies. The names of the publishers or owners and a list of their reporters. Men and women.

"I want a list of all the radio stations, also TV stations. Their hours of broadcasting and their rates. Find out which ones have mobile units equipped with TV cameras. Get me the name of some big outfit which has public address systems for rent, with operators to man them. I want at least ten pickup stations with about twenty-five loudspeakers.

"Please read that back so I will know you have been paying attention."

She read it back without a flaw, a rising lilt in her voice. She added surprisingly,

"Apparently you have been attending to business between times."

I couldn't help asking,

"Between what times?"

Her reply was thoughtful,

"I suppose even you must take time out to recuperate."

"Your mind is a thing of beauty Darleen. One of these nights we will go to my apartment where you can cook me a good dinner, and after dinner I can tell you how wonderful I think you are."

"I wouldn't go to your apartment alone with you if you were starving to death." There was a long moment of silence then a low barely audible whisper drifted out of the receiver,

"We could invite your landlady to dinner with us."

The phone didn't click as she laid the receiver very gently on the instrument.

I heard voices shouting in the driveway and car doors closing. I didn't want to meet the men who were going to spearhead the party. Not yet. That was the Sergeant's job.

I sat back and took stock of the day's plans.

Six thousand men and women from all parts of the state were going to be a formidable group to work with. There were some who wouldn't go along with the Colonel on party lines of course. Others would not take any interest one way or the other. But on the whole there would be a tight group who owed much to the Colonel. These would be the workers to depend on. I would work my own men into each section of the state and they would lead the way. By the time the party was over, Colonel Morley would be known by pictures, TV and radio to every voter. He would be a man who was liked enough to draw six thousand friends to his birthday celebration.

Best of all, there could not be a single hint of political publicity in the whole affair. Barring an accident, I would be able to pull off the slickest publicity stunt on record.

The opposition would be snowed under before they knew what hit them or picked their man.

That brought up another thought. I had to find out who the opposition was planning to run. The present Governor would automatically go out of office in January having served two terms. A new man would take his place on their party ticket. I was woefully ignorant of the machine politics in the state because my clients, so far, were all small fries compared to the Governorship.

I had a moment of truth as I realized my clients had almost no opposition for their respective offices. I wondered if I had been used so subtly by the machine I hadn't been aware of the fact.

I laid that thought aside instantly. All my clients had been young, fired with enthusiasm to make the state a better place to live in. Fighters, every one and since their election they had raised hell with the old time order of state and civic government. Each one had an enviable record in public affairs. The whole state was rotten with graft from top to bottom and the machine would fight with tooth and claw to maintain their hold on the public purse strings.

I had to get an intimate look at each and every man connected with the machine.

That brought Captain Downs into the picture. Sweet Amy with soft and yielding body, twisting, reaching and moaning in my arms.

Tough Amy. Captain Downs with a mind like a steel trap, hard and experienced, searching out the hidden secrets of men.

Secrets hidden deep in their guts. Secrets they hoped to keep hidden from the world. Those were the ones I had to know.

At the same time I had to protect Jennifer Morley from the prying eyes which would be focused on her from this day on.

Her every move would brighten or blur the image of a happy and contented woman, a queenly woman to occupy the great place as first lady in the state.

There had to be a way to make her see the importance of her actions. I had to find the way, but first I had to know her secrets. What inner tensions were driving her with such ambition to "Show them." She was obsessed with hate, distorting her thinking processes. Yet to all appearances she was a young, vivacious, happy child. Much in love with her husband, a charming companion and dutiful wife. The people who lived beside her day after day, told me so.

There was a way to draw her secrets into the open. She must be loved and give love. Her dogs, her horses, her husband, at odd moments me, all bespoke her need for love. She was a sensual little animal in every fibre of her body. Perhaps in a moment of physical release if she were exhausted enough, she would unburden herself of the nightmare in which she lived.

I thought of the consequences, but first things first. I had to know in order to protect her from herself.

In answer to my unspoken wish she came through the door like a whirlwind and slammed it behind her. She plumped into my lap with reckless abandon smothering me with her hard round breasts, then sliding down between my legs kissing me all over my face until I was on fire. She pulled at the back of my neck, her hands locked in my hair, mashing her hot mouth against my lips, pushing me away, pulling me close.

She was beside herself with excitement, laughing and crying at the same time. She freed one hand, opened the front of her dress and forced my face deep into her bared breasts.

"You smart son-of-a-bitch. What a wonderful idea. Ouch. Not so hard. They're tender. A party for Bart with half the population of the state here and not even Wells knows why, but I do.

The sneakiest stunt ever thought up. M-m-m-m- I could eat you. Move your hand away, you're driving me crazy and we don't have the time now. No. Chris. Stop it."

She wriggled out of my arms coming to a stand out of reach. Dress open, skirt awry, tousled hair, flaming face.

Like a street urchin on a windy corner she stood feet wide apart, braced against her gusty breathing.

"You are no gentleman. Chris Howard. A wise bastard you are. When do you spring the announcement?"

I grinned at her mockingly,

"Just stay close beside me, be a sweet wife to your husband and you will find out."

"I am a sweet wife to Bart. I intend to stay beside him. Right now he is in New York and you are here. I'm not going to wait any longer."

She lifted her skirt above her waist, straightened her lacy panties, sliding her hands down her thighs. Then she deftly patted her hair in to a semblance of neatness and danced out of the room, opening and closing the door with a whirling, dancing motion.

She left me in a whirling, dancing state too. Her kisses clung to my face like drops of water, her feminine perfume clinging to my clothing like a mist. I closed my eyes and leaned back to stifle my sobbing breath. It was no use.

I could see her, feel her, and taste the sweet moistness of her delicate nipples.

I had to get the hell out of the house and not come back.

I decided suddenly to buy a new car. I could work here days and spend the nights at my apartment. She was the Governor's wife and needed as much protection as a battle wagon in peace time.

I reached for the phone and called a cab.

CHAPTER THIRTEEN

By dark I was the proud possessor of a new cream colored Plymouth and short in the Howard Trust account by three thousand dollars. I used the campaign fund to pay for the car knowing it was a legitimate expense. I had no social life and all the car would be used for was transportation about the state in connection with Colonel Morley.

I thought about calling Darleen and asking her to have dinner with me. I changed my mind on second thought. Our dinner together would be in my apartment, very cozy, very private. What happened then would be of her own choosing.

She would walk up the stairs with her eyes wide open. If she closed them later. Well. I wouldn't pry them open.

For an hour I drove about the city enjoying my new car. I felt secure in the knowledge no one would recognize me in the car and take pot shots at me. I found a little smart restaurant on the outskirts, went in and ate a tasty broiled steak. I finished the meal in relaxed weariness. God I was tired. Good hard physical labor is easier on me than mental.

The emotional storms Jen had built up in me the last few days hadn't helped either. Every time I came in contact with her, she left me weak as a wet rag. I would go to my place and sleep off my emotional jag, but first I wanted to tell Wells where I was going to be.

I parked in front of the Morley house, locked the car and went into my office. A soft glow lit up the room. A TV set had been moved in and was placed against one wall, turned on low, the music of a famous band filled the room with soothing music. A long, wide, brocaded couch was placed in a corner, the foot pointing toward the TV.

Jen was curled on the couch with a glass in her hand. She waved the glass at me without taking her eyes off the set.

"Mix yourself a drink and join me. The music is dreamy."

I groped my way to the refrigerator and turned on the kitchen light. I found the makings for martinis and made two.

I switched off the light, went back and handed her one. She murmured a "Thank you" and sipped it slowly, her eyes still glued to the TV screen.

I sat carefully in one of the chairs across the room from her and gulped about half my drink before I glanced at her. She had moved and was sitting on the foot of the couch with her knees drawn up, her chin resting on them watching the show. At first glance I thought she was naked.

Then I saw she had on the tiniest bikini I had ever seen. I couldn't see any cloth around her waist. It looked like all she was wearing was a narrow strap between her legs.

She watched the show with concentration just tasting the drink with the tip of her tongue. To save my life I couldn't keep my eyes away from the bit of strap. When the show ended I felt like a towel in a washing machine, tumbling from side to side. I was just as wet, too.

I stood up hanging on to the chair to keep from falling down, and said as soft as my panting breath would permit,

"I just came here tonight to tell Wells I would sleep at my apartment tonight. It's late. I'll go now."

She opened and closed her legs in a waving motion of "Goodby," the strap glistening in the dim light,

"It's the best idea. You won't be afraid to go alone?" Her voice was deep and mocking.

"No. I know the way."

She asked softly,

"Will you please make me another martini before you go?"

I went back to the kitchen, dug the liquor out of the refrigerator and mixed another pair. I tipped one of them into the sink and watched it run down the drain. I had enough liquor and enough of her too. I switched off the light and carried the glass back to her.

She was standing at the side of the couch with her back toward me. She took the drink from my hand and walked to the TV. Close to the light the suit looked flimsier than before.

She changed stations, took a drink then turned around. I sucked in my breath and held it. What I had thought was cloth, was only strips of white flesh normally covered with the suit. The whole of her was Jennifer, tanned a golden brown from head to feet. The only thing she wore was a pair of diamond earrings. She was naked as a newborn baby.

I froze in my tracks absolutely stunned.

"You like what you see, darling." Her voice was like honey.

She walked purposely to me, threw back her shoulders. Standing on the tip of her toes and taking a deep breath her breasts were almost touching my face, hard and taut.

She changed hands with her glass and laid her cold one on the side of my neck. She was hardly breathing as she murmured,

"My hand cold darling? The rest of me isn't. Touch me. Touch me down there. I'm warm all over."

My body was paralyzed. Every instinct told me to run. Run. Run. I stood still unable to make my legs function.

In a fury she threw her glass across the room, gasping,

"You dirty bastard."

She moulded her body against me, her hands caught my shirt below the collar ripping it apart, the buttons flying around the room with little bouncing sounds. She slid her hot hands under my undershirt at the waist, spread her fingers wide, sliding her hands up the curve of my ribs. She pressed my nipples gently into the palms of her hands, then let them creep around me, closing them behind my back in a tight grip forcing the tips of her breasts to dig little holes in my chest.

I lost my mind and responded in a crushing hold, straining with all my strength to weld her against me.

I bent down and found her hot, moist mouth, bruising her lips and tasting the blood from the bruising. She moved against me seeking a union through my clothing, she moved her mouth from side to side moaning,

"Please darling. Please my dear one."

"Where?"

"Upstairs. In your bed. My dear one carry me."

Through that wonderful night another picture slowly formed in my passion drugged mind. A picture of Jennifer Morley as she really was.

She was without shame or mercy. In her wantonness and craving she drove me to heights of physical passion I never dreamed a man could be capable of. She was the master. I the slave. Every moment of the night she was pleading, urging, demanding. In sheer exhaustion I would momentarily drowse against her perspiring flesh, only to waken with the blood pounding in my body in a fresh storm of desire as her delicate hands, knowingly stroked and caressed my entire body, her hot wet lips and flame tipped tongue following the pattern of her hands. After our minutes of delirium she would cry and murmur like a person under the effect of an anesthetic. Her words uncoordinated, rambling.

Not once did she get complete satisfaction from our physical union. She only gave it. Each time left her unsatisfied, with a terrible yearning to keep reaching for that one thing she was unable to attain.

Toward morning her physical strength began to weaken, her mind becoming clearer, her murmured words beginning to tell her story. Piece-meal the hidden memories and thoughts torturing her came from her bruised, swollen lips in a torrent of words.

Word sentences filled with hate, intermingled with soft words of love and devotion. As she murmured on I listened with bated breath fearing to disturb her train of thought, my mind alert to catch her every meaning. As though a ticking clock had suddenly run down, her words run out.

She leaned over me, resting on one elbow and said in a fear ridden voice with tears gently falling on my face,

"Oh my darling. I have just had the most awful dream. I dreamed I was a little girl again, and you had just run away from me, leaving me all alone in a dark forest. I called and called for you to come back but you just kept on running till you were out of sight. Oh darling just love me. Love me with all your might. I need your love so."

She moved into my arms, no longer the fierce demanding female, but a sweet submissive woman, seeking only to give and receive pleasure in our union. A union that ended all too soon in a mutual spasm of ecstasy.

After all the years and after the long hours of seeking in my arms she had found what she was seeking for.

She drew away from my body gently and said in a hushed, delighted, small voice,

"Thank you dear one. Thank you. For the first time in my life I know what it is to be a woman. What a wonderful feeling it is. Thank you. Thank you My darling."

She found my hand and moved it over her breast closing my fingers around the soft mound, holding it there while she looked at me from under her deep purpled eyelids, a tiny smile uplifting the corners of her swollen lips.

Her face was pale and drawn but over it was a look of perfect contentment. She moved her head slowly from side to side in wonderment,

"My dearest. I have been dead all my life. Dead. Dead. Now I am so alive. You my darling have made me live. Thank you. Thank you."

She raised over me and kissed my eyelids one after the other, then softly touched her lips on mine for a fleeting second, sliding to the side of the bed in one graceful motion,

"It is daylight my love. I will leave you now so you can rest. Sleep darling. I will still be by your side."

She rose to her feet and tiptoed toward the side of the room. I called softly,

"Jen."

She came swiftly and nestled her face in my throat.

"Jen. How can you walk through the house without any clothes on?"

She chuckled delightedly like a child,

"I know a secret. When Bart's father had these rooms made into an apartment for himself he added a closet over the lower hall. The other end of it opens into my dressing room. I can go in your closet, sneak the length of it and I am in my own. Aren't I a smart girl. Even Bart doesn't know about it. I fixed a board so I could move it."

Her pale face actually glowed with mischievousness. I had to laugh,

"I'll remember that and use it often."

She glared at me fiercely,

"Don't you dare. I'd have to shoot you and say I thought it was a burglar." She kissed me tenderly,

"I'll use it every night I can. Bart sleeps alone in his own room. He says I keep him awake."

I leered at her,

"You wouldn't do that. Not you."

"You're a stinker Chris Howard. A real stinker."

Her quick sweet kiss belied her words and in a flash she pulled a pillow over my face and mashed it down. I pawed it away in time to see the closet door close.

I would have given a year out of my life to lay back in bed and go to sleep. I couldn't do it. I had too much to do.

I had to try to remember all she had told me and I had to get it down on paper. I took a cold shower remembering all the times when I had stood watch aboard ship unable to take a moment for a wink of sleep, expecting every second to see the phosphorus trail of a torpedo plunging into the bowels of my ship from a hidden submarine. Those nights I lived in a frenzy of excitement which left me weak and trembling from tension. I felt the same way now. I couldn't sleep then I couldn't now. I must remember.

I went downstairs and pushed the button connected to the kitchen. I hoped Mary was there that early.

In a few minutes she came in with a wonderful breakfast.

"A lovely morning Mr. Howard. You should sleep later, you look peaked. You work too hard."

I grinned to myself. Ah Mary. If you only knew.

"Lot to do this morning My love. I have to get at it."

"Yes I know. But you should have some fun, too."

She went out of the room, as usual, humming a little tune. I ate as quickly as possible and sat down to the typewriter. Closing my eyes I allowed my thoughts to drift back into the night to a warm, sweet smelling naked girl crying salty tasting tears while she painted a word picture that shocked me to the very marrow of my bones.

In a moment of self appraisal I knew myself for a monster who was even lower than some of those who filled the background of her picture. To ease my conscience I tried to think I had not willingly seduced her. She had been the aggressor in every single instance since the first moment she had walked into my office and told me she was all mine.

Even at the last second of leaving me she had thanked me. Actually thanked me again and again for the animal use of her lovely body.

There wasn't even the flimsy excuse of love. Morally I was guilty of adultery in its worst form, if there is any distinction. Yet, under my self castigation I could hear her whispering softly,

"Thank you dear one. Thank you. For the first time in my life I feel like a woman. I am a woman. I have been dead and you have made me live. Thank you. Thank you."

Other words she had mumbled in her sleep came to me. Words muttered in a childish voice, a loving voice,

"Daddy. Where is my Mommy? I'm so lonesome. I love you. I'm a big girl now. What is school? Will you give me a pretty dress? You are so nice and I love you Daddy. Come back to me. Please come back to me. Why did you die and leave me all alone? I'm so little to be left all alone and live without you. Please come back. I want to die too. I can't live without you My Daddy."

Scalding tears had streamed down her wan face as she lived in agony those fleeting moments of her childhood.

"Oh, thank you. I will love to live at your house. My new brothers? I never had any brothers. I love all of you. I've been so lonesome all by myself. Please. Please don't whip me any more. I'll work harder. I will. Please don't whip me."

I felt again the cringing, shuddering body, re-living in terror, her whippings. Sobbing in my arms she went on,

"I like to sleep with you my dear brothers. So warm. I like to sleep warm. What are you doing to me? Please don't tickle me. Your fingers hurt when you tickle me there. Please. Please don't. You hurt me. Please don't. It hurts so. Don't hit me. Oh, please don't hit me again. I won't tell. I promise I won't tell. I won't tell. I won't tell. I won't tell."

Once more the trembling girl was crying in fear. Her hands pressed over her face to ward off blows. It was the terrible crying of a little girl in terror and loneliness.

I had put my arms around her and gently cradled her head against my chest, whispering softly to waken her from her nightmare. In a convulsive movement she had wound herself around me still only half awake,

"Chris. Chris. Oh God. Make it go away. Hold me tight. I'm so frightened. Love me. Love me."

A half hour later she had drifted back to her world of heartbreak and terror. She sobbed softly as she mouthed words filled with vindictiveness and a new fierce purpose,

"Yes I'll let you. All three of you dirty bastards. But first you pay me. Pay me first. You are all dirty liars. After I let you, you never pay me. Pay me first. I must go to school. Going to be the smartest girl in school. Pay me first. Pay me. My God how you hurt me. Got to see a Doctor. Sick. So sick.

"Doctor. Will it hurt? Every month? I'm a woman now? No. You can't. No. Please don't, Doctor. You son-of-a-bitch. I know what they do to bastards like you raping a little girl. I'm only twelve years old. I'll make you pay, or rot in jail. Pay me or you'll be sorry you did that to a little girl. Pay me. Pretty clothes. Pretty shoes. Money. Money. Money. I hate you. You can't run. Take me with you. Take me to New York. Make me a lady, Doctor. I want to learn how to be a lady.

"NO. NO. I can't have your baby. NO. NO. I'm going to die. Now you dirty old man you can pay to make me a lady. You are a murderer. You murdered my baby. Pay me. Pay. Pay."

I had watched her keenly as she mumbled through this part of her life. Her hands clenched in the pillow, her teeth grinding angrily. I had laid very quiet lest I disturb her train of thought. Soon she had continued with a small child's wonder in her muted voice,

"What a beautiful house. I love the garden, Such a big house. Yes. You can do it to me whenever you want. I'll be naked whenever you want me too. Yes. First you give me a lot of money. I'm going to be a real lady. You'll see what a fine lady I will be. I'm sixteen, Uncle. You think I'm beautiful do you? You like my beautiful naked body. Use it. Kill yourself over it. I hate you but you can use my body as long as you give me lots of money.

"Going to be a wonderful actress. Rich now. Famous. Dear God. Going to have another of your dirty brats. Take it away. You put it there. You're a murderer again. I hate you. I won't die because I hate you so. God how I hate you.

"Going to kill you. I want you dead. Dead. Dead. Know a man. He'll kill you. He wants my beautiful body to sweat over. I'll drive him crazy with my beautiful body. I'll make him kill you. I hate you."

She had screamed the last part of her recital, then subsided into a quivering beaten small woman, her breath coming in choking sobs,

"Yes. Uncle. I'll come back. You killed him. I know. I wrote it all down and put the paper where you can never find it. You kill me and the paper will be found and you will die.

"If you ever touch me again you'll hang for murder. As long as you live you will give me all the money I can ever use.

"I've always hated you. See my beautiful body. Look at it. Think of all the times you raped it. Now you can never touch me again, I'm free. Free from your slobbering rape. Free.

"I'm a lady and you can never hurt me again. Now I can be happy and not live in fear of you. Ha. Ha. Ha. I'm free."

Her body had slowly relaxed when she stopped talking, her breathing became regular. I had laid quiet wondering if the memories would continue, but she was cleansed of all her hidden terror. The telling in a half drugged sleep of physical exhaustion had set her free. Her hands had wandered over me, tender and loving. Suddenly she had caught her breath and the wells below her closed eyelids had filled with tears. She had leaned over me on one elbow, with tears falling in my face and she had said,

"My darling. I have just had the most awful dream—

"Love me. I need your love so."

I had loved her with all the vigor of a first love and she had given herself with all her heart. Free from fear and terror.

She had found her first complete ecstasy in my arms in the loving.

It was almost noon when I finished typing. She had told me what I wanted to know. Her immature body had been raped at the age of seven or eight by the three loutish boys, and the act had been continued until she was past the age of puberty.

Then the monstrous rape by a Doctor to whom she had gone in her childish ignorance of the facts of womanhood had left an indelible mark in her mind. It had filled her with a consuming hatred of all the males she had known in her early life. The woman she had known as a foster mother had mistreated her to the point where, to this day, she hated and mistrusted women.

No wonder she didn't have any friends. Close friends. She didn't dare trust either, men or women. It had been beaten into her with lash and fist.

This was Jennifer. The woman who would be the Governor's lady the first of January. I thought of the last moments she had spent in my arms. A sweet, submissive, gentle, loving woman. A real lady such as she had always dreamed of being.

For the first time in her terror ridden life, her mind was free of all hate filled emotion. She had been a woman giving freely of herself with no motive other than to serve. In so doing she had tasted the golden fruit of ecstasy and complete satisfaction. The fact it was me was beside the point. I had been only the instrument within reach at the exact moment of her freedom. She loved her husband, of that there was not a single doubt in my mind.

But through the years she had been constantly on guard to conceal from him the facts of her former life. Outwardly, she had been a loving and dutiful wife. Always seeking to give him pleasure in her companionship and luscious body.

Inwardly, she had seethed with hate, not for him, but for those who had castigated her very soul.

When she was near the breaking point, she had met me. She had recognized at once that here was a man she could use to vent her spleen on all the men in her past.

She had set about using me in a methodical manner, but by some strange alchemy of nature she was the one who had been transformed after hours of violent and physical effort into a weakened state of mind and body. She had lost her will to fight back the terrible memories and they had come tumbling out in a torrent of spoken words. Words which she had kept bottled inside her mind like a banked furnace fire.

When the fire was allowed to burn brightly the tension was released also. Her mind clear and no longer afraid, she had turned to me with her heart bursting with love and asking nothing in return but to be loved as a woman. Her reward had been a tremendous burst of applause from her Gods of the universe. Applause which left her breathless with wonder, melting with tenderness, keenly alive with well being.

I wondered what she would be like when next we met. Would she be the aggressive female? Or the sweet, tender woman who had left me with a mischievous secret between us?

I could only pray it would be the latter.

CHAPTER FOURTEEN

There was one thing that kept prodding at my mind. How did the gangster friend of Jen fit into the picture? Was he connected in some way with her racketeer friend, Tony Athens?

Was Tony Athens the man she had meant when she had said, "Know a man. He'll kill you." Was he the man the Doctor had killed? Did this man have some knowledge of Jen which he could use to blackmail her? Could he blast Bart Morley's political ambitions before they got well started?

I picked up the phone and dialed the police department.

"Inspector Rodgers, please."

"Rodgers speaking."

"Hello Inspector. Chris Howard. Just fine. Thank you. Do you know anything about a character the government indicted a year or so ago on a tax charge? He beat the case——

"Yes Inspector. That's the man. Leon St Clair. I'd forgotten his name. Front man in the Eagle Club? Vice? Narcotics? What a sterling gentleman, Inspector.

"The hell he is. Mike Flynn. Hu-uh. No. Nothing yet. As soon as Captain Downs reports in I'll put her to work on it. Someone doesn't want Bart Morley elected. Thank you, Sir. I'm allergic to bullets. I'll be careful. Good-by."

In my mind a pattern was beginning to form. Was it possible all the rackets in the state from the Governor down to the back alleys were tied together under one head man? What man could weld together such an organization?

Not a single person I knew or had heard about could fit the bill.

I gave up, rummaged around in the refrigerator for a quick snack and went to bed. My mind wasn't up to sorting out all the facts which were piling up.

I woke long after dark. I turned on a light and looked at my wrist watch. Nine thirty. I felt like a new man. While shaving I noticed the swelling was all gone in the side of my face, but what a beautiful blue-black it was. Just the color of a beetle. My shower refreshed me and I felt like a new man.

In the kitchen, I found a plate full of roast beef, potatoes, vegetables, a pot of coffee, and a slab of apple pie. The dinner was still warm so I ate the whole thing.

What a cook that Mary was. I could love a woman like her.

Suddenly I thought of my new car. It was late, but a short drive would do me good. From a distance the car looked like it listed to starboard. On closer examination it sure as hell did. Both front and back tires on that side were flat. I stepped back into a shadowy bush and looked cautiously around.

In the light of the house I was a sitting duck for a man with a rifle. A new car doesn't have two flats at once. It was a setup if I ever saw one. I got down on all fours and crawled deeper into the bush. I heard a slight click like the cocking of a gun and froze instantly. From the balcony a choked giggle and then a low voice,

"Which are you? The big bear? The middle bear? Or the baby bear?"

I sucked in a gusty breath and in two seconds I was in my bedroom. Jen was in the middle of the bed with her feet curled under her and she was bouncing up and down, howling with laughter.

She wasn't even wearing earrings. The dark frothy cloud of her hair cascaded around her shoulders waving in rhythm to her laughter, her face a pool of merriment. It was too much.

In a single motion I sat on the edge of the bed, flipped her across my knees, face down, and whacked her pretty little rump. She slid back far enough to get a good grip on my leg and sunk her teeth in the fleshy part of my thigh clear through the pants.

My second smack wasn't half as hard as the first one. My hand refused to raise again for the third try, remaining flat on the reddening flesh with a will of its own. She said in a sultry voice,

"Beat me big bear. I love it."

I jerked her roughly against my chest,

"I ought to tan your britches good. Two flat tires on my new car."

She took one of my hands and slid it downward,

"What britches?" She asked in mock innocence.

Her arms stole around my neck,

"I was afraid you would leave me alone tonight so I fixed your car good. Oh, Chris, darling. I've been in here twice this afternoon but you were sleeping so soundly I didn't have the heart to wake you. I wanted to feel your arms around me again. I've been in a rosy dreamy all day."

She tugged at my belt buckle,

"Take your clothes off. Please. I want to lay close to you and feel your arms around me. No darling. Don't kiss me. Just hold me tight."

My heart leaped. She was sweet. Supple and yielding as a reed in a summer breeze. She cuddled in my arms, burying her face in my throat, making little whuffing sounds.

How long we lay quiet, I have no idea. My blood was pounding in my body like waves on a rocky shore. Beat. Beat. Beat.

Every time I tried to kiss her, she burrowed deeper into my arms, holding herself in check, but the delightful, delicate touch of her fingers caressed me, drove me crazy.

Still, I wanted to humor her until she came to me of her own will. She suddenly slipped away from me and walked to the long door mirror. She turned about, studying her body.

There were no flaws in the reflection. She was the perfect sexual female—full bodied, ripe and warm looking. She faced me and said, with a bit of amazement in her voice,

"All my life I've wondered why I never could get worked up to real passion. I've always had to pretend I loved it, even with Bart. To me it was just a ritual I had to perform to help the man of the moment. I've hated the act all my life but when I was very young, I learned I could use my body to get what I wanted from men. It has never meant a thing to me. Now, in a single night, you have made me feel like a different woman."

She came to the side of the bed and knelt, laying her cheek on my chest.

"Chris, tell me what has happened to me."

Carefully I asked,

"Don't you remember what you told me last night?"

She started upright, with fear in her eyes.

"No. My God, what did I tell you?"

I drew her close, repeating all she had told me of her past. She sobbed quietly, but listened attentively. At the last I told her,

"You must never think of that part of your life again. It is gone forever. When you told me, you got it all out of your mind. You have been ill with the thought of it. Please try not to remember again. You are a lovely, wonderful woman, the wife of a man who loves you. Please, Jen, never look back again."

She moved away and walked slowly around the room, head bowed in silent thought. Presently she lay beside me, raised on one elbow, then said softly,

"Dear one. I'm very grateful. Very grateful to you. I have never told a soul about myself before. I have lived in hate all my life. Bart has been the only person I ever trusted, or wasn't afraid to love. But I knew if he ever found out about me, he would leave me and I have lived in daily fear of losing him. I know he loves me, he's proved it many times.

"Since we have been married, he has had other women. I've known every time, but he has always come back to me. Each time I have died, but I knew it was my fault because of the hate and fear I have been filled with. Now, someway I am not afraid any longer."

She closed her eyes for a moment, then looked at me steadily and asked,

"Chris, do you love me?"

I answered honestly.

"No, Jen, I don't love you. I like your sweet lips, your loving arms, and your luscious passionate body. But love you, I do not."

She rolled on top of me in a quick smothering embrace.

"What a delightful bastard you are. You are not even gentleman enough to lie to me. I'm glad, Chris. I'm so glad you are not going to be hurt. I can enjoy you all the more, knowing you are just loving me with your body instead of your heart."

I ventured a query.

"Don't you have any conscience?"

"Not a bit where you are concerned. What I give you is apart from my life with Bart. You are the only man that has touched me since I met Bart. The only man who ever will, besides my husband. That I promise." She laughed softly,

"Bart will think he has a new woman in his bed."

She thought for a minute.

"Chris, there is a man who knows about the way I lived. His name is St. Cyr. He told me the night of the party if I didn't return the paper containing the facts of Tony Athens' murder, he would tell the newspapers about me. He is a foul animal, involved in all the dirty vices in the city. I know enough about him to put him away for life, but in so doing he would ruin me forever. Rather than hurt Bart I would kill myself first." She shuddered in my arms, crying in desperation.

"Jen, dear, I know about St. Cyr. You remember the lovely woman Bart was friendly with the night of your party?"

"I sure do. The undressed bitch."

I chuckled.

"For your secret information, she is a private investigator. Captain Downs. She is working with me. Also her uncle is Inspector Rodgers of the police department.

"The Captain is in Washington now. When she returns tomorrow, her assignment will be St. Cyr. She is clever and has a world of experience along those lines. She will have the help of all the city police, also the Federal Agency. The Tax Department is most anxious to get their hands on St. Cyr and all his henchmen. Will you tell the Captain what you know?"

"Oh, Chris. You know I can't. It would destroy me."

"Jen, think. Isn't there some way? You can trust the Captain with your life. She thinks Colonel Morley is the finest person in the world. She will protect you, never fear."

"It is impossible. You know it is," she moaned.

"Please, Jen. Before you say no, think about it. The things you know may be just enough to put him away far enough to make you safe the rest of your life. You trust me, don't you?"

"Chris, how can you say it. Look at me—naked, wanton, and shameless in your arms. Of course, I trust you."

"All right for now. But think about it. Captain Downs is devoted to your husband. Believe me she is a wonderful woman. She will do everything in her power to see the Colonel is elected Governor."

She looked at me accusingly.

"Just how well do you know her?"

"Why?"

"Why? You give yourself away. When you speak of her, your eyes light up like a lamp. Is she as good in bed as I am?

"Don't answer that, you snake. I know she isn't. The bitch sure gets around. First my husband, now you. It is comforting to know who I am sharing my men with."

I laughed until she pounded me with her small fists.

"So you think that's funny? Please put your arms around me. Please hold me. Please run your hands over me."

Her hot lips pulled at my mouth while she murmured,

"Funny. Funny. Funny. I love it. Slide a pillow under me, it will be easier."

The bright sun awoke me, shining through the window. The rays made a mottled pattern over Jen. I was reminded of a new born fawn I had once found in the woods. She had one arm over her face as though she was hiding. But I knew she would never hide again. That much she had told me in the night.

I kissed her breasts gently, and instantly her arms were around me, wide awake in a twinkling.

"Good morning, my very dear. What a delicious way to be awakened. Kiss them some more."

I bit her. She curled her fingers in the back of my hair and jerked my head back.

"Damn you. That hurt. Now make it well again. Gently."

I was most happy to oblige. An hour later she bounced out of bed, fairly dancing with vitality. It made me weary just to watch her. She said scornfully,

"You look all drained out, dear. You've lost your stamina, I hope. Your other woman is sure going to be disappointed when she comes back to you."

"You're a merciless wench. I have no other woman, for which I'm thankful. Don't you ever get enough?"

She laughed low and happily as she bent over me.

"Not of you, big bear. Not of you."

My arms were too leaden to reach for her again, so she kissed me chastely on the forehead and said,

"Meet me in the dinette in an hour for breakfast. We have a lot of work to do today."

I piled the pillows atop each other, jerked the covers over me and went to sleep.

Mary shook me roughly,

"Get up, you big ox. Mrs. Morley has been waiting for you in the dinette. Hurry. Your breakfast is getting cold."

I said grouchily,

"Mary, I'm dead for sleep. Leave me alone."

"Shame on you. It's nine o'clock. You're just lazy. Get a move on or I'll take a broom to you."

She waved her broom dangerously near my head.

"All right. All right. I'll get up, but I won't be happy about it."

She said in a motherly way,

"What you need is a good woman to make you toe the mark. You've been a bachelor too long."

I groaned aloud.

"A woman is the very last thing I need right now. I have work to do. Get out of here and let me alone."

She headed for the door, laughing,

"Says the man, bashful, too."

When I made it downstairs, Jen was at the typewriter, her fingers flying. Mary was in the room dusting the furniture. Jen glanced at me.

"Good morning, Mr. Howard. Sleep well?"

I had a ready answer, but I didn't dare say it. I nodded and settled down to eat my breakfast while Jen went on with her typing.

When Mary left the room, Jen joined me at the table. She poured a cup of coffee, lifted it to her lips, grinning over the rim.

"Was it such a bad night, darling? Did I poop you all out?"

I gave her a twisted smile.

"That, my dear, is the understatement of all time. Frankly, I'm dead. How you can be so damned full of vitality is beyond me. Are you made of iron?"

She said impishly,

"Want to feel and find out?"

I gave up.

"Please, Jen. Just let me rest a little while. Let me think of something besides you today. You have me wrapped in such a fog, I can't think. When I close my eyes, all I see is you."

She cooed with delight.

"Why, Chris, how gallant you are. I believe you could be a gentleman if you tried."

She came around the table, kissed me thoroughly, then went back to the typewriter. I followed and sat down.

She said,

"Chris, what I am writing here could get me killed. I know others who have been killed for much less. The men's names who are here are all men who live beyond the law.

"They are all dangerous. When I give you this paper, I am placing my life in your hands. I am doing this to help and protect

Bart. If he should find out all I have told you, I would certainly die anyway. We have lived a quiet life since we have been married. We haven't gone out too much or made any close friends. I couldn't, knowing that sooner or later I would have to face up to my past. I want desperately to have Bart become a power in the land. So great that when he learns the truth of me, he will be beyond the reach of their slimy hands."

I asked her,

"Are you sure you want to do this? I think I was wrong when I asked for your help. Bart can withdraw from a campaign that isn't even started, and no one will be the wiser. You can continue to live as you have in the past—quiet, peaceful, happy with your husband in this beautiful home."

She answered with force and vigor.

"That time is past, Chris. I haven't told you before, but I have half a million dollars in bonds in the bank. Bart doesn't know a thing about them. It is all mine. I earned it, as you well know. I am going to place it all to your account and you must use it any way you see fit. Please, Chris. Save me some shred of decency if you can, but first of all use it to silence these men at any cost. If necessary, I will leave Bart and disappear from sight forever rather than hurt him by having him held up to ridicule in the public press.

"He is a proud man, a fine man. If I left him he would get over it in time. If he was hurt by my past, he would never get over it. It would hurt his pride."

"You are a wonderful woman, Jen. You love him very much, don't you?"

"I wonder, Chris. I admire him above all men. He was the first man in my life who treated me as an equal. He was the first man who came near being my ideal of a knight on a white charger. He was the first man I ever met who was kind and gentle with me. Not once did he try to get me into a bed with him before we were married. We met, of all places, at a church social the day Tony Athens was killed. The fact I was with Bart Morley kept me from being questioned by the police. Only a few men knew I was Tony Athens' woman. One of them was a commissioner of police. When he found out I had been with the famous Colonel Morley all afternoon at a church social, he forced the others to keep silent. I will not write his name, but I will tell you. If necessary you can talk to him, he's a power in New York politics now, and clean of any gangster connection." She paused, then said softly, "You asked me if I loved Bart. I would gladly die to make him happy. I know he loves me, but I don't think honestly I know what love is. You have given me the first physical satisfaction I have ever known. At the right time, I could have loved you to distraction. You are the second man who has been kind and understanding. For those two things, I wish I could say I loved you. In a small way, I do. Right now, my body is crying out for you to hold me in your arms. That is the first feeling of its kind I have ever experienced. I wish it were real love. In your arms, I have a feeling of security, no fear, no emptiness, just a marvelous sense of aliveness and well-being. It is a thing I will always be grateful for. The money I place in your account is part of my past. I never want to see a penny of it again. If you can save my life, it will be well spent. Through the years, I will be yours any time you want me. I know I will want you physically all the rest of my life."

She bowed her head on the typewriter and sobbed. I lifted her into my arms, rocking her like a child. My God. What could I do to comfort her? Hire guards for her? Send her on a long tour? Ask her to return the incriminating paper? I racked my brain for the answer. I didn't love her, but by heaven I would protect her some way if it killed me. Underneath her polished exterior, she was still lonely and frightened.

My first thought was to present Colonel Morley with all the facts, relying on his honor to stand by her, but I rejected the thought because it would be against Jen's wishes. All of a sudden I realized I didn't give a damn about Bart Morley's campaign. Jen was the focal point of the whole situation. Without her, there would be no campaign. Without her, Bart Morley wouldn't want to be Governor. Without a wife, he couldn't be elected. The voters won't go for a man who is mixed up in national scandal.

I stroked the lovely head lying so trustingly on my shoulder. Half a million dollars would build a big fence around her. I sure as hell would need a lot of help to build it, but that kind of money could hire a whole army. I had a happy thought. With all those dollars, I was a very rich man. I could be a powerful enemy, myself. The thing to do was get to work.

Jen turned her head and looked at me.

"You have thought of a way out, Chris?"

"I think so, Jen. But how did you know?"

"I have been listening to your heart beat. It was running wild, now it is a steady beat. I know."

"You scare me, Jen. I can't even think without you knowing what I'm thinking about."

She pressed her nose into the hollow of my shoulder with a contented sigh.

"Hold me, dear one, just a minute longer, then you can get to work. Squeeze me real tight so the feel of your arms will linger. Oh-uuf. Woosh. That's enough. I'm a softy, you know."

She was out of my arms in a second and walked out of the office without another word or glance.

I picked up the paper on which she had written the names. There were eight names of men, names of five banks, names of two hotel room numbers with men's names after them, two girls' names with addresses, four safety deposit box numbers, and ten business addresses. All but two of the men's names listed New York addresses. The two exceptions were here in the city. As I read these names, I almost had a heart attack. I knew them both. I was sure Jen was out of her mind when she wrote the name of one of them.

I took my knife out of my pocket and cut that name out of the list, chewed the small piece into bits and swallowed it. I was actually afraid to think about him in my own mind. I wasn't going to trust any other person with that bit of information. At the proper time, I wanted to get him alone where I could get his neck in my hands and slowly strangle him while I gloated over his puny struggles. I wondered how I could keep from jumping down his ugly throat if we ever met face to face before it was the right time to expose him. That was one son-of-a-bitch I wanted to finish off in my own good time.

It was late afternoon when I finished my paperwork. It was all in shape for Captain Downs to go to work on. How her eyes would bug out when she saw that file of information which had been so carefully hidden that all the Tax Department men, with all their Government resources behind them, had been unable to uncover. Where it came from would remain a secret. She could think what she liked. I thought wryly, she wouldn't like what she thought.

I pulled out a desk drawer and taped the file to the under surface of the desk top and shoved the drawer back in place. The bomb was loaded and the fuse was set.

CHAPTER FIFTEEN

Jen walked into the room, wearing a lovely creation of an afternoon dress, gloves, hat, fashionable purse under her arm with shoes to match on her tiny feet.

She was absolutely gorgeous. Even her face was aglow with a new radiance. She said abruptly,

"I've just come from the bank, Chris. The bonds are in a deposit box in your name. Here is the key. I thought it would be better that way, so there will be no question of taxes. The bonds are tax-free Government bonds. All you have to pay is taxes on its earned income, which I have never collected. That amounts to something over fifty thousand dollars. You can find out what the tax is and pay it. The rest is all yours. I never want to see a cent of it again."

Her matter of fact statement took my breath away. She had just given me over five hundred thousand dollars like she was handing me a bon-bon. She noted my consternation.

"It is dirty money, Chris. I feel like I had just stepped out of my bath. I feel clean for the first time since it was given me. Believe me, it wasn't given willingly either. I only pray you can use it wisely, and at the same time get some measure of enjoyment out of it yourself."

She gave me a special kind of a look, then chuckled,

"Remember the first time I came to your office? I told you you loved two things. Money and women. In that order. Now you're almost a millionaire, which is enough to keep you in pocket money for a few months. Next, you have me. More woman than you can handle. It is going to be interesting to see how you are going to react to that combination."

Until that moment, the thought of the money being actually mine had not entered my mind. It was only money to be used to protect her. It was still her money, yet here she was, telling me she hoped I would enjoy it myself. On top of that she was telling me I couldn't handle her. Hell's fire. I'd already handled her to perfection. She had told me her story, hadn't she? I had stayed with her physically till she was weak as a rag doll. I had news for her.

"You're a beautiful doll, Jen Morley. I adore every inch of your lovely skin, but let's get some things straight.

"The money is all yours. The fee you pay me is enough for me to struggle along on. I will use your money to get you out of trouble of your own making, and to keep you out of future trouble if you do as I tell you. From now on you are a little lamb following its mama. You will be a sweet, shy, loving wife to your husband, a busy little homemaker, the woman's ideal of the proper kind of a wife to be the First Lady of the state. That is the picture of you I'm going to plaster in every public place in the country.

"What you do in your bedroom is no concern of mine, just be damn sure you confine your antics to your own bedroom, not any place else where the tiniest bit of suspicion could be pointed at you. What money is left over, I will return to you intact. I only hope there is a wad of it left."

She opened her mouth, closed it, shook her head, then said softly,

"Chris Howard, you are the most gentleman I ever knew. A real stinker of a gentleman. God bless you. I promise with all my heart I will be just what you ask, with one exception. There is another bedroom I will visit often. I wish I were there right now.

I would show you some antics you haven't even dreamed about. If you want me to be shy and a plain housewife, that I will be. A loving wife, I will try to be. I will even be a little, gentle lamb following its mama, or should I say papa?" She grimaced in distaste, then bent her head and let out the three amazing sounds.

"B-a-a, B-a-a. B-a-a."

I burst out with a bellow that could be heard for a block. She joined in with a joyous laugh which rang against the walls echoing her freedom at last.

The door suddenly opened and Colonel Bart Morley was in the room, his face wreathed in smiles.

"Jen, darling. Hi, Howard. That laughing was the best thing I've heard around this old place. How are you both?"

Jen was all over him in a twinkling.

"Bart, Bart. Oh, Bart. How wonderful. You are home."

He swung his briefcase around her and hugged her tight with both arms. He winked at me over her shoulder.

"Worth coming home to, Howard."

"She is that, Sir. I was just leaving. I'll see you in the morning. Everything is going according to schedule. We have a lot to talk about, but I know you want to spend some time with Mrs. Morley, so I'll be on my way. Good-by, Sir. Good-by, Mrs. Morley."

Jen gave me a quick look and nodded her head as I went upstairs to dress for the evening. I wanted to get out of the house in a hurry in order to give Jen time to collect her senses. We had been so close in the last three days, I was afraid she would give herself away if I were around to distract her attention from her husband.

When I went to my car, the tires were repaired, and it took but a moment to start the motor. I swung out of the driveway and drove to my office.

From the outside of the door, I could hear the typewriter humming. I opened the door and stepped in, pausing just inside. Miss Dahl looked up inquiringly, her eyes blinking.

"May I help you?"

"Whose office is this?"

She said with perfect courtesy,

"Mr. Howard's, Sir. But he is here so damn seldom, I'm sure I wouldn't recognize him if he came in the door."

I went toward her, around her side of the desk. She rose from her chair and kept the desk between us, her face lit up like a string of Christmas tree lights.

"Keep away from me, you stinking wolf. I'm delighted you found time to pay us a visit, but just stay away from me. I have no inclination to be bitten."

She was right on the ball, dangling the bait in front of my eyes. I looked her over happily.

"The same, sweet wholesome girl, with the kind thoughts for her boss. Will you do me the honor to have dinner with me tonight, then do the town?"

She eyed me like I was a specimen in a zoo, then queried,

"Just what does 'doing the town' consist of?"

"Well, I thought we might go to some swanky place for dinner, then take in a good show. After that we could go to my apartment to talk over our evening's entertainment."

"No, thank you. The start was fine. The finish was your finish. It was a nice thought, anyway."

She said briskly,

"I have the reports on the newspapers and stations all completed. They are on your desk. It will take another day to get the names of all the reporters you asked for.

"There are three firms in town who can furnish the public address systems. I have written down their names and phone numbers, so you can make the arrangements you wish. Their prices are all about the same."

"You are very efficient, Darleen. I couldn't possibly get along without you. In the next months, please stick with me even if you think at times I'm off my rocker. I will have a purpose in every action I take. It is not going to be easy for you to understand. I want your trust and your confidence. When the campaign is finished, I'll give you a paid vacation at any spot in the world you choose. I promise."

She leaned on the desk with her elbow, her chin resting in her hand. She said dreamily,

"I know just where I'd like to go. To a little island off the coast of Florida. There is a big wonderful hotel, clean white beaches, warm moonlit nights. How I'd love it there."

She moved her head from side to side.

"That is something you wouldn't understand."

Just for fun I said,

"I've been thinking of the same place lately. I think maybe three or four months would be about right."

Her eyes grew big as silver dollars, her face flushed. Then she said in a hushed voice,

"No, you're not thinking of the same thing I am. All you think about is chasing women, and there are no naked women there for you to ogle."

"Why, Darleen. If you just happened to be there on your vacation, how could I see any one else?"

"Simple. You'd just look past me into the next green pasture. I'm only your secretary."

"What a twisted mind you have under that mop of lovely hair. Afraid of competition?"

Her look was unabashed. She walked to a chair, lifted her foot to the edge of the seat, bent over straightening the seam in a stocking. Her pose was perfectly natural, but the view was entrancing. Under the dress, the long curved leg above the foot resting on the floor a model of perfection. The top of her stocking was fastened to a slender garter, the upper end hidden in a band of lace.

The inside of the pink, warm thigh was all Darleen. She laughed softly as she saw the flush spread over my face, tucked her dress around her carefully, and sat down. She said,

"Captain Downs called. She said to tell you she would be back tomorrow." She studied me a moment,

"I have changed my mind. I would love to have dinner with you. Only I am not dressed to go to a fancy place. I'd like to have you come to my home. I'll cook you a steak."

I jumped for joy, went around the desk reaching for her. Picking up the chair, she fended me off like a lion tamer.

"None of that, Cassanova. I'm only going to cook your dinner, not feed your ego. Put your hands in your pockets and keep them there. I want mine to work with."

I stuck my hands in my pockets, giving her my best smile.

"I'm a lost child. Lead me home."

When we reached the car, she said happily,

"Why, Chris, what a beautiful car. Is it yours?"

"Yes, indeedy. All paid for, too. It came out of my expense account."

She said sarcastically,

"My, my. You must be quite a man if your services are that valuable. I've underestimated you. She must find you very entertaining."

"Keep thinking those sweet thoughts, my dear. You will soon learn all about me."

I thought for a few moments she was going to walk away, then she slid into the seat. I went around the car, eased under the wheel and started the motor. I reached over her thigh, pulled her close beside me, then drove on. She pointed the way to a small white old-fashioned house set well back from the street, almost hidden by shrubbery. The lawn and the trees were carefully tended, apparently with loving care.

She said simply,

"I was born here. I've never lived in another house. My parents are both gone, so I live here alone. Please come in."

Inside she said,

"Excuse me. I will get dinner, then we can talk. Look around if you wish." She added softly, after a slight hesitation,

"I've wanted you to see my home for a long time, Chris. Thank you for coming." She walked rapidly away.

I looked around. The room was large and spotlessly clean. The furniture was the old-fashioned kind, solid, the upholstery slightly worn, still lovely. A tall radio sat against one wall beside a new, large screen TV set. The tables, coffee, and end, were polished like mirrors. Off a short hall, the bathroom was tiled from floor to ceiling in a pastel blue, the tub, lavatory and stool to match.

Beyond that were two bedrooms. One was unmistakably Darleen's—modern from floor to ceiling, coloring perfectly matched, even to the great doll sprawled on the pillow. The other bedroom was simpler, but decorated in excellent taste.

Through the glass in the back door of the hall, I could see into a flower garden filled with rows and rows of various flowering plants. It was costing the gal a small fortune to keep up the lawn and gardens. No wonder she wanted more money.

Back in the large room, I turned on the TV. On the opposite side of the room was a deep cushioned lounge with pillow arms. I flopped there and stretched luxuriously. I had come home. I closed my eyes to think about it.

Darleen shook me awake.

"Wake up, lazy. Dinner is ready."

She was cute as a baby chicken, fluffy hair, fluffy apron, shining eyes. I swung to my feet.

"Remind me sometime to tell you how adorable you are."

She caught her breath, but led me by the hand into a small dining room without a word.

I knew she was a good cook, but this meal was a gourmand's delight. I like good food, also I like to eat without a lot of unnecessary conversation. Darleen was very quiet all through dinner. I ate ravenously, enjoying every mouthful, her pride in her accomplishment rising at every moment as she watched me stow the grub away. I made a few inane remarks out of courtesy, but the way I ate was all the compliments she wanted. I swallowed the last bite of a delicious peach cobbler topped with whipped cream and straightened up.

"Little one, you are too good to be true. How do you do it? Who helps you take care of all your flowers and lawn?"

"Just me. I like all kinds of housework and gardening. If I didn't have that I would go crazy living here alone. I've tried having another woman live with me, but it didn't work out very well. I'm too much of an old maid, and too set in my ways I guess. I have a lot of company, so it is not so lonely. Then I have my work. I get along just fine."

"Forgive me for asking, but what about boy friends? You are a choice morsel as I well know. Don't you have a lot of men dying to move into a superlative set up like this?"

She bubbled with laughter,

"Oh, no. I've had a few men who were interested for awhile. I could tell by the way they looked at me, they were more interested in my home than myself. I want a man to love me, not my house. I would live in a paper shack if my man loved me enough. I want very little out of life. Mostly I want love. My parents were very much in love with each other all their lives. They passed away within ten minutes of each other. I guess I'm just spoiled. I only want what they had."

I stared at her so hard, she flushed a deep red, then turned toward the front room without speaking.

I said lightly,

"I'll wipe the dishes if you'll wash them."

"Not now, Chris. You are not going to stay long. After you leave, I'll do them." She motioned toward the lounge.

"Lay there if you wish. My father always took a nap after a big meal. Said it was good for his stomach."

I asked her,

"Will you sit near me? Please, Darleen."

She held her breath so long I could see a deep throbbing in her throat from the pressure. All at once she let go with a trembling sigh, as she made up her mind.

"Of course, Chris. Lie down. I'll sit there with you."

I propped my head up on a pillow, opened my arms toward her, and she came into them, murmuring small sounds of happiness.

She refused me her mouth, saying softly,

"I've never done this before, Chris. Please be gentle."

I drew her close, buried my face in her hair, whispering,

"This is all I want now, precious girl. Just to hold and kiss you. Just hold you in my arms."

She wriggled tight against me, lifting her face.

"Oh, Chris. Now I know you love me. I know it. You don't have to say it yet, but I know it."

I pushed her away roughly,

"You're crazy. I don't love you or anyone else. I'm a sensual moron. I chase women. I like money. I got no time to love one woman. I'd go nuts with just one woman."

She crawled back inside my arms, pinched my knee between hers, saying throatily,

"I know all that. You're a genuine no good, sex-crazy, worthless, and stupid. In spite of all that you love me just the same. If you had a lick of sense, you'd kiss me, then you would know it, too."

I let all holds go and kissed her. I mean I kissed her. I kissed her until she cried for mercy. Still I kissed her.

She put her hand over her mouth, fingering her lips.

"Chris, darling. Please. They're all puffed out. Doggone it, why are you so rough?"

That I could answer,

"You wanted me to kiss you. I kissed you. I still don't love you."

She emphasized her words.

"Oh, yes, you do. Your heart is beating like a drum. Your face is hot. Your hands have made black and blue marks on me. You're trembling all over. It's not sex either, I can tell."

She jumped up and said, laughing,

"Go soak your head in cold water in the bathroom, then come back to me. I'll still be here."

My mind was blank, so I did as she told me. It made me feel better, too. I had a faint suspicion she was half right because I hadn't got all worked up. She was sweet, tender, loving, and all mine for the taking. Why not? Yet all I wanted to do was kiss and love the daylights out of her. The sex angle hadn't been stirred up at all.

She was waiting for me by a big chair. She pushed me into it, sat in my lap and her arms went around my neck, pulling my face into her breasts. Her legs lay across my lap and over the arm of the chair, slightly parted. Only a tiny tightening of her muscles showed her reaction as my hand moved over her.

Her lips rested on mine, soft moist, quivering, as I touched her. Her breathing was uneven, with quick indrawn gasps, then slowly released in long audible sighs against my mouth. She moved almost imperceptibly against my hand, murmuring,

"My wonderful darling. What a wonderful sensation. So sweet, so gentle, your hand. Oh, Chris. I love you so."

Carefully, I drew her arms from around my neck, held her hands in one of mine, pushed her away. She sagged in my arm, eyes closed, lost in dreamy remembrance. I said firmly,

"Wake up, monkey. It's your turn to soak your head in cold water. I'm going home before I forget I'm a gentleman."

She leaned into my arms as though she didn't have a bone in her body, seemingly incapable of movement.

I shook her roughly,

"Stand up, wench, and pull your dress down. I can see your legs."

She looked at me from under her droopy eyelids.

"I don't give a damn if you can. You said you liked them."

"Darleen, I think they are beautiful, but right now, stand on them, way over in the corner before you get pregnant just from my thoughts."

She swayed uncertainly as I walked to the door.

"Thank you for a delicious dinner, and for everything. You're a delightful female to be with. I adore you, but I don't love you. I'd lose my mind if I had to live with you."

She caught my sleeve.

"Oh, yes, you do. I know you love me, so I'll wait. I'm bright enough to know you'll be thinking about me all the time, even when you are with some other woman."

She stood on tiptoe and hugged me.

"I've never been so happy in my life, Chris, darling. Go away, so I can think about it."

CHAPTER SIXTEEN

I n the morning when I entered the Morley house office, Colonel Morley was seated behind the desk. He greeted me with a smile.

"Top of the morning. Jen tells me you have been busy. Like to tell me about it? She says you are the greatest publicity man she has ever known. She was in show business for a while so that should be quite a compliment."

"She has worked hard herself, Colonel. I talked it over with her and she thought the idea was worth trying."

He nodded. I explained just how the birthday party would work out. I hoped. I went into great detail about the arrangements, also why Sergeant Wells should be the leading figure leaving my name out of it altogether.

"With a thousand of your friends scattered in strategic spots in the state, you will have a powerful ready-made organization to start with. Most of them will work like hell to see you elected and they will influence others to support you."

He chuckled,

"The old infiltration tactics. How are you going to keep this out of the papers until the proper time?"

During the night I had given that considerable thought. I said frankly,

"You are the main stumbling block. With you here there can be no question but what the reporters will smell out the truth. If you and Jen were to take a trip, say to Hawaii for two weeks, it would solve the problem. When you returned on the twenty-fifth of May, a good share of your friends would already be here. Sort of a welcome home committee.

"The whole thing would jell in a natural way and seem spontaneous when your name was shouted out for Governor."

He gave a long steady look, then smiled,

"Wells told me you had a devious mind. Now I understand. He cautioned me to listen and not let you prod me into blowing my top. Seems you got under his skin a couple of times."

"I was just having fun. He doesn't like Navy men so I used that as a lever to jockey him into position for a sneak jab. When he recovered he was so fighting mad nothing could stop him. In two hours he had the project under way before he realized what he had committed himself to do. Then he was mad all over again and I had to needle him again."

Bart roared with laughter,

"So he told me. He'll get the job done but grumble all the time he is doing it. Many is the time I have asked for an opinion before making a difficult decision. Also he saved my life a couple of times. He has a genius for details and he isn't afraid of the devil himself."

He leaned back and thought for a long time while I waited. He suddenly laughed,

"Wait till Jen hears about this. She'll bust wide open. You want to be around, or shall I tell her privately?"

"No, thanks, Governor. You tell her. I'm leaving right now before she can let me have a few not so choice words about my ancestry."

"Tell her what. You conniving bastards. What is it you want to tell her that will make her bust wide open. Tell her to her face."

We both started guiltily. Jen was standing just inside the door with her hands on her hips in a belligerent attitude.

Bart reached her in two jumps, lifted her in his arms and swung her round and round the room,

"Sweetheart. How would you like to go to Hawaii for a couple of weeks?"

"Put me down, damn you. Put me down. You're both crazy. With the campaign about to start you want to go on a trip.

"Why? Just tell me why?"

Bart set her on the desk near me saying,

"Tell her, Howard. It's your idea."

This called for diplomacy, something I am short on so I put her on the spot,

"As long as it was your own idea to give Bart the party, he must naturally be surprised. Right?" She nodded.

"If he is around here while all the tents, equipment, and supplies are rolling in, how could he not know about it?

"Don't you think it would be a good thing if both of you were far, far away while this is going on?"

She looked at me curiously but her eyes showed anger. She swung her legs, each time her toes coming closer to my face. I almost laughed because I knew how she wanted to land one on the button. She stifled the impulse with a sigh and said,

"I'm a very obedient housewife. When do we start?"

Bart was as surprised as I was at her meek words. I could have kissed her. She was fine and hadn't blown up without thinking.

Bart looked at her as though he couldn't believe his ears. She must have given him some rough sessions at times and was wondering what had come over her. I said positively,

"Tomorrow morning. I will get your plane tickets and make all the reservations. I wish you would leave quietly and please try to avoid all publicity while you are in Hawaii.

"If you are questioned by reporters, tell them you are on a second honeymoon. That always sounds good to the press.

"After the announcement of your candidacy for Governor I will see your every move is publicized to the utmost."

Bart asked,

"Any particular reason why you picked Hawaii?"

"Yes. You can pick up the paper almost every day and see where some prominent couple has returned from there, complete with pictures of them with garlands of flowers around their necks. You seldom see where any one is planning to go there. You can bet I'll have photographers on hand when you return. Also I'll have a big crowd at the airport to meet you. From there, the publicity will carry right on to your surprise party. Someone in the party will think you will make a hell of a good Governor and the whole idea will start from there.

"Six thousand people shouting your name for Governor will be hard for the press to ignore. In the excitement they won't take time to analyze the situation and ask questions, and later when they do take time to think it will be too late. Your name and pictures will be spread over the front pages of every paper in the state. You will be the people's choice.

"From that point on, you will be seen and heard in every place where two or more voters get together right up to the night before election."

Bart said quietly,

"It's quite a plan, Howard. If you pull it off there will be a place on my staff for you. If it backfires there will still be a place where you can become independently wealthy in my business organization. I'm always looking for bright young men with ideas."

"Thank you, Governor. You will be elected without a doubt, but I'm happy with my own business. The fee you are paying me will be sufficient to keep me contented for a long time.

I've suddenly discovered I'm more interested in accomplishment than money."

Jen piped out,

"I told you he was unbalanced, Bart. He looks so normal, too."

Bart laughed,

"You're right, sweetheart. We'll have to see he doesn't go hungry or get himself committed to an institution."

He thought a moment then straightened,

"All right, Commander. We will leave as soon as possible. At this time I am free of all business and a trip to the islands will be wonderful. I'll show Jen the time of her life.

"Coming, darling?"

He grasped my hand almost breaking my fingers and walked out of the room.

Jen brushed close to me, whispering fiercely,

"You sleep here tonight or I'll kill you." She trotted away after Bart.

I called a travel agency and in an hour all arrangements were made for their trip. I thought how good it would be to be able to pick up the phone and ask for reservations to any place in the world without having to worry where the money was coming from. Just think of a place I wanted to go and take off like a duck. Money and women. Darleen. I'll bet she would love a trip to Hawaii. How her eyes would bug out at the sights.

I had a warm feeling just thinking of her. I called my office. Instantly her voice answered,

"Mr. Howard's office."

I spoke through my pocket handkerchief, folded over the mouthpiece,

"Howard about? May I speak to him?"

Her voice was lilting and soft,

"He's all about me. He's all around me. If you wish to speak with him, you will have to come to the office."

"You're too smart for your lacy pants. How are you?"

"Oh, Chris. If you only knew how good I feel."

"I know exactly. Have you forgotten?"

"You're mean. You make me blush all over."

"Keep your sensual thoughts to yourself and tell me, has Captain Downs called again?"

"No. She said she would be here tonight. Why?"

"I need her urgently. Ask her to call me as soon as she checks into the office. The Morleys are leaving for Hawaii in the morning so I will be busy here the rest of the day. By, hot stuff."

She gasped,

"You dirty—" as I cradled the receiver.

Except for a short interval while I ate a quick dinner which Mary served me at my desk, I worked steadily until midnight. My work was through, my plans for the campaign were completed. I had nearly two weeks in which I had nothing to do. I sat back contented. I had a new car, pockets bulging with green backs, no personal ties. What a life. I'd go hunt up some beautiful women and enjoy myself.

For a moment I thought of Darleen. Nope. If I took her along I would come back married for all time. If I gave her that much time to work on me. She had too many persuasive baits to tempt me with. I would go alone.

I went upstairs, stripped off my clothes and settled in a tub of hot water. I reviewed the last weeks. I felt smug indeed. The Morley contract had pulled the plug out of the barrel. Now all the things I'd always hoped for were falling in my lap. I envisioned my future with glowing satisfaction and on that happy thought I dropped off to sleep, the warm water in the bathtub caressing me like a woman's arms.

I came out of it with a jerk and cursing. Water was spraying from the shower head, icy cold, sharp as needles. I turned the damned thing off and hopped into the bedroom dripping wet and shivering. I should have remembered.

Jen was in the bed, shaking with silent laughter. She held up one side of the sheets and beckoned with a forefinger,

"I'm so warm," she whispered. "I'll lay next to you and get you warm, too."

Those were the only words she spoke the rest of the night, except for soft murmurings of ecstasy when she fulfilled her role as a woman. When daylight came I was past caring whether I was warm or cold. I had no feeling in my body, my mind was blank and I was physically exhausted.

At the last moment she ran her hands lovingly over me from head to feet and kissed me gently, her lips ever following the touch of her hands, then she bent over me, gave me a lingering kiss on my lips, silently pressed my eyelids closed and was gone.

It was nine o'clock before I was able to come alive enough to make it down to the office. I had just made it when Bart and Jen came in. She looked like she had slept for a week. Dewy skin, fresh clear complexion, sparkling eyes and her movements were lithe and full of vigor. She was a sex machine if I ever saw one. Nothing fazed her. I was still droopy.

Bart was happy as a kid at a taffy pull. He said in lieu of greeting,

"Just got a confirmation on the plane tickets, Chris. We leave in an hour. We will see you on the twenty-fifth. Thanks for the suggestion. With Jen by my side we'll have a ball." He said laughingly to Jen,

"Don't you think you could spare a kiss for the man? After all it was his idea we're going."

She actually blushed a deep red from the vee of her dress to the top of her head,

"You wouldn't mind, Bart?"

He shook his head and she came shyly into my arms and kissed me on the lips, holding the kiss long enough to tickle the inside of my upper lip with her tongue. With Bart looking on it felt like a bee sting. I looked at her as she stepped away. Her eyes were misty but she was smiling in secret thought. Bart gave my hand another of his bone crushers,

"We'll write, Chris. Keep out of trouble."

"Thanks, Governor. Phone me the hour your plane lands here at the airport and be surprised as hell at your reception."

He laughed heartily, took Jen's hand, and together they walked away leaving me standing like a wooden Indian with Jen's kiss still burning on my mouth. She was quite a gal.

Wells came pacing up the hall with a sober look on his face,

"You sure suckered me into a hell of a mess, Howard."

I grinned at him,

"Want some Navy men to take over?"

He sat down and sighed,

"Don't try to pull any more of that crap on me. That's how I got took." He pouched out his lower lip thoughtfully,

"Mrs. James has located over two thousand of the old bunch and has talked to most of them. They been having kids like rabbits so there will be nearly eight thousand here. I can handle the grown-ups, but what am I going to do with a passel of kids?"

I had another bright idea,

"How about a carnival? All the city folks would like that. You can buy the tickets for your kids and the locals can buy their own. Let the locals eat for free. Those that want to and that will create a lot of good will for the Colonel."

He said curiously,

"You got the least idea what it's going to cost to feed eight thousand people for three days?"

I figured quick in my head,

"I'd say about twelve thousand dollars. Why? You broke?"

He replied promptly,

"No, by God, I ain't. And that ain't the last verse. I ain't put-ing out a cent of my own money either."

I wrote a check and handed it to him grinning,

"Here is another ten thousand. Go ahead and be a big shot on my money."

He rubbed the check between his thumb and forefinger,

"Keep it up, swab. You'll need a dentist to put back your front teeth. Besides it ain't half enough. Shell out another ten thousand while you're at it, an' maybe I'll make it do. A lot of them will stay at hotels an' pay their own way."

He added with a crafty look,

"The Wells hotel is going to pay expenses for a change after I get through filling it up."

I tore the check in half and wrote another one for double the amount.

"That's thirty thousand. Have yourself a time, Sergeant, it's only money."

He said surprisingly,

"This is a smart stunt. I've got to give you credit, Commander. I've had a hand in some of the politics around the state for some time because I don't like the thieves that are in office, but we couldn't get to the first trenches.

"Bart Morley will be one hell of a leader if he gets elected. He'll send half of the bastards to the guardhouse and shoot the rest, I hope. Mike and Fred are willing to bet two to a plugged nickel he makes it after this stunt makes the newspapers."

He studied a while and then went on,

"Howard, I'm going to tell you something. If you open your ugly face about it I'll make you dig latrine ditches for the rest of your life." He paused and eyed me suspiciously.

I waited, wondering what he was about.

"It just happens there is about fifty thousand dollars available for the campaign fund." He grinned at my start, and went on,

"Don't ask where it came from, just use it and keep your damned lips buttoned. Say you won it in a crap game or something."

He delved into a pocket and came out with a check and handed it to me. I looked at it closely. A cashier's check made to me personally. The signature was that of a bank official which meant nothing as far as learning who had made up the amount. I had a good idea but it was none of my business.

Ke-rist. I was standing under a full grown money tree in a wind storm. All I had to do was bend over and pick the stuff up. Over a million and a half had fallen in my hands in less than a week, and me a poor ex-Navy deck hand.

The thought of all that money made me tight as a drum head. He was watching me as I mentally struggled, so I told him,

"Sergeant. When Bart Morley hired me, he paid my first year's fee in advance. Ten thousand dollars. That is my own money for the services of my organization. He contracted with me for a quarter of a million more for expenses. That is his money or what is left will be.

"Sergeant. This amount will be added to the campaign fund which is in the National Trust bank and every cent will be accounted for. The Colonel can draw out the full amount any time he wishes. It is a joint account subject to both his and my signature. There has been another sizable donation to the fund also. You realize of course I could pocket thousands of dollars and there would be nothing you could do about it. All the money is in a personal account."

He held up his hand,

"Bart told me all that. He also told me just this morning if you need any amount while he was away to fork it over and keep still about it. If you come out of this deal with a neat little nest egg it will be all right with all of us. Bart gave us a start and not a damn one of us can spend our incomes. The damned Government gets the most of it besides."

He waited a moment and then leaned toward me confidentially,

"Jen cornered me this morning and poured out her heart. She said she trusted you enough to place her life in your hands. How you forced that little fiesty woman to tell you her story I don't want to know. I only know I love her. I do know she is in big trouble but has left the whole mess in your hands. Her word about you is all the proof of your honesty we need. I get a kick out of making money but I'm too old to enjoy it. Repeating your own words, Commander. Have yourself a ball. We'll see you have the money to flatten out her troubles and mop them up. She is my heir when I kick off so I'd rather she had some use of the money now while she can enjoy it, and I'm alive and can see her happy."

"Did she tell you what she gave me, Sergeant?"

"No. Just that she had given you some names and dates that could get her murdered if it became known she had given them."

"That's fine. You and I are the only ones who know that. She has been living in fear ever since she married Bart. Afraid she would lose him if her past came to light. In the next week I hope to be able to clear her so completely she will be free of all past associations. She is a fine woman in every way and will make a splendid Governor's wife."

DON LEE

Wells said, curiously,

"You know, Commander. When I first saw you I figured you were just smelling around her like a dog after a bitch in heat. She's always in heat so I couldn't blame you. I know how hard she has tried to keep herself in hand and not let a man next to her. She's had a problem. I know. I know what she was before she met Bart. A woman like her can handle a dozen men and not feel it because of the way she's made.

"If I had been younger I would have made a play for her myself and to hell with the consequences. I'm damned glad you are devoted to her whatever your motives. I asked her point blank if she was in love with you and she laughed like a kid. She said you were one hell of a fellow but she was all Bart's for all time."

He got to his feet like he was tired.

"Usually this time of day I can sit in a chair and read the paper, but since you egged me into this fracas I haven't had time to get any rest. Now I got to go to the State Capitol and put a burr under the General's tail or he won't get out the paper work in time for us to get the Guard equipment."

The telephone rang, so he waved his hand and walked out of the room.

CHAPTER SEVENTEEN

I picked up the receiver,

"Hello,"

Darleen said breathlessly,

"Chris, Amy Downs is here. You want to talk to her?"

"Not on the phone. Tell her to come out here."

"I will, Chris." Her voice sank to a barely audible whisper.

"Hands off, Chris. I like you with both your arms. I don't want her to have to twist one of them off."

"Why, my right hand is all I need. Remember?"

She must have hissed into the mouthpiece because the sound went clear through my head.

I thumbed the button in the kitchen. Mary came in expectantly.

"I'm having a lady visitor. May we please have some lunch? She eats like a ranch hand so you be the judge of what we have."

"Glory be. The man's got a girl. I'd given up all hope."

"Not my girl. Mary, my darling. She is a Captain in the Army."

Mary asked, with a twinkle in her eye,

"Is she female and kind of pretty?"

"Both."

She clucked approvingly,

"Tell her to come see me. I'll give her some motherly advice." She hurried away muttering. "Wh-o-o-o, wh-o-o-o."

I went out to the driveway to meet Amy. She came in a taxi and I hurriedly stuck a big bill in the driver's hand and jerked open the rear door. She said in a way that made my heart leap,

"Oh Chris." That was all, but instantly I wanted to sling her over my shoulder and go hop, skip and a jump to my cave. As it was I almost dragged her into the office and slammed the door.

She was just as avid as I was. We clung together in mutual passion, mouthing crazy things which were senseless to anyone but us. When we finally tried to step apart, we both leaned forward, our lips still glued together. She stuck her tongue in my mouth to break the contact and I almost pulled it out of its socket but my lips slipped off the end of it and she let it lay between her teeth with the tip exposed twitching suggestively.

Again she said, happy like,

"Chris. Chris. Are you going to take me to your apartment?"

"Right away, sweet girl. First I have some papers to show you." She let me set her on the desk with her legs swinging over the edge. Her fingers pinched my cheeks while I run my hands over her thighs, under her dress. She cried softly,

"Hurry, hurry. I'm in no mood to listen to business so get it over with."

I got the file from under the desk top and handed it to her without a word. She took one fast look then sat in a chair and reread it a dozen times, her eyes devouring every word I had written.

She raised her eyes to mine. I shook my head at her unspoken question. She made a decisive movement, and said,

"You have a private wire outside?"

"Yes. That one is an unlisted number."

She dialed a number then told the operator,

"Get me Bureau 20 in Washington. Reverse the charges. Captain Downs. D-o-w-n-s. That's right."

While she waited she looked at me intently. Her face was still flushed from our love making but her eyes were cold as ice reflecting her thoughts. She suddenly smiled at me,

"What a son-of-a-bitch you are. It don't seem possible you could get there so fast. How you get around women is absolutely beyond my comprehension. Oh, I know I was a pushover, but her. My God——."

"Hello. Ray? Captain Downs. I have all the pieces in my hands. Names. Dates. Bank accounts. Witnesses. I want ten men tonight. I'll brief them. Just a minute."

She asked me,

"Where can we meet? Some quiet place."

"My apartment."

She spoke into the phone,

"Send four to this address." She gave my house number.

"The rest to the Wells Hotel."

"Yes. Private house. Stairway at right side, top floor. I'll be there. No mistake, Sir. I have it all. Thank you, Sir."

She replaced the receiver, glanced at her wrist watch and said in a sultry voice,

"Now take me to bed. Here. In the bushes or anywhere you can undress me. I'm going to tear you into little rags."

"Come along woman. I like you too."

She didn't even notice I had a new car, she was cuddled so tight against me as I drove to my apartment.

Just before midnight she said in a slow, drowsy voice,

"If I had any secrets, deep, dark secrets in my mind, I would spill them now. No wonder you got information the whole Service wasn't able to dig out in four years of intensive work. You wear a girl down in the most wonderful way. I'll get a promotion out of this and you'll get a big reward."

I chuckled,

"I just had my reward. If I got any more I wouldn't live to enjoy it. You wear a man down too."

Her kisses were like apple cider. Sweet, sticky.

"Lover. Lover. You are a good man. I hope the woman you marry will be female enough to keep you at home. I envy her from the bottom of my heart."

She sat upright and said abruptly,

"Darleen turned red all over this afternoon when I asked about you. Have you been fooling around in her panties?"

I could answer that honestly,

"I went to her home the other night where she cooked a luscious dinner for us. I kissed her some, then left. My powers of resistance are very weak and I'm no gentleman. I don't want to hurt her."

Amy said thoughtfully,

"She's ripe as a peach and some man will get to her one of these days sure as shooting. I believe I would forgive you if you were the man. She loves you so much I'm sure she would think she was doing you a favor. She might even make you want to marry her to keep her honest. You couldn't find a more perfect wife."

"Shut up. You say another word and I'll throttle you. I'm a bachelor and I'm going to stay that way. I told Darleen if I had to live with just one woman I'd go nuts. This arrangement is perfect as long as you are satisfied. In my own way I'm crazy about you. I'd like for you to move in here and live with me till you decide to move on. I'd be faithful too. I wouldn't have the energy to be otherwise."

"Why what a bastard you are. That is the most indecent proposal I ever had. Kiss me while I decide to say No, No."

She clutched at me,

"Wh-e-e-e. Stop it, you almost bit the tip off. I'm going to have a bath and get dressed. You take off. This meeting is strictly for us working people. All on account of you I'm going to be a sensation in the office in Washington. I'll make Colonel out of this sure."

She bounced out of bed and lit running. At the bathroom door she winked at me,

"I like our arrangement too, lover."

At daybreak the next morning I left for a round of places where I could find some fancy women. For two weeks I traveled.

Lakes. Mountains. Beaches. Hotels. Motels. Bars and night clubs. Not in a single place did I pick up a woman. They didn't ring a bell in my sex organs. I came to the conclusion I was spoiled. When one of them gave me the eye I thought of Jen or Amy and most of all Darleen. The kind I could get were bags compared to those three wonderful gals. I bought a few drinks for some of them and I even broke down and bought a meal for a lush redhead. When she suggested I might like to get a more intimate view of her obvious charms, I bolted like a schoolboy and left her standing on the curb viewing my vanishing taillights as I drove out of the town in a hurry to get far, far away.

On the thirteenth day I headed for home. Heavier by ten pounds and filled with vim and vinegar. I hoped Amy would be waiting for me at my apartment.

I went to my office first and hardly recognized the place. Darleen was the only familiar sight. She glowed all over when I stepped through the door, but she said demurely, as though I had only been away a few minutes,

"Captain Downs is waiting in your office, Mr. Howard."

I winked at her and looked around. Extra desks almost filled the room space. There was a man behind each desk and two teletype machines were clicking at a great rate.

Not a man gave me more than a casual glance as I opened the door and entered the inner office.

Captain Downs glanced up and her eyes blinked happily. She rose and offered me her hand in greeting, saying easily,

"Mr. Howard. I would like you to meet Mr. Robbins."

As we shook hands formally I sized him up. His head came only to my shoulder, thinning grey hair, hard compact body, piercing blue eyes above a slit of a mouth which was smiling faintly. He said,

"You arrived just in time Mr. Howard. Tonight we move. The Captain has told me you have a personal interest in this business."

"What business?" I looked to Amy for information.

He said to both of us, his eyes twinkling,

"I'll be in the outer office while the Captain briefs you." He looked at each of us in turn, gave a little snort then went out, carefully closing the door.

In a second we were tearing at each other like strange cats. Her mouth and arms were possessive and demanding as she stood on tip toe turning her body against me in fury and tugging at the back of my head. I run my hand down the front of her dress and squeezed gently the lower part of her abdomen. She stepped out of my arms with a sibilant breath, straightened her wrinkled skirt and resumed her seat behind the desk. Her glance was warm and appraising, her voice uneven,

"No—women—lover? I'm glad. It's been so long. If I hadn't have been so busy I would have found you. I'm a shameless hussy since you came along. I think about it every minute."

I asked her,

"Can we leave and go to my place?"

"No. Damn it. I have to stay by the machines all night. By morning we should have a hundred men locked behind bars from New York to San Francisco. This time they can't beat us.

"The evidence is conclusive enough to keep them locked up from now on. The file you gave us could only come from a person who knew all the facts. Have you taken any steps to protect your informant?"

"Not at the moment. How about a man named St. Cyr?"

She gave me a veiled look,

"He will be charged with first degree murder. He can't make bail. That help?"

"Anyone else connected with him?"

"All of his collection men. Every one has a previous record. But he has a boss, right here in the city. We haven't been able to get a single line on that man."

She bit her lower lip and asked abruptly,

"You know him Chris? One name was cut out of the file. Only you could have done that. If you are trying to protect him, I'll have you locked up for obstructing justice. You'll be a fool if you think I won't."

I parried the question,

"You know about the birthday party for Colonel Morley?"

"Certainly. We know all about it. It's a publicity stunt you cooked up yourself. We dug into that first thing and came out with Chris Howard, boy wonder."

She smiled with her mouth only,

"Robbins thinks it's a great stunt but that won't let you off the hook. We want the name of the man you cut out of the file. I want it now."

I leaned back and closed my eyes, thinking. Of lovely Jen Morley crying her eyes out and tossing in the bed beside me while she poured out her story. I thought of Bart Morley. Proud, fine, and honest who loved her even though he was surely aware of her secret fears. A man couldn't live with a woman for years without knowing something was wrong with his loved one when she reacted like Jen.

I thought of his unspoken trust in all his friends and how he was ready to go to their aid at the drop of a hat.

He trusted me. Jen had given me all she possessed. Affection which was part love, and physical satisfaction beyond my wildest dreams. I thought of the beating I had been given at a time when I was wholly ignorant of its meaning. I thought of the bullet which had come within a hairsbreadth of ending my life which was just beginning. Only one man could be responsible for all that.

First of all I must protect Jennifer Morley. I must see no taint or suspicion was directed at her. A man had to die that very night. Perhaps two men. I could only hope I wasn't the second one.

Amy said impatiently,

"I'm waiting Chris."

"Who is Mr. Robbins?" I asked,

"He is head of the Bureau of Internal Revenue for this district."

"Please ask him to come in. I don't want you mixed in this dirty business."

She hastened to obey, pausing to kiss me,

"That's my boy." Her voice was filled with suppressed excitement.

He came in promptly seated himself and leaned toward me expectantly.

"Mr. Robbins. If there were a man, rich, with hosts of powerful friends, every legal device at his command, with an unimpeachable character, yet he was the head of all the vicious rackets in the country, could you handle his arrest quietly and take him out of the state where his subsequent actions would not become a local scandal? Would it be possible to silence him?"

He answered quickly,

"No. Such a man knows more devices to beat the law than we do. He would be out on bail in an hour. He would delay the criminal action against him for months, even years.

"However in this instance, I think we can bring this man to trial in a matter of weeks. We have all the evidence we need to convict him. He has been an accessory to murder, aided in the violation of the narcotics law. Received large payments from gambling, vice and has conspired to evade the tax department. We have the whole picture with only the face missing. He is a clever man to have kept his identity hidden all these years."

I glanced at Amy. She was tense, her hands clenched on the desk top, her eyes pleading with me.

Robbins said quietly,

"Captain Downs has given me a hint of where your concern lies. We are not interested in your personal business and we will do our best to protect your friends from injury. With your cooperation we can in one move expose the head of the combination, then the rest of the small fries will start bleating like sheep."

He studied the watch on his wrist, waiting.

I made up my mind. I knew I had to kill a man or force him to make a break where he would be killed trying to get away. He had to die. Tonight.

"Give me a man to make the arrest. I'll take you to him." He sprang to his feet, and grasped my hand. Amy came around the desk with tears running down her cheeks.

"Chris lover. You're wonderful."

Robbins cleared his throat loudly, then chuckled,

"Your emotions are showing, Captain. Haven't I taught you better?"

She glared fiercely at him,

"I don't give a good Goddamn. I told you he was a man."

He said gently, almost sadly,

"I've been trying to make her look at me like that for years, Howard. I didn't think she had it in her."

He went toward the door, saying,

"Don't get any notions yet. I'll be right back."

He wasn't out of the room over a minute, coming back with a sheet of teletype in his hand,

"In one hour we will start picking up men all over the country. It's a big operation. The first raids are aimed at key figures only. Once we have them in custody we can pick up the rest at our leisure. The bail bonds will run into astronomical figures alone. They will need time to get up the money."

He said crisply,

"You will stand by Captain. Have the girl out there make minute reports. I'm going with Commander Howard. We won't be long."

Her eyes never left my face as she nodded. I said,

"Mr. Robbins. I would like to go to my apartment for a minute. I'll meet you at the door to this building in ten minutes."

He said, giving me an odd look,

"Be sure you know what you are doing Commander."

I drove home, carried my grips upstairs and in the alloted time I was waiting in front of the building as prearranged.

Robbins came up, and without a word, led me to a rental agency car. Two men occupied the front seat. Robbins said,

"Where to?"

"The Wells Hotel."

The driver swung the car around, and in a moment parked under the canopy. I walked to the private elevator with Robbins close behind me. I asked the operator a question. He nodded indifferently. Through the closing door I saw Robbins men leaning against separated pillars casually watching the crowd in the lobby.

The elevator lifted swiftly to the penthouse. I silently dismissed the operator and he closed the door, the elevator dropping downward without a sound.

I pointed to the knocker on the entrance door. Robbins lifted it and soft musical chimes sounded inside the room.

The door opened wide. Kurt Avery stood facing us.

He said heartily in some surprise,

"Mr. Howard. Won't you come in gentlemen?"

We followed him into a small room overlooking the wide terrace which surrounded the entire penthouse. There he turned,

"How is the campaign going Mr. Howard? I've been too busy to make inquiries."

"Mr. Avery. This is Mr. Robbins."

Mr. Avery asked questioningly,

"Another Public Relations expert to help create a new Governor?"

Robbins said clearly as he extended his wallet, opened where it showed a gold shield.

"Bureau of Internal Revenue, Mr. Avery. We would like to talk with you if you have the time."

Avery laughed shortly,

"Certainly gentlemen. Would you like a drink?"

We both refused his offer. He motioned toward chairs, seated himself, and sat waiting. He was an old hand at that game. He was motionless as a statue, his eyes unblinking.

Robbins eyes slowly moved around the room, noting every detail. Finally settling on Avery's face with a steady unwinking gaze, he said,

"The Department has had men checking into various tax accounts throughout the city for some time, Mr. Avery. We have come up with some startling deductions. Like to hear some of them?"

Avery just barely tipped his head in assent. Robbins took a sheet of paper from his inner coat pocket, unfolded it, paused, then said,

"This is a summary. The story begins about fifteen years ago. It is a long story and I will not drag it out. At the moment this summary will suffice. Let us begin here.

"A gentleman came from the East coast with a large amount of money accumulated from several unlawful enterprises.

"He was looking for legitimate outlets for this money. He wanted a prominent attorney to represent him in these transactions. He soon found the man he was looking for. A young, struggling attorney with a cultural background. By careful planning this Eastern man soon had a finger in all the vices of man. The original investment grew into the millions. The attorney reaping a harvest for his services.

"The legitimate investments were relegated into the background as the unlawful ones grew. The original investor became the victim of old age, his perceptive powers dimmed.

"Unable to protect his vast holdings any longer, his friend the Attorney, who knew every detail of the business, by threats or force took over his business lock, stock, and barrel.

"It wasn't easy. Along the line there were at least three murders. Men left the country to seek other fields of endeavor. But in the long haul the Attorney became the head man.

"Since then, under his able management vice has flourished, gambling has run unchecked, narcotics have flowed into the city and country in a stream. If a man or a woman disappeared suddenly there was always a ready answer. Friends who trusted him

214

were ruthlessly swept aside in his grab for money and power. Innocent people were subjected to a life of terror and want."

Robbins stopped abruptly. There was a moment of terrible silence, then he went on,

"In order to substantiate these deductions, Mr. Avery, we have names, dates and checks. We have checked hidden bank accounts opened safety deposit boxes, and by this time we have a hundred men in custody. Men whose livelihood and lives, hang by a thread on the whims of this one man."

His voice broke loud and clear,

"Mr. Avery. I have here, ten warrants for your arrest.

"They range from simple violations of the state laws to accessory to murder. Also Federal warrants charging violation of the narcotics act, and tax evasion. You may examine them if you wish."

CHAPTER EIGHTEEN

Kurt Avery never moved a muscle. Only his eyes changed. They burned with a hell of hatred, moving slowly between us. A slight contraction of his lips marked his tension.

He turned his head in a gradual survey of the room, then his eyes focused on the distant horizon visible through the window.

I felt my body break into a clammy sweat making me itch across my belly and between my legs. I glanced sideways at Robbins. He was poised on the edge of his chair for instant action like a racer waiting for the starting gun.

Kurt Avery said in a clear precise voice, biting off his words in his clenched teeth,

"Only one person in the world could have given you that information. In a moment of weakness, the only one I ever had, I boasted of my success and my achievements. It was without avail. The person rejected me scornfully. I should have had that person killed long ago. I regret my mistake. I can say truthfully it was my one and only mistake in the last fifteen years."

He was silent a long time then turned toward me and fastened his eyes on mine,

"I realized the day I met you Howard, I couldn't buy you off. I should have killed you on the spot. One honest man is more dangerous in this business than a thousand hired thugs. You were just lucky the rifle bullet missed you. The man who fired it never missed before."

The telephone on his desk rang stridently. He let it ring until Robbins motioned him to answer it. He picked up the receiver,

"Yes?"

He listened with closed eyes, then spoke,

"No. I can do nothing for you."

He cradled the receiver precisely, his hand resting on the instrument. He waited a long time then opened his eyes and spoke to Robbins,

"May I speak privately with the Commander?"

Robbins straightened up, opened his mouth, closed it. He went out of the room, closing the door behind him.

Kurt Avery said pleasantly,

"Give that person my regards Commander. I bear no ill will. That person was the only thing in my life I wanted and couldn't have. Your gun Commander. I don't own one."

Instantly I knew he had seen the butt sticking out above my belt where I had placed it. I laid it on the desk in front of him,

"One cartridge only, Mr. Avery."

"Thank you. You are very thoughtful and also careful."

I turned and walked to the door, opened it, stepped through, and closed it. Robbins motioned me to join him at the window.

The sound of the shot was muffled by the walls in the small room. Such a small sound to send a man into eternity. I walked to the entrance door while Robbins entered the room of death.

He came out in a few minutes with a brief case crammed to the bursting point with files of papers and small note books.

He said exultantly,

"Enough here to clean out the entire rats nest. Thank you Commander."

We walked back to my office in silence. I was trembling from head to feet, my knees knocked against each other in weakness.

Outside the door Robbins touched my hand said wonderingly,

"How odd a strong healthy man like Avery should suddenly drop dead of a heart attack. No doubt it had been bothering him for a long time."

I leaned against the door jam and mopped the sweat from my face with my sleeve. A heart attack. How in the name of God could Robbins——?"

He said real low,

"Go home Commander. Forget it. I will do what is necessary. Men die every day under strange circumstances. He was a festering animal not fit to live among decent people. He knew it and took the only way out. I can even admire him for that.

"Had he chosen to fight he would have dragged down dozens of innocent people with him.

"With these records we can ferret out the guilty in short order." He gripped my arm, "I'm mighty glad he didn't force either of us to shoot. You are a fine man Commander."

I stood woodenly until he added,

"Would you like some one to go home with you for companionship?"

I thought for a moment,

"Send my secretary to me. I'm not up to talking to anyone else at the moment."

He went inside. In a minute Darleen came out with her handbag under her arm. With a gentle tug she led me out of the building. At my car she said,

"Get in on this side. I want to drive. I haven't banged a fender for a long time. It might be fun."

I watched with misgivings while she started the motor, then spun the rear wheels getting into the stream of traffic.

"Take it easy. This thing won't fly."

She chirped happily,

"Fasten your seat belt Christopher. I'm in a hurry."

She drove like she had been trained on hot rods. In a skidding squeal of rubber she came to a stop in front of her house. She hopped out and trotted toward the front door, calling,

"Come in. Don't just sit there."

Inside it was dark. Darleen turned on a tiny candle light on the far side of the room which gave out just enough light to keep me from bumping into furniture.

I sat on the couch, hung my coat on a chair back, unbuttoned my shirt collar stripping my necktie through the knot. I kicked off my shoes and stretched full length, weary in every bone and muscle.

Darleen came from another part of the house treading softly in bare feet.

"Hungry? Darling."

"No. Just tired. Darleen I want to tell——"

Her slim fingers covered my mouth,

"Mr. Robbins said you were not to talk. He said for me to make you be quiet."

Her hands moved at the front of her gown before she came against me, pressing my mouth on one of her incredibly firm breasts. The nipple was hard, erect. The touch of my tongue made her tremble but she didn't draw away. Her thighs parted slightly for my hand then she closed them, making my hand a prisoner in her soft femaleness. We lay quiet, savoring our intimacy. Only her mouth moved bit by bit over my forehead, until she caught her fingers under my chin, raising my mouth to her own.

Moving her soft moist lips to the corner of my mouth she said in surrender,

"If you want me, my darling. Show me how."

I held her freshness and sweetness in one arm while I removed the gown. Her lovely body vibrated with desire and love and she drew me over her in fierce appeal. I tried. God how I tried. It was no use. I was limp, impotent, and frustrated.

Even her trusting helpfulness created not a single spark of desire in my body.

With understanding, she held me, crooning softly,

"It's all right, my love. All right. We have all the time in the world. I love you. I love you."

In the shelter of her loving arms, with my face nestled in the warmth of her breasts, I went to sleep.

Hours later I woke sluggishly. My thoughts slow to assemble, until I remembered Colonel Morley would be home tomorrow.

I raised from the couch. One hand was pinned down. Darleen rested partly on the floor, partly on the side of the couch in a kneeling position. The side of her face was in the palm of my hand with her fingers clasping my wrist. She was sound asleep.

My eyes smarted as I looked at her in that position. In spite of my bumbling attempt to take her virgin body, she had gone to sleep loving me enough to want my hand for a pillow.

I jostled her head. Instantly she looked at me, her wonderful eyes lighting with happiness. I lifted her. She stepped back smoothing her rumpled gown.

"Hi. Please don't look at me. I'm a mess."

She ran to the bathroom door, and called back,

"Give me ten minutes then I'll get us some breakfast."

I could hear the shower running. I had a notion to walk in on her and offer to scrub her back but before I could carry out the thought, she dashed out, running down the hall with a big towel wrapped around her. Only she forgot to wrap it below her waist. She had the cutest little rump.

In the bathroom I found a new, woman's electric razor. It did a good job on my two days growth of whiskers. I showered, dressed in my baggy trousers and wrinkled shirt, pulled on my socks, feeling right at home. I like being untidy in my own place. She yelled from the kitchen,

"Soup's on."

For breakfast, I had scrambled eggs, bacon, toast with honey, coffee, kisses, loving hands on my cheeks, rounded mounds under cloth pressed against my shoulder, knees touching mine, and little bare feet firmly holding my toes down on the floor.

She pulled out all the stops, letting the music of her mind and sensual body fill the room around me.

You're damn right. I loved it. I ate a big breakfast too. Between her own bites of food, she gurgled, whuffed the side of my face, chuckled deep in her throat, bit me on the ear, and made sounds I couldn't understand. She was crazy as a honey bee in a tub of sugar water. I never wanted her to stop but I had to get to work. I asked her,

"Can you be sensible enough to go to the office?"

She answered with a delightful whinny,

"No sir-e-e-. I haven't a lick of sense, but I'll go anyway. How do you expect a girl who has just had the most wonderful night of her life to be anyway but delirious?

"Chris darling. I've wanted to lay in your arms all night since the first moment I saw you. I've got one of your coats you left in the office, in my bedroom. I've imagined it was you lots of times. I've gone to sleep with it in my arms.

"I'm without a speck of shame or decency telling you such silly things. You can tell me you don't love me if you want to lie about it, but I know you do. You love me in your heart but are too damn stupid to admit it. You can live here with me all the time if you want to. I'd be happy, because sooner or later you are going to make me a woman. I hope I get pregnant. There. Think about that. I mean the act, not the result."

She kissed me with sudden tenderness,

"I love you so, Christopher. I love you.

"Now that is out of my system. What do you want me to do at the office?"

"I'm going to the Morley house office. You get all the information on the papers, radio, and TV stations you have. Grab a taxi and go there. For the next four days I'll be there all the time."

"Right, Commander."

She went down the hall singing,

"More of his lovin, more of his arms, more of his heavenly, manly charms, more of his——." The closing door shut off the sound.

I laughed like hell, and went to my car.

Wells was walking across the garden when I parked the car.

He motioned for me to follow him, saying,

"Where the hell have you been? There's been dozens of phone calls for you."

"That's the main reason I took off. You're the goat in this parade for the sheep to follow. Remember?"

He gave me a sour look and walked on. Back of the barn he watched me get my first look at the pastures. He grinned at my amazement.

Big Army tents were everywhere, set far enough apart to give the people who were to occupy them plenty of privacy.

A wide space for a street divided the rows. For every four tents there was a neatly painted Chick Sale. Portable bath houses were ranged in order at strategic points.

Across the fence from the tents a circus tent was stretched. He said proudly,

"That's the eating tent. Seats and tables too. The kitchens are in the next smaller tent, hot and cold water in the bath houses."

He pointed to another pasture,

"See all them seats? We can set a whole Army there at one time. I got an outfit to set up a bunch of speakers all around the joint. By golly you can hear a pin drop on the platform, clear back to the woods. The carnival will move in tonight and be ready to go in the morning."

He eyed me with an anxious look,

"You sure the Colonel and his woman are going to get here?"

"He'll be here Sergeant. If I wasn't a Navy man I'd shake your hand. This is beyond my expectations. I'll ask the Colonel to make you a Second Lieutenant. You certainly deserve it."

He spit on the ground viciously,

"I wouldn't be a shavetail even in your Goddamned bath tub outfit. Keep your dirty suggestions to yourself."

I laughed like crazy but he remained stone faced,

"Sergeant. I want one man who is well known in the bunch to get on the platform at the proper time, swing his arms, jump up and down, and then ask the crowd if they didn't think Colonel Morley would make a fine Governor. Know a man like that?"

He pulled a piece of grass, stuck it in his mouth chewing reflectively, he shook his head, then said,

"One of my First Sergeants owns a string of banks in the Southern part of the state. He's got a voice like a bull, also a good education. Thinks he might have been a great actor if he hadn't got caught in the Army. I'll bring him to you. If he balks I'll part his ears with a club. A good man for the job. His name is Ames. Jeff Ames."

"One last thing Sergeant. Late tomorrow, the Colonel will land at the airport if he is on schedule. I want every man, woman, and child to be there in cars to meet him. I'll have reporters, cameras, and TV mobile units to cover the reception. Make it a big thing. Savvy?"

He grunted and for the first time he smiled happily,

"You're a sneaky bastard. Good luck."

Darleen was waiting in the garden for me. She said in a voice filled with awe,

"Gee whiz, isn't this a grand place? Will you show me around?"

"Not now. Close your mouth and follow me."

Inside she took one look,

"Shu-s-s-s. Shu-s-s-s-. A soft couch, TV and everything. No wonder you were too pooped to stagger down to the office. What a bouncing you must have had."

I answered her caustically,

"To relieve your pretty mind. I haven't had time to sit on the thing. I've been too busy.

"Darleen. Take that phone. Call every reporter whose name you have. I'll tell you what to say. Then call the radio and TV stations, ask for the manager and tell them the same thing, or approximately. If they ask questions, hang up."

She made ready while I wrote her little spiel. I handed her the paper. She read it then looked at me,

"Do I start now?"

"Read it aloud to me. I want to see if I could believe you are sincere."

"Hello. Mr. —————.

"There is a rumor the famous Colonel Morley is going to be a guest at his own surprise party at his fabulous estate.

"Have you heard about it?—————

"I understand it will last for two days, beginning Saturday morning the 27th. I hear everything will be free to all the people who wish to join the party. Food, lodging, even transportation. His old friend, Sergeant Wells, of the Wells Hotel is sponsoring the event. Wouldn't that make a wonderful story for your paper especially as hundreds of his friends from your city will be there.

"A man just told me there's going to be over six thousand guests at the party. I'm trying to find out about it. I wondered if you knew?"

I listened with my eyes shut. She tickled the hell out of me. I felt like saying I'd love to go myself she was so convincing. She looked at me,

"Would you come to my party? Mister."

"Yep. Try one now. Take the Gazette, ask for Barney. If he listens, you got it made."

She dialed the number and did her stuff. She winked at me while she listened a couple of times, then laid down the receiver. She was jubilant,

"He said he would run out to the Morley place and look over the joint. If what I said was true it was the biggest story that had come his way in months. He even thanked me."

"Good girl. Call one other paper here, then switch to the outlying towns. They will call the local papers for confirmation. By that time Barney should be back in the office of his paper with all the dope and the balloon will burst with a bang."

I hurried to find Wells. He was sitting on the corral fence with about a dozen men, directing the first of the visitors down the tented street. He saw me coming and came to meet me.

"Sergeant. There will be a bunch of reporters here in a hurry. Give them the whole treatment but do not mention anything about the campaign. Tell them to invite their friends. It's on the house."

He grinned,

"Will do Commander. You bastard."

I grinned back at him and ducked back into the house in high glee.

I stood at the front window waiting impatiently. Five minutes later two cars parked in the driveway. I recognized Barney.

He was an old friend but if he saw me now I would be on his crap list forever. He got out of his car, looked around, listened for a second then veered across the garden heading toward the barn and the sound of men shouting. The rest of his crowd followed. Four men. Two women. I hoped they were the most excitable reporters on the staff.

I would have given a chocolate cookie to have seen their faces when they saw the setup in the pasture.

I waited by the curtained window, listening to Darleen make her calls. Her diction was good, just enough reflected curiosity, with a tiny lilt in her voice. She had perfected her story until even to me she sounded sincere.

Just then Barney came tearing around from the back of the house and cut across the garden, running like he had a hornet under his tail. I laughed out loud. His car lurched over in a tight turn and he was away. He was going to be the first to splash headlines across the state. I was all for it.

I suddenly wondered how Wells had moved all that equipment into the place without the whole countryside knowing.

The other six reporters straggled along, stood at the curb gesturing, then piled into the one car. It took off in a screech of burning rubber. More headlines were in the making.

Almost immediately a Western Union messenger came to the door. I sent Darleen to get the message. Colonel Morley wasn't wasting words.

"Three-forty-five-B." That was it.

I almost jumped for joy. The Governor was in for a hell of a surprise.

It was two hours before Darleen was through with her calls on the telephone. All we could do now was wait and hope for the best. I asked her,

"Would you like some lunch?"

Her reply was emphatic,

"Lunch? I could eat a horse. I don't remember even having breakfast." She added with a sly look, "Where is the bathroom?"

"Through that door. Upstairs. Find it."

I went to the big kitchen. Mary was pleased when I asked her to serve us a meal.

"I see you fattened up on my cooking. You're a handsome brute. Is this a new girl?"

"Nope. My secretary."

She clucked,

"Female and pretty?"

She was a romantic creature for sure.

"You might think so. I haven't noticed."

"Then why are you getting red in the face? I wish I was a young chick again. I'd teach you the facts of life."

"You can try anytime you feel like it, my love."

Her merry laughter was wonderful.

"At my age? A couple of drinks, a big lovin' an I wouldn't be able to cook for a week. Get along with you. You tempt me."

I walked away from her cackling laughter.

Through the window I could see several cars parked at the curb.

While I watched, a field radio unit pulled up, the large letters, "KRTV" printed on the panel side. Hot damn. The biggest station in the county. Now the ball was starting to roll. Wells sauntered across the garden as though such an event was an everyday occurrence in his life. He talked with the driver a minute then the truck moved on down the driveway toward the entrance to the barn.

He came to the office like a man with a problem on his mind. He said abruptly,

"For Chrisake Commander. How many reporters have you told about this shindig?"

I consulted Darleen's report sheet,

"Fifty-seven, Sergeant. Forty-eight radio stations, and seven TV stations. Why?"

He sat down like he had weak legs,

"Over a hundred. There's only about ten out there now already raising hell with me, because they weren't notified ahead of time. So they could set up their equipment and get the whole story. You're a damn fool if you think I'm going to put up with all their cussing. You get out there and make 'em be reasonable."

I held my hands like I was reading the headlines in a newspaper,

"Surprise."

"Colonel Bart Morley, returning from Hawaii with his beautiful wife will be the guest of honor at his estate, where a crowd of six thousand of his friends have assembled to honor him on his birthday.

"The great party was conceived and planned in the fertile mind of his long time friend and business associate Mr. Justin Wells."

I said as nasty as I could,

"Shall I read more Sergeant?"

He squared his shoulders as he stood on his feet and bit off his words,

"When this is over, I'm going to drag you out back of the barn. I've got one more good one left in me, and by God you're going to get it."

He strode forcefully away, his voice was low but distinct,

"Bastard. Just a waterlogged bastard."

I laughed until the tears ran down my cheeks. Wells was the kind of a man to ride the waves with.

Darleen stopped beside me,

"That's the biggest bedroom I ever saw. What a lovely room. Is it yours?"

"Yes. Temporarily. This part of the house was used by Bart's father before he passed away. Bart wanted me to stay here during the campaign. This room was simply luxurious until the furniture was moved out to make room for the office equipment. I have all my meals served here too."

She said with a little laugh,

"I can see why you like it here. You live like a king."

Mary came in, pushing a rubber tired, wrought iron tea cart. She gave Darleen a frank look and said to me,

"You're a terrible liar Mr. Howard. You had reason to blush."

She smiled at Darleen,

"I'm the cook. This is a grand boy but he needs his eyes examined."

"Mary, my love. My secretary, Miss Dahl, Darleen, Mary wants me to make love to her, but she stuffs me with such wonderful food I haven't the energy."

Darleen giggled,

"He thinks all women are a menace to his bachelorhood."

Mary looked Darleen up and down,

"You look a first rate mantrap yourself. Keep the bait dangling in front of his eyes and he'll take it. Maybe he's just bashful."

"Don't rush me Mary, I like living with you in sin.

"The Morleys will be home tomorrow about four or shortly after."

Her face lit up,

"Glory be. I miss them so. I've got to hurry. Just push the cart out in the hall when you finish."

She ran away, humming happily.

Darleen said thoughtfully,

"Every woman who sees you, falls for you. I hope you can be faithful to the one you marry."

"I haven't the slightest intention of getting married so don't worry about it. Let's eat."

She said softly,

"Whu-f-f-f, whu-f-f-f. I wonder."

In the middle of the meal she said unexpectedly,

"We've been together a whole night and day. Isn't it heavenly?"

I almost choked, but I didn't answer. Presently she said,

"Do we stay here tonight?"

"I do, but you're going home. I know when I'm well off."

She said musingly,

"Mu-m-m, mu-m-m. So big and soft. Such a big soft bed and I don't have a nightie to sleep in."

CHAPTER NINETEEN

After I pushed the tea cart out in the hall and closed the door again, she had such a "cat that ate the mouse" look on her lovely puss I was scared.

I called a taxi and when it arrived I ushered her out the door and across the garden, slamming the door on the cab after I forcibly hoisted her inside. She threw a first class tantrum during the process.

I ignored her struggles. The cab driver looked at me wide eyed when I gave him a five dollar bill telling him to drive her home. He said out of the corner of his mouth,

"You must be sick, Mister. She wasn't fightin' you off."

I waved him away and turned back into the house without looking around. I could hear her yelling some very uncomplimentary remarks at my flapping ears. I slept alone but I dreamed of an angel who wasn't wearing a nightie.

Early in the morning I called a news agency that specialized in out of town newspapers. I had every available paper that was printed in the state delivered by special messenger.

For three hours I gloated over the news of the party. There were some caustic remarks in a few of them regarding the use of Guard equipment, but on the whole the reporters were favorable to the idea.

The Gazette carried a half-page picture on the third page of the entire tent city. Below that the page was filled with a complete story of Colonel Bart Morley. That page alone would have cost a thousand dollars at regular advertisers rates. Old Barney would tear me apart joint by joint and hide the pieces when he found how he had been suckered.

Wells stopped by long enough to tell me the reaction from downtown,

"Just came from downtown. Every son-of-a-bitch I met like to pounded me to death. Looks like you pulled a fast one and got away with it. I'd hate to be in your shoes when the news men discover it's all a putup job."

"Too late now Sergeant. Look at these papers. They won't admit they fell for a sneak punch. Besides, after the Colonel is shouted into running for Governor by all his friends, how are the reporters going to learn any different?"

He grunted,

"You make me think of a bug. A spider."

"The Colonel will land at the airport at three-forty-five. You ready, Sergeant?"

"Yep. Been up half the night hiring a band and talking the police department into furnishing a proper escort, while you been getting your beauty sleep. Why in hell you stickin' in this office like you was hidin' out?"

"Sergeant. Get this through your thick skull. If one reporter saw me here he would start looking for the reason. My business is running political campaigns. The whole thing would bust wide open. You run the outfit till Monday morning and then I'll give you some help. Until then I'm afraid to step out in the hall."

He asked, hesitantly,

"You got a man picked for Lieutenant Governor?"

"No. I was hired by the Colonel. I don't know who he has in mind or if he gives a damn. You have a man in mind?"

"Had a long talk with Jeff Ames. He's made a pot full of money in the last ten years, but mostly he likes farming.

"Owns a lot of land and he likes to be known as a hell of a feller. When I asked him would he get up and off hand like tell the crowd what a Governor the Colonel would make, he jumped at the chance. Said he would put on the show of his life. He said he would like a crack at the crooked politicos in the state himself. I'd back him for the second spot an' so would the rest of the bunch."

"I'll talk it over with the Colonel, Wells. All I'm interested in is getting Bart Morley elected. Believe me, he will be too."

"A good strong running mate would be a big help. Let me know how the rest feel about Mr. Ames, but keep it quiet until after the Colonel announces his candidacy. A few days after the big blast in the papers die down, we can spring another surprise by having Ames come out for Lieutenant Governor with all the publicity necessary. I'll handle his campaign without fee. I'll try to do it in such a way that the papers will eat it up."

His face twisted like he was trying to smile but all he did was grunt,

"I got to admit Commander, I didn't know a man could have such a crooked mind and still be honest. It makes me wonder."

"Thanks for the left-hand compliment, Sergeant. I wouldn't trust you either."

That got him. He let go with a belly laugh and walked away.

I wanted to be on hand at the airport when Bart and Jen came out of the plane but that would be committing suicide.

I wondered how I could see all the events and see all the pictures on the TV. I settled that in a hurry.

I called one of the Radio Supply houses and ordered two large screen TV sets and a radio. There were three different network stations in the city and I wanted to see the next three days action on all of them. The supply house promised they would deliver the sets within the hour.

Darleen run in the door looking like a cover girl, big smile included. I had a flash thought, wondering if she would be as beautiful without her nightgown. She was a lollipop. Good enough to eat.

"Chris darling. You put it over. I'm so proud of you."

"I'm proud of me too. There will be a delivery truck here in a few minutes with two TV sets and a radio. Have the man set them along that wall beside that one. I can watch all three from the lounge. I'm going upstairs until he leaves, then call me."

She said breathlessly,

"Wh-e-e-e. I'll call in person."

"Damn it, just call me. Take this money and pay for the sets and sign Bart Morley's name with yours. I've got to keep out of sight till Monday."

She squealed with delight,

"Goody. I love to play hide and seek."

I waited impatiently while the sets were carried in and connected to the electric current, and adjusted.

From upstairs it sounded like bedlam with all three sets operating at once then they were turned down. Presently I saw the truck drive away.

I went down the steps on the jump just as Darleen came up the same way. We met halfway. I tried my best to break our fall but we ended on the bottom in a tangle. I felt around the legs to determine if any were broken. Mine were all right and the other pair were in perfect shape clear to the top where they came together. So soft and warm.

I lifted her to her feet,

"You all right?"

She leaned against me,

"I think so, but I'm kind of dizzy and hot all over. You better carry me to the couch."

I had a moment of panic as I laid her gently on the couch. Her clinging arms dispelled that in a hurry. Her warm mouth covering my lips took my breath away. I jerked back,

"Damn it. I thought you were hurt."

She half closed her eyes, squinting at me,

"Would you have cared so much?"

I roughly shoved her over and scooped her in my arms,

"You're driving me nuts. Why can't you be a sweet little virgin and not keep me all worked up."

"Cause I love you. Cause a virgin I don't want to be."

"You crazy dame. Didn't your mother ever tell you not to chase a man?"

She run the tip of her tongue over my lips experimentally,

"I'm not chasing you. You're holding me."

She had a point there so I just held on. She was contented as a kitten although little trembling movements ran down her body from time to time as we watched the scene unfolding at the airport.

The networks must have had a dozen cameras set up. From the moment the plane landed, the crowd surged forward and Colonel Morley stepped through the plane door holding Jen by the arm. Every move was visible. It was a publicity man's dream.

They were a handsome couple if I ever saw one. Bart waved and smiled like a professional, while Jen clung to his arm. A perfect picture of the devoted wife. At the bottom of the loading ramp the amateur photographers almost mobbed Jen in an effort to get close-ups of her.

It was fifteen minutes before the police could clear the way to the waiting cars. The crowd jostled and pushed around the Morley car after Bart and Jen were seated inside, yelling, shouting and waving.

Wells had the band seated in a flat bed truck which led the string of cars away from the airport. Portable camera trucks ranged alongside the car the entire trip until the caravan entered the tented city behind the house.

In close-up pictures of Bart I could see he was actually bewildered by the tremendous reception. Jen was having the time of her life, waving and smiling at the people who crowded around her.

She might not be much of a wife to Bart, but she was the best candidate's wife I had ever looked upon. The crowd loved her. Even the women.

It was the same thing all over when Bart and Jen left the car, walking up the street between the tents toward the house.

One of the announcers said with awe in his clipped speech,

"In all my years of broadcasting, I have never seen such warm affection shown to a man. Colonel Bart Morley, distinguished gentleman. The man of the hour."

The stations abruptly switched to their regular programs. I got off the lounge, turned the sets off. If it would have been possible, I would have yelled, run, and jumped like crazy.

In my intense excitement I broke into a sweat, my shorts were wet with perspiration, my groin ached. I had to get rid of my energy some way and Darleen was there waiting.

I lifted her into my arms and swung her wildly around the room. She lay limp in my arms when I eased her to her feet. With my free hand I caressed the inside of her thighs with a boldness I had not attempted before. I hooked my fingers in the narrow strap of her panties and jerked. The silken cloth parted, leaving the tender flesh exposed to my exploring fingers.

She moaned softly, half in pleasure, half in sadness, elbowed herself away from me and began walking nervously about the room. Pressing her hands to the side of her face she said unhappily,

"I think you are the most wonderful man in the world and I want you to love me. But right now I'm going home. If I stay we may both be sorry. I want to be loved, tenderly, gently, with your heart as well as your body. If I don't leave now you will simply rape me. There will be no thought of tenderness in the act. Chris darling. I've waited a long time. I'll wait some more. Good night, my love."

She caught her breath in a sob, ran out the door, across the garden, then walked on down the driveway toward the city.

I watched her through the window feeling like some slimy monster of the deep. She was right as hell. I would have tom her wide apart in my animal lust without a single thought of her feelings. I would have hurt her womanly sensibilities beyond repair. Thank God she had stopped me in time. What a wonderful, intelligent woman she was.

Her abrupt departure following her soft words of love calmed me. I wanted her again so I could beg her forgiveness, but for the moment she was gone. I cursed myself bitterly for acting like a damn fool.

I could hear many voices in the hall outside the door. Women's shrill voices raised above the clatter of the crowd, laughing and shouting. Bart Morley was being welcomed home in grand style.

I was struck with an odd thought. Here I was. The man responsible for the whole shebang, a prisoner in my office.

Unable to join the crowd because some eagle eyed reporter would spot me and see through the fabrication in a single glance.

Wells opened the door cautiously and stepped in, grinning from ear to ear,

"Wasn't that something, boy?"

His eyes took in the three TV sets. "I see you had a first row seat."

"It was a ringtailed performance, Sergeant. You should have been a General."

His grin widened,

"The Colonel didn't have to act surprised. He got the surprise of his life." He chortled,

"Could you see the expression on his face when the old bunch damn near tramped him to death?"

"Yes I could. How does he feel about it?"

"I haven't been able to talk to him alone yet. We just had a few quiet words in the crowd. The old boy had tears in his eyes when he saw how many of the old gang was there. There's two thousand out there now and that ain't a fraction of them.

"There was thirty reporters and camera men. I counted them."

He had a pleasant far away look on his face,

"I'm enjoying myself more than I did when the Colonel and me landed in North Africa. By God we're headed for the capitol in a clean sweep. The old bastards will follow the Colonel to hell if he asks them to."

"That's the way I like to hear you talk. You sound like a man with a mission. Be damn sure you get a few of your cronies to help tomorrow when Ames starts shouting. That will be the decisive point to put over."

He said confidently,

"Just sit back in your easy chair, swabbie. I got her all lined up. They'll tear the goddamned tents down when they get the word."

"Thank you Wells. You make my job a pleasure."

He said gruffly,

"I'm having a hell of a good time. The Colonel said to tell you he would see you in the morning."

Alone again I cleaned out the refrigerator to see if there was anything edible. There was. I didn't have the heart to buzz Mary. She would be busy.

I watched TV until midnight then went to bed, but I couldn't sleep. I could hear sounds coming from the pasture in waves. Music, singing, snatches of boisterous laughter, and now and then the sound of a revved up motor as new guests drove in and parked.

I wondered what in hell had become of Captain Downs. Not a word from her since Avery had taken his well deserved departure.

Not a word in the papers about the nation wide raids on the gangsters. Avery's demise had been noted in a very small space in only one of the local papers. A brief notice that the Eagle Club was closed for alterations. That was a laugh. I wondered if St. Cyr was having champagne and pheasant under glass for dinner in his cell.

These days were enough to drive me nuts cooped here in the office. Maybe tomorrow I'd drive to my apartment and get a girl to keep me company. I wondered if Darleen was snug in her virginal bed and fast asleep.

I never gave a thought to Jen, until suddenly there she was leaning over me.

She had come into the room like a ray of moonlight, silently, and all aglow.

She bent over me, her warm lips softly touching mine. I threw back the covers and pulled her down beside me. With infinite tenderness she moulded her lush body against mine, her knee wedging between my thighs. Her murmurings were like the music of tiny birds at dawn. Through her parted lips I tasted the sweetness of her mouth. She wasted no time in preliminary love

DON LEE

making. Turning slowly, she pressed her hand against the small of my back, then sighed, arching her body to meet my descending weight.

Long after we had reached our perfectly timed mutual climax she lay trembling, her throbbing breath audible.

Winding her fingers in my hair she pulled my ear to her lips and whispered,

"Only you, lover. Only you can do it. I've tried so hard, but I just tighten up inside and nothing happens. I've nearly killed Bart in the last two weeks trying to get some satisfaction from his love making. I've forced him time and again to love me. He thinks I've suddenly gone crazy about it. But darling, I only wanted to be a good wife."

I held her tight. With me she was perfect. In her moment of orgasm she was torn from head to feet like lightning striking a tree. What could I say? I wisely kept silent.

She murmured fiercely,

"I'm nothing but the lowest kind of a bitch. A dirty filthy bitch. I made one of the bellboys, in the hotel where we stayed, get in bed with me. All I got out of it was dirty.

"A beach boy took me sailing. He was big and strong. When I left him, he was exhausted and sound asleep. I still wanted more. Now you know all about me. I hate myself except when I'm in your arms. I hate you too, but I love your body."

She cried softly, her body trembling under me. I was shocked into sober thought.

Bart Morley was going to be elected Governor as sure as day followed night. What would his wife do to him?

She didn't know the meaning of conscience. In one of the great moments of his life, here she was in my arms. She had crawled into my arms to satisfy her female desire. I drew my arm from under her. She whispered softly,

"Please don't send me away darling. I know what you are thinking. I know. Please let me stay in your arms. If only you could understand how I feel. Time and again, hundreds of times men have used me. I didn't care. I hated their guts. I used them too. I hated their sex organs, but I used their money. I had to, to live. Please lover, hold me. You're the only one I can cling to."

She clasped her arms around my neck in desperation. Her crying went on unabated.

The stark truth hit me like a fist. We were birds out of the same nest. I wanted money and women. She had given me half a million dollars. She had given herself. I hadn't used any of the money, but I had used her at every opportunity without a twinge of conscience. With her husband just on the other side of a wall I had just completed the act of coitus with her in unbridled delight. She had soaked me up like a sponge in the same passionate embrace.

It is said that a man passing over a woman leaves no more trace than a ship passing over the sea. The men who had passed over Jennifer Morley had left a dark stain on her mind. I had left a stain of another color. Physical satisfaction, and orgiastic completion. The stain was there, obscuring her vision of reality. At the moment her sensual body was in command. Only a miracle could save us from disaster.

My eyes burned with the thought. Unconsciously I hugged her tight. She raised over me, gently licked the moisture from around my eyelids.

She whispered, but the soft sound was strong,

"There is nothing anyone can do, my dearest. I will be everything you want me to be. I will be a good wife to Bart. Not by look or deed will I hurt him in the campaign. You can trust me in that. Only this my lover. When my body cries out in sickness for you, please be kind. Take me in your arms and make me well again. Please my lover. It's all I ask."

With a cold fear in my heart I drew her into the shelter of my arms in silent promise. She kissed me with her heart in her lips. Not a heart filled with love, but a heart filled with physical well-being. Almost instantly she went to sleep, clinging to my hand resting on her breast. Her regular breathing lulled me to sleep beside her.

When I awoke, she was gone. Only the woman scent of her lingered.

Waiting is the hardest kind of work in the world. What do you do? You eat, you drink all kinds of bellywash. You pace the floor like a caged animal. You think of all the women you have had. Hell. I nearly went out of my mind until shortly after noon.

Darleen came in then happy as a lark. She was a bit wary for a while but when she saw I had no designs on her beautiful self she became a wonderful companion. The times she came within reach of me I kissed her thoroughly. Each time she submitted willingly, breaking away before I could work on her in earnest. She seemed to glow with an inner light that set her face aflame. Her returned kisses were tantalizing, promising, but she held herself in check every minute.

I turned on the TV sets just flicking the switches so the picture would form but no sound would come. At two o'clock after a windy commercial, a panoramic view of the tented city behind the house filled the screens. My waiting was over.

Turning up the volume I settled down to watch what I hoped would be, the crowning achievement of my misspent life.

Darleen helped herself to a cozy position in my lap with a series of little wriggly motions, captured my roving hands, and held them firmly in both of hers. She explained the action with a throaty chuckle,

"We want to watch the pictures. Remember?"

She was holding my hands in such a position I could press downward and make her squirm. I made her squirm a lot of times in the next two hours.

The cameras panned all over the pastures, giving us a complete view of every detail. Inside the tents were suitcases, and clothing strung helter skelter over both tidy made up cots and untidy ones with the bedding trailing off on the ground. One tent was crowded with a group of young women, each holding a small baby in every manner known to mothers.

Lush breasts filled with sweet milk were being bubblingly sucked on. Baby clothes were upended, held in half security by a pair of pigeon toed feet. Beaming mothers bent over a naked form, belly down, while he got a coat of soothing powder patted on with a kiss across his heaving little butt.

Darleen said with a merry laugh,

"I'll bet the cameraman sneaked in on that tent. See the expressions. They don't know there is a man anywhere."

She added musingly, giving me a flick of a glance, and gently pressing one of my hands over her own delectable dinner mounds,

"I'd love to have a baby. It must be fun trying to make one."

I agreed with her, silently.

The dining tent got a full share of the picture, half filled with men, women and children, eating, coming in, or moving out, shouting and having the time of their lives.

The kitchen tent was shown inside from end to end. Big pots bubbled, filled with all kinds of food fit for a king. Busy cooks lifted pint sized spoons of the ingredients, letting the contents slowly fall back into the pots for the edification of the viewers.

The Chick Sales brought another laugh from both of us. Women wandering innocently toward their doors, glanced over their shoulders then ran pell mell inside, or turned, flying back into one of the nearest tents, their mission, hastily abandoned.

Simultaneously all three screens showed about the same view. A slow panning of the pastures where thousands of people were seated in a semi-circle around an improvised platform. On the platform a man and a woman were just ending some sort of a performance which brought the crowd to its feet in a burst of applause.

A man walked to the platform and held up his hand to silence the crowd. He motioned to a man standing behind him.

By some hidden wire, a cloth as big as a small tent was whisked off the top of a truck parked directly in front of the platform. On the truck, resting on snowy linen, was the biggest cake in the world.

It must have been twenty feet from top to bottom, and ten feet across. Electric candles twinkled all over it. Around the sides in letters formed from rose buds, were the words.

"HAPPY BIRTHDAY BART."

The band struck up. "Happy birthday to you—"

The mob went crazy. It was fifteen minutes before Bart Morley walked across the platform holding Jen firmly by the hand. She was bawling like a baby, struggling to get away from him. Unashamedly he pulled a handkerchief from his coat pocket and blew his nose and wiped his eyes, then stuck the kerchief back in his pocket. The cameras caught the reaction of the crowd. There wasn't a dry eye in the lot.

A long, slow rumble of sound swelled over the area. The sound of the band became louder. In a minute, thousands of husky voices, intermingled with the higher voices of the women were singing in unison, "Happy birthday dear Bart—."

With Jen securely held by one arm, Bart Morley faced the crowd. The mighty sound rolled across the countryside in a great tribute to the man they loved and admired.

My own eyes were wet and Darleen was crying softly.

When the song ended there was silence. Bart caught the microphone with his free hand to steady himself, and squared his broad shoulders. He opened his mouth to speak, but no sound came out.

CHAPTER TWENTY

He stood for a moment then turned away with bowed head and walked to the back of the platform, leaving his wife to follow alone.

A host of eager hands lifted him to shoulders which materialized from behind the platform. He was carried back to the microphone, held high like a conquering hero.

A man's voice filled with excitement, shouting into the microphone quieted the throng,

"This is our Colonel. Remember?"

There was a surge of sound from the men,

"Every man here followed him across Africa, and Europe. Remember?"

Again the long surge of sound from thousands of throats.

"How many of you would follow him again?"

This time the crowd came up standing in a single move, yelling their heads off.

"Now. I ask you. Would he be the man to be our leader in this state?"

Without hesitation a roaring chant began,

"Yea. Yea. Yea. Yes. Yes. Yes."

The man speaking held up his hand,

"How would you like to see him Governor?"

This was the great moment. Even the TV announcers' voices were stilled. The cameras caught the action as the crowd let go. As a single voice they roared their unqualified approval.

In that moment their voices carried to every city, town, and cross roads in the state, spilling across the borders into the states adjoining our own.

In that moment with the cameras focused on Bart Morley's smiling face, with tears running down that face, with thousands of faces lifted toward his in adoration, the image of a great man was created in the minds of all who were watching in the four corners of the state.

My mind flashed back to my father. He often told me, "only a man who was great and strong was weak enough to cry."

The screens pictured a last view of the crowd streaming forward in a close packed mass around the platform. Bart was hidden in the men around him. Jen was nowhere in sight.

The announcers' voices were raised as they voiced the scene in its most dramatic moments. Their usual calm, familiarity with many different moments of excitement was broken by a human emotion beyond their control. Their voices came out in jerky sentences as though they were fighting for breath.

On the hour the stations resumed their regular broadcasting. Darleen turned the sets off, placed a pillow on the floor in front of my chair, sat on it, laying her head on my knees. Her look was eloquent of her love.

The last two days had been hard on my nerves. Now I was at peace with the world. Now I could go back to work.

Beginning Monday, counting holidays and Sundays, I had four months and nine days to put on the damnedest political campaign ever seen in the state. Bart Morley was a dream of a candidate. His beautiful, gorgeous wife was the only drawback.

With the morals of a barnyard hen she was a real problem. Damn her little hide I'd keep her under control if I had to take her to bed every night and wring her dry. After the election I could leave her alone. She would be much too busy to think about every man that took her eye.

By then maybe she would have some sense.

I groped in thought trying to think of some way I could get her out of the way until after the election. There was nothing I could do. I was committed to being her stud.

From the very second she had spread her thighs, closed them over me and drawn me into her passionate body there was no turning back. The way was ahead at all costs. You win the battles first, then count the dead. I had the unhappy thought that I would be the first counted.

I thought of Amy Downs,

"Where is Captain Downs? Why hasn't she called me?"

Darleen said quickly,

"In New York. She wrote me a little note, said to tell you 'hello.' "

She looked at me curiously,

"Did you like loving her, Chris?"

"What a stupid question. Where do you get such crazy ideas?"

"The way her eyes followed you around. She kept licking your kisses off her mouth. I wanted to slap your face."

I couldn't help laughing at her fierce expression.

"Is she coming back soon?"

"I hope not. Let her sleep with the army."

I dragged her onto my lap,

"Is it possible you are the possessive type?"

She fought me with all her strength then gave up with a sigh,

"I've nothing to be possessive about yet. I know you are a sexual moron. I only pray you will be true to the woman you marry."

"Put your mind at ease kitten. I'm not married. Period."

From under lowered eyelashes she gave me a melting look,

"Pet me darling. Try to imagine I'm the one and only in your life. Not just some female you are trying to get into.

"Chris darling. Close your eyes and try. Kiss me gently with your heart in your kiss."

She was so sweet and appealing I did exactly as she asked. In a crazy flashback of thought I remembered the first time I had tried to kiss one of the little girls that lived next door when I was a kid. I had puckered against her face but somehow my mouth had hit her behind the ear. I didn't try to kiss another girl for a long time.

Darleen's mouth was easy to find. She placed it hotly on mine. I rubbed my hands over the outside of her clothing from her shoulders to her knees with no hesitant stops in between.

In spite of all I could do I kept drawing her closer, and closer, until she was grasping for breath. I was drunk as a Lord on the sweet nectar of her mouth. My head was bursting.

Little black spots danced before my eyes, and I was suffocating from lack of breath. From the back of my brain I got the message. I was a dead duck. I knew it right then.

My God, how I loved her. I almost burst with the joy of knowing. I repeated over and over to myself,

"I love you. I love you. I love you."

I held onto her like a drunk hanging to a lamp post.

She lifted dewy eyes to mine. Deep shining pools of love.

"Say it darling. Say it. Tell me. You have found out at last how much you love me."

I closed her mouth with my lips unwilling to utter a word. I knew it. She knew it. Why should I make a big production out of a thing we both knew.

I dropped her on the pillow at my feet and straightened up.

I walked as fast as my wobbly legs could carry me toward the stairway door. There I turned to look at her. She was kneeling at the edge of the chair with her hands pressed together in front of her, steeple fashion, and with her head tipped back and eyes closed, her lips were moving in silent conversation with an unseen figure.

The next four months slipped by like a single night.

A hazy blur of meetings in drafty halls, great sports arenas, hotel rooms, county fairs, state fairs, grange halls, big banquets, little banquets, and small suppers in some isolated little farm community.

We rode trains where we got no sleep, and planes that roared out of the clouds to land on a runway lined with dense crowds yelling their lungs out at the sight of Colonel Morley.

There were automobiles that got stuck in the muddy roads, a thousand rickety platforms where we sat under hot lights while cameras and microphones registered every movement and expression of Bart Morley's expressive face and every gesture of his hands.

Jennifer Morley wore every costume she could lay hands on. Blue jeans, calico shirts, straw hats, Lily Dache hats, and cow girl hats. Ballroom gowns worth a fortune, overcoats in stormy weather filched from her husband.

She paraded in clear cold creeks wearing a silver bathing suit. She rode horses, mules, tractors, and even had her picture taken astride a prize bull at a stock show.

In our tour of the state whenever possible we made a swing close to the Morley mansion. These nights were filled with more excitement as everyone wanted to see the future Governor in his own home and talk with him.

During these times I tried to have as many of my own people as possible come in from the towns and cities around the state. I kept a tight rein on their optimistic thinking discounting their probable estimate of the voting results by half. They were enthusiastic as hell, but most of them only saw our side of the campaign. I knew it was going to be close.

The incumbent machine was fighting a life and death struggle. If they lost the fat was in the fire. In our travels, we had learned of the wholesale graft that was taking place in every office in the county and state.

We had facts and figures to prove it. Men and women came to our hotel rooms at night, or openly met us and told us of the things going on in their communities. The list was too long to even mention in the publicity.

Colonel Morley poured it on as the campaign came to a close. He called the men's names out in a loud and clear voice, defying the men mentioned to get up in public and deny the facts as he presented them.

I was in a publicity man's heaven from start to finish. I poured out money like I owned a money factory but always more was added to the supply. For the last two weeks of the campaign it was impossible to listen to any radio or TV station in the state without hearing the name of Colonel Morley mentioned.

Jeff Ames on the second spot for Lieutenant Governor was on the road every day, Sundays and holidays included. We tied his campaign to Colonel Morley's in all our publicity and in language and personality he was no shrinking violet.

He ranted and raved in a manner well known at the turn of the century. His words at times bordered on the obscene but the voters through the state loved to hear him give the opposition their comeuppance. He seemed at all times to be ready and willing to take on any one who opposed his thinking in a free for all fist fight. The reporters who followed him around the state loved him and consequently gave him a lions share of the free publicity.

The newspapers got their huge cut of the money also. There wasn't a single paper in the state ignored. From the five or six hundred circulation weekly to the great metropolitan dailies, I fed in the notices, speeches and pictures. Sunday editions carried every aspect of the Morley's private life in full page splendor.

I often wondered if there wasn't some reporter or photographer watching Bart and Jen make love if they got the time and the urge.

On our tours Jen was the perfect Governor's lady. She didn't make any mistakes and her eyes had lost their natural predatory look. The women loved her and invited her to their homes in true affection. I saw her many times with a little apron wrapped around her luscious frame in some kitchen, hot faced and perspiring, working like a slave over a range or carrying great platters of food to adorn the tables where we were to sit and fill our bellies with food such as only can come from the kitchens of the farms where the women take great pride in serving their men folks.

Whenever we were at home, sometime in the night, she would hurry to my bed and curl her hot form around me.

We would lie quiet, savoring the closeness of our bodies until the pressure mounted beyond control. Then we would tear the bed apart in our love tussles, slowly unwinding the tensions in our exhausted forms. She said over and over,

"Oh Chris my darling, I've wanted you so. I need you so. Again, my love. Make me well again. Oh—I thank you. I thank you."

To each of us it was a wonderful moment. The next day always had a rosy look, the endless procession of people easier to meet.

I kept Darleen busy as a bee. In truth, she managed the campaign of Arthur Finley almost single handed. By election day he was a "shoo-in."

With me, she was a darling little female. She used every trick she could think of to keep me aware of her.

Whenever I checked into a hotel there was always some little reminder of her devotion. Once she sent me a lock of short curly hair tied with a tiny white ribbon. I carried it around in my wallet and I would have bet a dollar to a hole in a doughnut she blushed when she cut it.

Election day arrived in a bluster of storm. Wells expressed it forcefully,

"This day is a heller, Commander. I wonder if anyone will make the effort to get out and vote. What a son-of-a-bitch."

Rain and snow swept the state from stem to stern. When Colonel Morley came from the voting place he said,

"So far, it looks like Jen and I have been the only ones to vote." He laughed wryly, "Maybe it's a good thing I'll elect myself."

We sat glued to the TV sets all day and by evening the first returns began to come in.

At eight o'clock the Colonel was trailing by ten thousand votes with about half the votes counted.

I stuck pins in the big map on the wall as each precinct was tabulated. Soon there was a cluster of pins concentrated in and around our three largest cities. The opposition machine still had control of the cities.

The overall storms were getting worse and the vote was lagging. I had to act.

I called every one of my men and asked their opinion. The replies were not heartening. Storms and more storms.

I asked each man to get some cars and round up voters and drive them to the polls regardless of party affiliation.

By ten, our place was crowded with Bart's friends. Win or lose, he was still their friend and idol.

By midnight the picture was slightly changed. The small precincts with only a handful of voters were solidly behind Bart. The farmers were ploughing through snow and muddy roads to vote.

The men working with me were hauling voters in by the hundreds. Bart's old buddies were apparently making a house to house canvass, furnishing their own cars and gasoline to get the laggard voters out into the storm.

Sitting in a nice warm house by the TV sets we could hardly visualize the discomfort the workers were going through. The old Army spirit was beginning to make itself known. They'd worked in mud and snow for Colonel Morley before, another night was nothing to fret about as long as they got the job done.

In a single half hour the picture changed for the better.

Almost like watching a slow motion action, Bart forged ahead and suddenly the election was in the bag.

When the final results were flashed on the screens, you could almost hear the cheers from the thousands of the Colonel's friends shouting from every fireside in the state. The winning total was not impressive but very satisfactory.

Twelve thousand votes on the winning man. Twelve thousand voters Bart's friends had hauled to the polls in the storm and machine politics in the state was history.

Arthur P. Finley beat his man ten to one for State Representative. I was a damned proud man. Chris Howard had done it again. A hundred per-cent record.

Darleen had been in the office all day working like a little beaver. Jennifer Morley worked by her side, the two of them giggling and whispering like they had been bosom friends all their lives.

A telegram came from the opposition candidate conceding the election. When Bart read it aloud everyone in the room went wild.

Darleen hung on my arm crying softly. Jen put her arms around both of us, kissed me vigorously while the crowd applauded her action. She said, with misty eyes,

"Happy day Chris. I knew you were the man for the job. Now listen to me you bastard. I love this girl. Be good to her or I'll kill you."

Her words shocked me into immobility. Christ. How she had changed. She further added to my bewilderment,

"She's going to stay with me tonight. I wouldn't trust you to take her home. We'll see you in the morning."

Bart and I were finally alone. He was tired but elated.

"I'm a bit late Governor. Please let me add my congratulations."

His eyes lighted with pleasure,

"Thank you Chris. I am perhaps the only man who knows that you alone are responsible for our victory. To try to thank you with words would be a waste of effort. I will try to repay you in a more substantial way."

He closed his eyes in silent thought then asked abruptly,

"What are your plans for the future?"

"Right now Governor, none. I'm dead from my rear-end both ways. I just want to rest."

He chuckled, letting the sound come without restraint,

"Two of us man. Two of us. Do you have any money?"

"Yes Sir. I spent the campaign money, keeping mine for my old age. You paid me ten thousand in advance. I have most of that." As an afterthought, I added,

"The Plymouth belongs to you. I bought it out of the fund also."

He grinned widely,

"For Christ's sake. It's all worn out and skinned up. Go buy a Cadillac tomorrow and send me the bill. The campaign's over and we can live like gentlemen again. Weren't some of those hotels hell?"

I agreed. He looked at me intently for a second,

"That girl of yours. Dahl. You going to marry her?"

DON LEE

"Not by a crockfull. I like being a bachelor."

"I did too. I was in love with a fine woman for years but never got around to asking her to become my wife. She is a wonderful woman too. Then I met Jen and married her in a few days. A man never knows when he might change his mind. I like the girl."

He laughed shortly and walked to the door,

"Take a long vacation Chris. You'll find a check on the desk in the morning. You earned it. Good night."

It was noon of the next day before I could wake enough to stagger into the shower. I dressed carefully and went down stairs. Darleen was sitting in the dinette storing away a ranch hand's breakfast.

"Help yourself to what's left, darling. Will you still love me when I'm a big fat cow?"

"What gives you the notion I love you?"

She oozed confidence,

"You. When you came in all you looked at was my eyes.

"Yours are all bright and shiny with love. You didn't notice my bare legs."

I peeked under the table. She squeezed her legs together quickly but not before I got a good look. She didn't have on pants either.

I went to work on my breakfast without a word.

She watched me with a happy smile, reached inside the front of her dress and pulled out a check. She looked at it, smoothing it between her fingers then held it for me to read.

My mouth was suddenly too full of food. I damned near choked.

Christopher Howard. Fifty thousand dollars. Bart Morley.

She laughed,

"I found it on the desk."

She held it tantalizingly before my eyes. I reached for it but slowly she drew it away returning it to the depths of her bulging blouse. She caught my hand, holding it firmly,

"Finders, keepers, darling. Jen said we could use it to go to Hawaii. She said there were the loveliest spots under the palm trees to make love."

I said absently,

"She should know. She's had the practice."

Darleen flamed,

"Chris Howard. Shame on you. I think she is the sweetest woman I ever knew. She said she has known for a long time you were in love with me."

"That is one woman's opinion. All women are natural match-makers. The married ones are the worst. They sucker some poor boob into giving up his simple life then look around for another one to foist off on one of their friends. Married life is not for Howard. I'd go blubbering mad if I had to sleep with the same woman every night of my life."

She toyed with her coffee cup, eyeing me affectionately,

"I never thought I'd see the day when you would admit a weak little woman would be too much for your manly strength to cope with. What's the matter Casanova? Afraid you couldn't keep her satisfied?"

I was afraid to reply. No matter what I said it would be the wrong thing. I shut my mouth tight and leaned back in my chair.

Her eyes were fairly dancing in anticipation as she waited for my answer. She had the look of a cat licking cream,

"You're a darling, Chris. You're cute when you act like a little boy. You want me to hold you on my lap and rock you?"

The mental picture I conjured up was funny. I went around the table, pulled her chair back and plunked my six feet of bone and muscle in her small lap.

She hugged me for a second then straightened her legs, sliding me to the floor with a jolt. She rubbed her thighs,

"You big ox. They're mashed flat."

I run my hands up their length. She crossed her legs squeezing them together. With one hand I held her, kissing her until I found what I was searching for. I drew away from her laughing triumphantly.

"See the pretty check? smarty, I'll teach you to use your feminine wiles on me."

She gasped,

"You dirty sneak."

She kicked at me with all her strength just missing my face by a whisker. I laughed at her,

"I'll take this check to the bank. It will make a healthy addition to my account and I won't spend it on a trip to Hawaii either."

She fairly sputtered in her fury,

"I hope you lose it on the way to the bank. I hate you. You're the most immoral bastard alive. I thought you were loving me with your hand when all the time you were hunting that damned check. Get away from me. You've got your last feel out of me. I'm too good for you."

She gave her clothing several vicious tugs then stalked toward the front room, her little round buttocks twitching in anger.

I poured another cup of coffee and chuckled contentedly. Old Howard was back on the beam again. In a few minutes I heard the office door slam. I looked out the window. She was walking across the garden like she was going to a fire. I loved the way she walked. So little, so stiff. She was so damn mad she was jabbing her heels into the sod and I knew she was wishing it was my face.

I loved her. Every inch of her taut, sweet body, but damned if I was going to admit it under pressure.

I had one last job to do before I was through with the Morley campaign. The accounting of the money spent on the campaign.

Two hours later Jen came in. She wore a tight fitting gown of silver cloth. No stockings. No shoes. When she passed in front of the window light I saw she wasn't wearing anything under the dress. Her form was clearly outlined, so transparent was the dress. She laughed softly at the flush that rose from my throat,

"It's been such a long time, my love. I'm glad you can get a thrill out of looking at me. Hold me."

It was quite a while before I could look at her again. She was all over me. By that time I was flushing in every pore.

She was sex personified and she laid it on. She said in a kind of wonder,

"I know I could never love you with my heart but I have no words to express how I feel about you. I don't love you. Yet, when I think about you I get sticky all over. Touch me with your hand. You'll see what mean."

She whimpered softly while I caressed her.

"You see? My body is crying for you to hold me in your arms. I should hate you. But Chris darling, you're the only one I'm contented with. I'd give my life if I could feel this way with Bart. Just one time. I try so hard while he is loving me. Nothing happens. When he is finished I want to run to your arms and bury myself under you for release."

Suddenly she was crying hysterically, moaning,

"My God Chris. What can I do? I want Bart to be happy with me. I'm so afraid. I'm afraid of what may happen sometime when you are not here. When I get this terrible burning I want a man. Afterward, I'm always sorry but at the time I go crazy. I can't help it. You are the only man I ever wanted again and again."

I held her tightly while she sobbed. She slowly quieted, then said,

"Darleen loves you very much Chris. Please marry her as soon as possible. The bonds you have can be my wedding present to both of you. After you are married I will never come to you again. I couldn't hurt her. She is a passionate, loving girl. Be gentle with her at first and give her time to learn the joy of sex without being afraid all her life. It is such a wonderful feeling."

"Jen. I don't want to marry anyone. I'm happy as I am. What if I felt about her like you do about Bart after a while?"

Jen said softly,

"You're a man. You get your satisfaction every time whether your bed partner does or not. She will love you just the same. Only this. Please take the time to make her enjoy you too. She will be worth it."

I said argumentatively,

"Suppose I were married to some woman, then sometime you came along, we looked at each other, remembering. Do you think for a moment we would give a damn about consequences? We'd be in each other's arms in spite of hell, whooping or hi-water. You know it. Just like we always have. We're a pair of alley cats without any conscience. The only conscience we have is between our legs and that hurts all the time. No Jen. Marriage is not for me."

She said gravely, with sadness in her words,

"I knew the minute I walked into your office you were a son-of-a-bitch. I could feel it clear down to my toes. I meant every word I said to you that morning. I wanted you and I wouldn't have said a word if you had tom my clothes off and stuck me to the floor like a butterfly on a pin. I'd have loved it. I'd love it now."

Her arms strained at my neck, her lips biting at the corner of my mouth. She said impatiently,

"Why do you wait? Take me upstairs to our big bed."

A few minutes later she said between gasps,

"Use your lips, lover. Use your lips."

She lay in my arms, softly singing. How the devil she had breath enough left to sing was beyond me. She said happily,

"I feel so damn good I'm going for a horseback ride. Want to join me? I haven't been on a horse for months. Come on Chris."

"No thanks. I've had all the riding I can stand."

She glanced at her wrist watch then swung her feet out of the bed,

"Please come on my love. We've been here four hours. Time you got a little exercise. You're getting fat and lazy."

"I'm not going horseback riding. I'm going to sleep."

"All right piker. I'll be back later. Get ready for a big night"

CHAPTER TWENTY-ONE

The piercing scream of a siren under my window brought me out of my exhausted sleep instantly. I rushed to the window in time to see an ambulance turn the corner into the driveway leading to the barn, followed by a police car.

An accident to one of the men on the place?

I turned away, absently wondering which one. My glance touched the pillow where Jen's head had rested just before she left me to go for a ride on one of the horses.

In a flash of thought I knew. Jen had been hurt. Lovely, warm, passionate Jen had been accidentally hurt.

I dressed in feverish haste. I had to get to her. I had to help her. I was the one she trusted.

I ran all the way. Past the kennels where the dogs were howling mournfully to where a white coated Doctor was kneeling beside a motionless form inside the gate of the big corral.

Bart Morley was standing beside the Doctor, his face a deadly white in the gathering dusk. Other men were standing in a tight little group, their faces twisted with grief.

No one noticed me approach. I looked down at the small form of Jennifer lying against a fence post, her beautiful head turned at an impossible angle to her body.

The Doctor raised slowly, looked at Bart with a compassionate sadness, then turned tiredly and began putting away his instruments.

I had seen death in many forms. This was the cruelest of all. That warm, passionate small form was still forever.

In her stillness she was a beautiful woman such as men dream about. Death had struck instantly, leaving the last spark of joyous life still indelibly printed on her features.

Her eyes were closed, the long lashes gently brushing the wells below her eyes. Her lips were turned up at the corners in a tiny provocative smile I knew so well. She was sleeping like a small child. Just sleeping.

Bart knelt beside the still form and laid his head on her shoulder, his laboured breathing making heartbreaking sounds in the stillness of the evening.

I walked away, blindly following the driveway out of the grounds. I had never loved her, yet, why was I crying?

I walked and walked. Unconsciously I walked straight to my apartment. I went in.

The womanly scent of her was on my body. Her fragrance was all around me. My arms had been the last to hold that luscious body, my lips the last to taste the nectar of her sweet mouth. She had left me, singing happily, her thoughts leaping in anticipation toward the next hour when she would be in my arms again. I had been the last to feel the quickened beat of her heart. That loving heart no longer beat.

I had never loved her. She had never loved me. We had been drawn together by the most primitive of emotions but she had taught me all the secrets of a woman in love. Joy, sorrow, forgiveness, compassion, strength and tenderness.

I knew now how much I had depended on her. Now I was alone. I couldn't stand being alone. I never wanted to be alone again. She had taught me that.

My eyes were still running hot tears when I thought of Bart. He was alone too. Governor Morley was alone when he needed his wife beside him. Since he had been married to Jennifer, he had lived for her. In all our travels during the campaign I had not seen him make a pass at another woman. In the months to come he would be alone. The Governor's mansion was built for a woman.

In an instant I decided to play a role beyond human strength. I felt I owed it to him and I knew Jennifer would approve. I reached for the phone.

I said to the operator,

"I want Bureau twenty. Washington. Ray. Mr. Ray. This is Howard."

I waited. I thanked God for being able to remember the phone call and bureau number I had heard only once before.

"Hello. Ray? This is Chris Howard. I want to find Captain Downs. It's very important."

"Thank God Mr. Robbins. Thank you. Colonel Morley's wife has just been killed in an accident. I want to talk with Captain Downs personally. MA 6-2345. Thank you, Sir."

I clicked the phone,

"Please get me Murryhill 6-2345, New York City."

In ten seconds I heard a soft voice speaking with authority,

"Colonel Downs speaking."

"Amy. This is Chris."

Her voice broke over the phone into a woman's voice filled with delight,

"Oh Chris. How wonderful. I was leaving tomorrow. I want to see you Lover."

"Amy. Listen carefully. Jennifer Morley has just been killed. She was thrown from a horse she was riding. Bart is all alone."

There was a long moment of silence, then she said gently,

"I'll be there in the morning. Please do not meet me."

Another silence which ended in a soft sobbing,

"Will you forgive me Chris? I know you will understand."

"Yes. Amy. That is why I called you. I've known since the first time I saw you two together. Bart told me he had loved another woman for a long time. Happy landing, Colonel Downs."

"God bless you Chris. Thank you, with all my heart."

I gently laid the receiver on the instrument.

Sometimes life is cruel. Perhaps I had been cruel and hasty. Only time would tell. I breathed a silent prayer.

The queen is dead. Long live the queen.

My thoughts slowly unraveled. I had over half a million dollars. I was alone in the world and I could travel to the ends of the earth, alone. I could build the most beautiful home in the city and live in it. Alone. I could buy and pay for anything I could wish for and enjoy it. Alone. The damned word drummed in my heart. Alone. Alone. Alone.

I picked up the receiver, hunting in the directory for a number, with impatience. I dialed the number, my heart pounding.

"Hello."

The sound of her lilting voice shook me to my toes.

"May I see you?"

"I know I'll hate myself, but all right, come to the house."

"Darleen. Do you know why I want to see you?"

"Yes, silly. You want me to cook all your meals for the rest of our lives. Hurry to me darling. Hurry."

Suddenly I got a whiff of diapers drying on a line. It was a wonderful scent.

THE END